THE RENEGADES

DEFENDERS OF THE PLANET

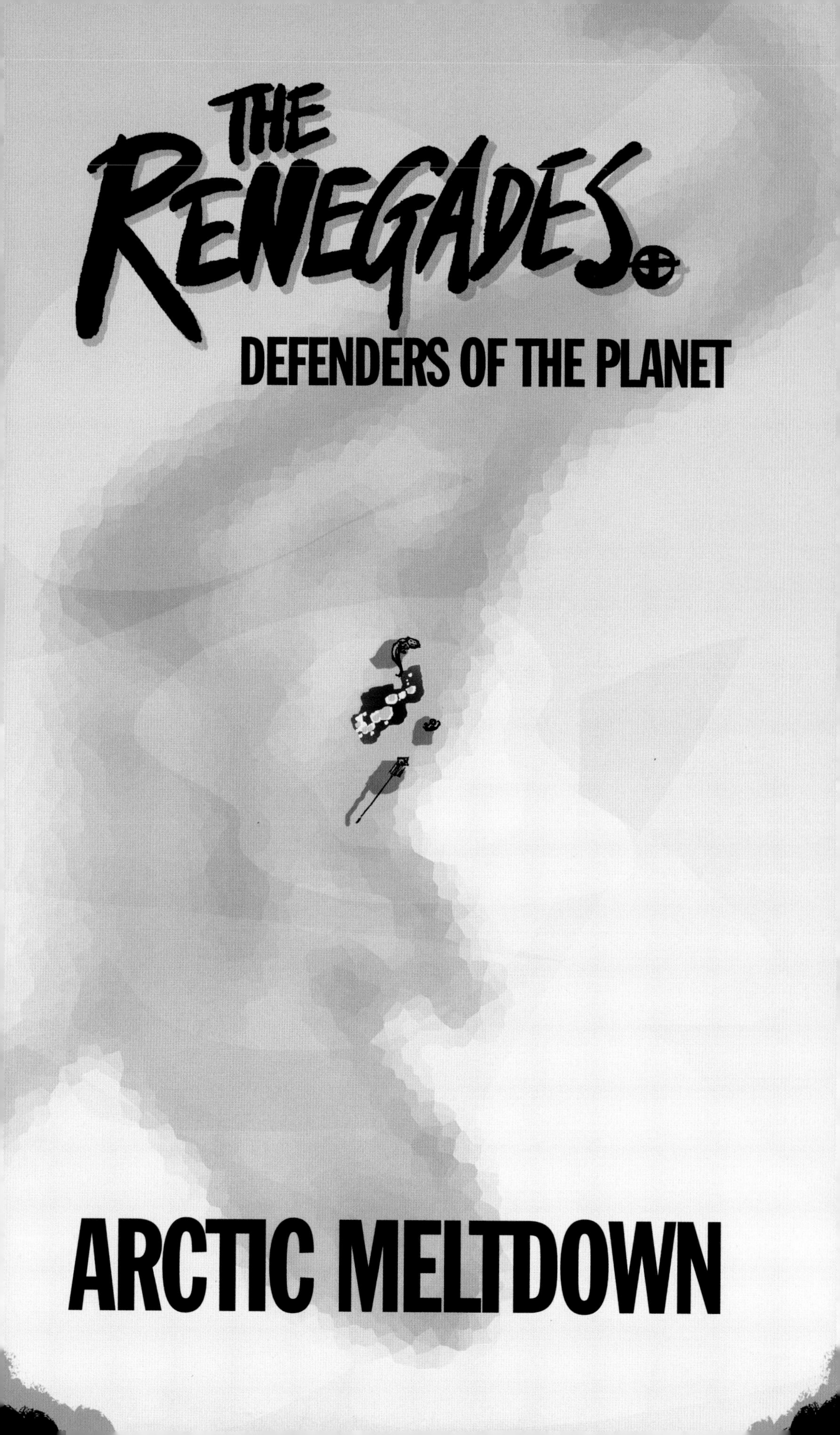

ARCTIC MELTDOWN

DK | Penguin Random House

DK LONDON
Senior Editor Ashwin Khurana
Designer Kit Lane
Editor Vicky Richards
US Editor Jennette ElNaggar
Managing Editor Francesca Baines
Managing Art Editor Philip Letsu
Production Editor Kavita Varma
Senior Production Controller Jude Crozier
Jacket Designer Surabhi Wadhwa-Gandhi
Jacket Design Development Manager Sophia MTT
Publisher Andrew Mcintyre
Associate Publishing Director Liz Wheeler
Art Director Karen Self
Publishing Director Jonathan Metcalf

First American Edition, 2020
Published in the United States by DK Publishing
1450 Broadway, Suite 801, New York, NY 10018

20 21 22 23 24 10 9 8 7 6 5 4 3 2 1
001-320948-Oct/2020

Published in Great Britain by Dorling Kindersley Limited.

A catalog record for this book
is available from the Library of Congress.
ISBN 978-0-7440-2454-8 (Paperback)
ISBN 978-0-7440-3250-5 (ALB)

Printed and bound in China

For the curious
www.dk.com

FSC
www.fsc.org
MIX
Paper from responsible sources
FSC™ C018179

This book was made with
Forest Stewardship Council® certified paper–
one small step in DK's commitment to a sustainable future.
For more information go to www.dk.com/our-green-pledge

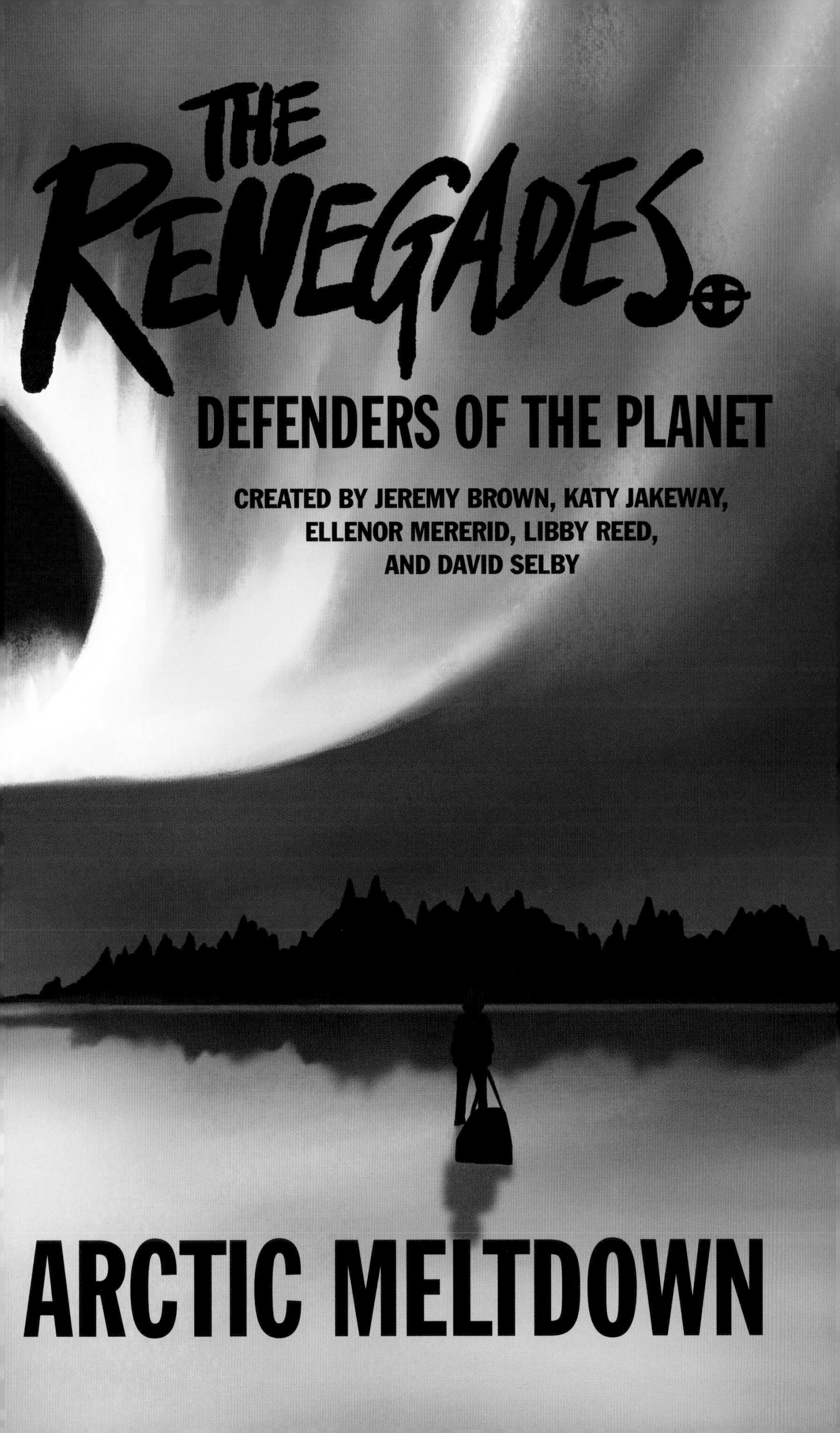

THE RENEGADES

DEFENDERS OF THE PLANET

CREATED BY JEREMY BROWN, KATY JAKEWAY,
ELLENOR MERERID, LIBBY REED,
AND DAVID SELBY

ARCTIC MELTDOWN

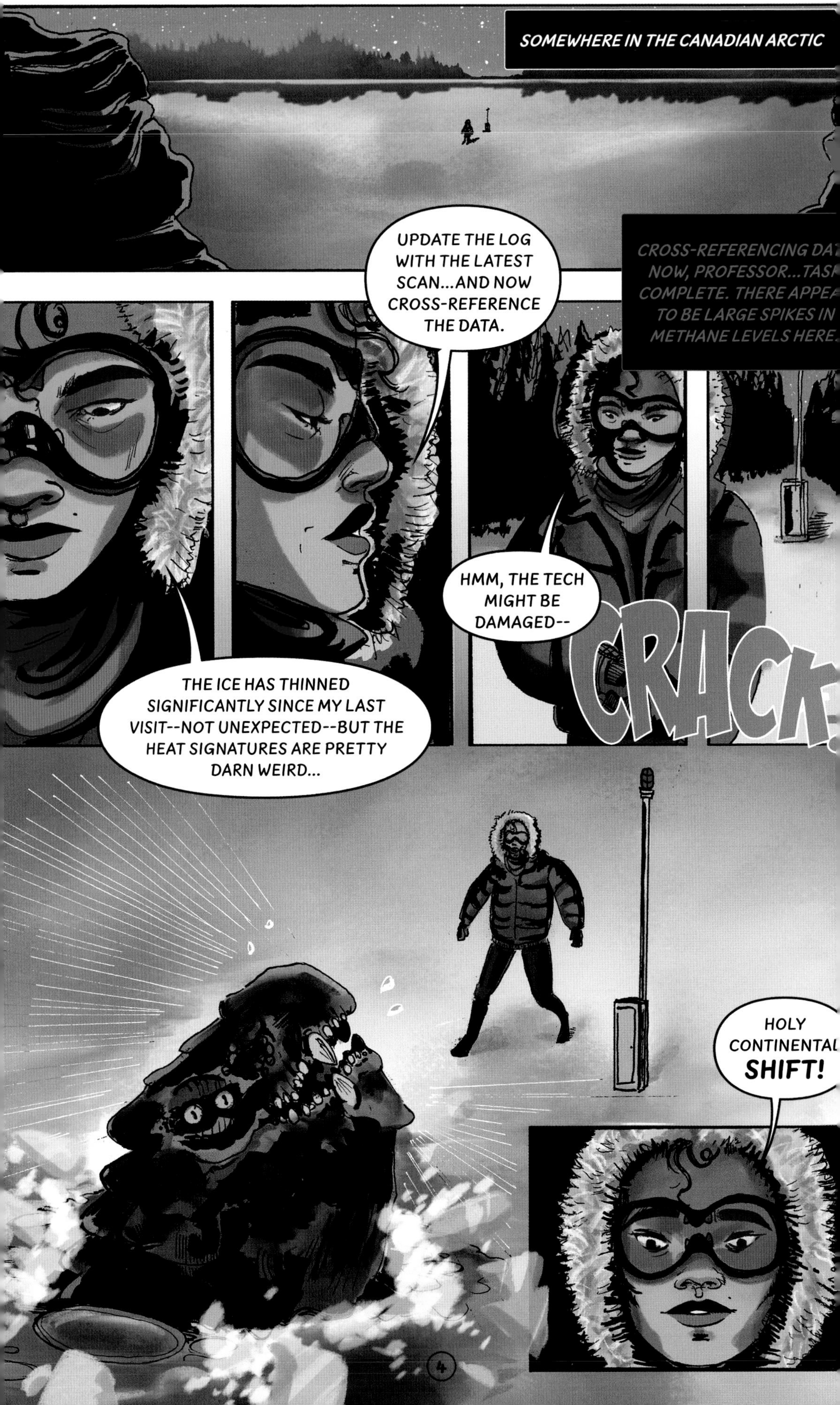
SOMEWHERE IN THE CANADIAN ARCTIC
UPDATE THE LOG WITH THE LATEST SCAN...AND NOW CROSS-REFERENCE THE DATA.
THE ICE HAS THINNED SIGNIFICANTLY SINCE MY LAST VISIT--NOT UNEXPECTED--BUT THE HEAT SIGNATURES ARE PRETTY DARN WEIRD...
HMM, THE TECH MIGHT BE DAMAGED--
CRACK!
HOLY CONTINENTAL SHIFT!

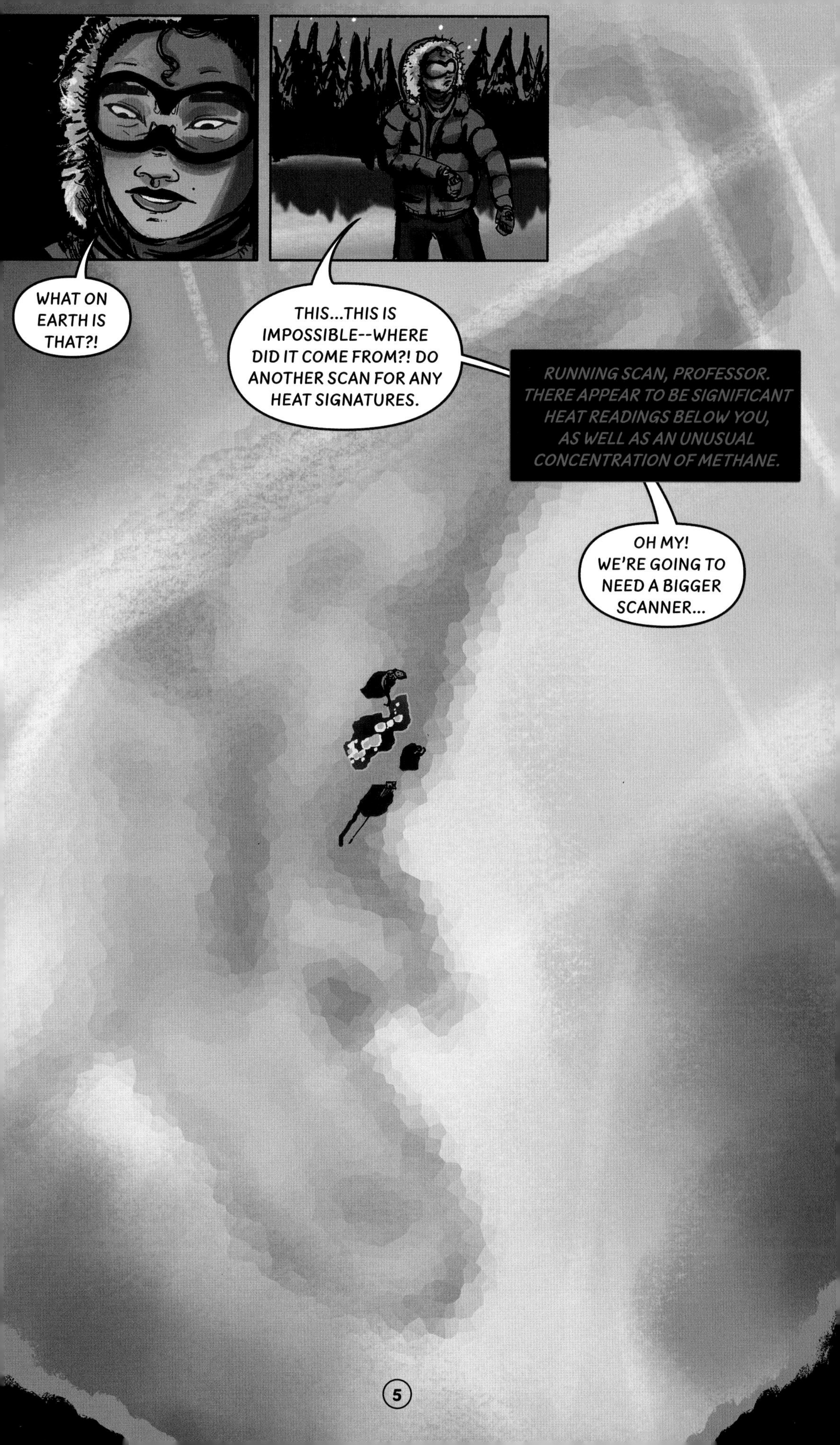

WHAT ON EARTH IS THAT?!
THIS...THIS IS IMPOSSIBLE--WHERE DID IT COME FROM?! DO ANOTHER SCAN FOR ANY HEAT SIGNATURES.
RUNNING SCAN, PROFESSOR. THERE APPEAR TO BE SIGNIFICANT HEAT READINGS BELOW YOU, AS WELL AS AN UNUSUAL CONCENTRATION OF METHANE.
OH MY! WE'RE GOING TO NEED A BIGGER SCANNER...

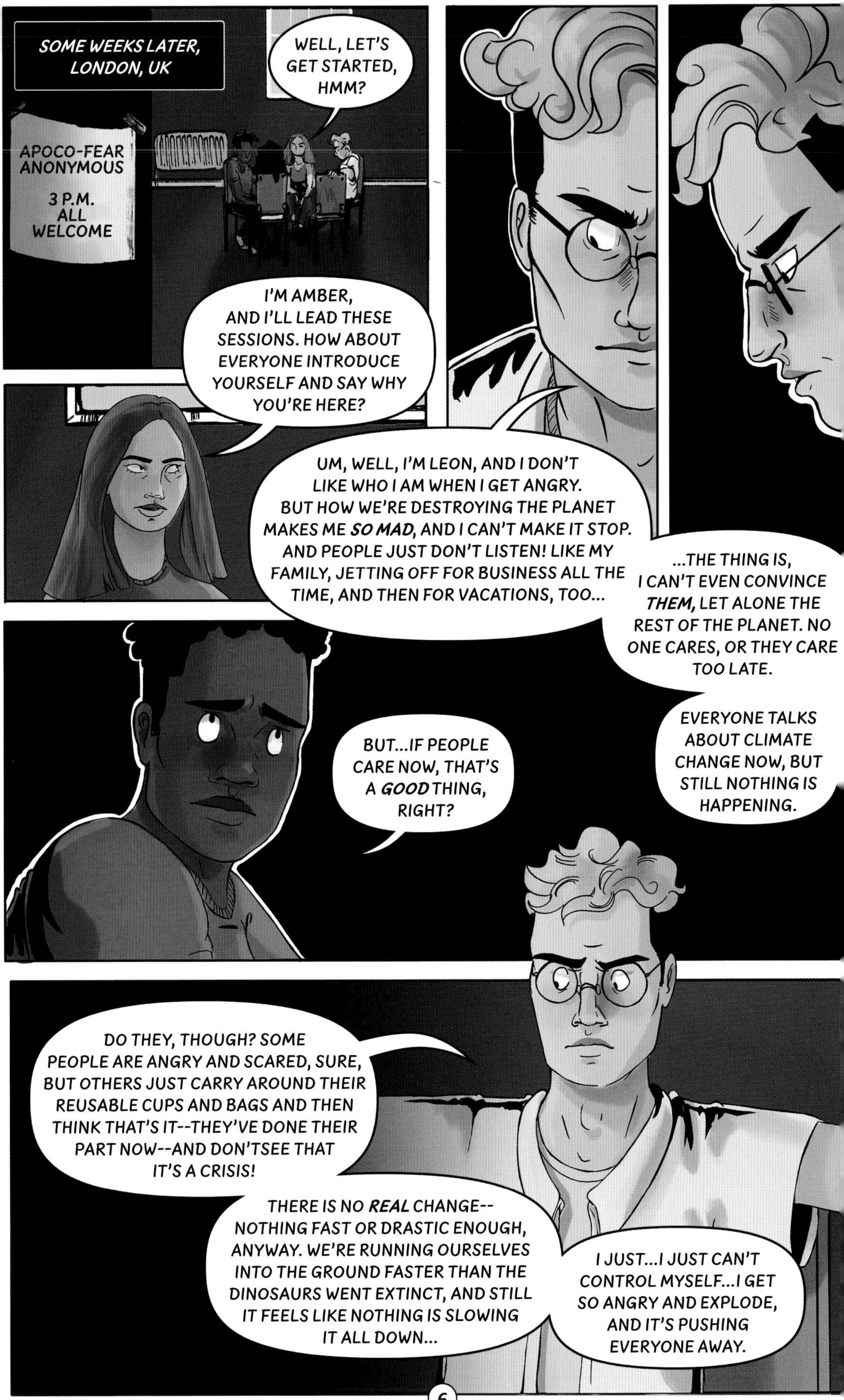
SOME WEEKS LATER, LONDON, UK
APOCO-FEAR ANONYMOUS 3 P.M. ALL WELCOME
WELL, LET'S GET STARTED, HMM?
I'M AMBER, AND I'LL LEAD THESE SESSIONS. HOW ABOUT EVERYONE INTRODUCE YOURSELF AND SAY WHY YOU'RE HERE?
UM, WELL, I'M LEON, AND I DON'T LIKE WHO I AM WHEN I GET ANGRY. BUT HOW WE'RE DESTROYING THE PLANET MAKES ME *SO MAD*, AND I CAN'T MAKE IT STOP. AND PEOPLE JUST DON'T LISTEN! LIKE MY FAMILY, JETTING OFF FOR BUSINESS ALL THE TIME, AND THEN FOR VACATIONS, TOO...
...THE THING IS, I CAN'T EVEN CONVINCE *THEM,* LET ALONE THE REST OF THE PLANET. NO ONE CARES, OR THEY CARE TOO LATE.
EVERYONE TALKS ABOUT CLIMATE CHANGE NOW, BUT STILL NOTHING IS HAPPENING.
BUT...IF PEOPLE CARE NOW, THAT'S A *GOOD* THING, RIGHT?
DO THEY, THOUGH? SOME PEOPLE ARE ANGRY AND SCARED, SURE, BUT OTHERS JUST CARRY AROUND THEIR REUSABLE CUPS AND BAGS AND THEN THINK THAT'S IT--THEY'VE DONE THEIR PART NOW--AND DON'TSEE THAT IT'S A CRISIS!
THERE IS NO *REAL* CHANGE--NOTHING FAST OR DRASTIC ENOUGH, ANYWAY. WE'RE RUNNING OURSELVES INTO THE GROUND FASTER THAN THE DINOSAURS WENT EXTINCT, AND STILL IT FEELS LIKE NOTHING IS SLOWING IT ALL DOWN...
I JUST...I JUST CAN'T CONTROL MYSELF...I GET SO ANGRY AND EXPLODE, AND IT'S PUSHING EVERYONE AWAY.

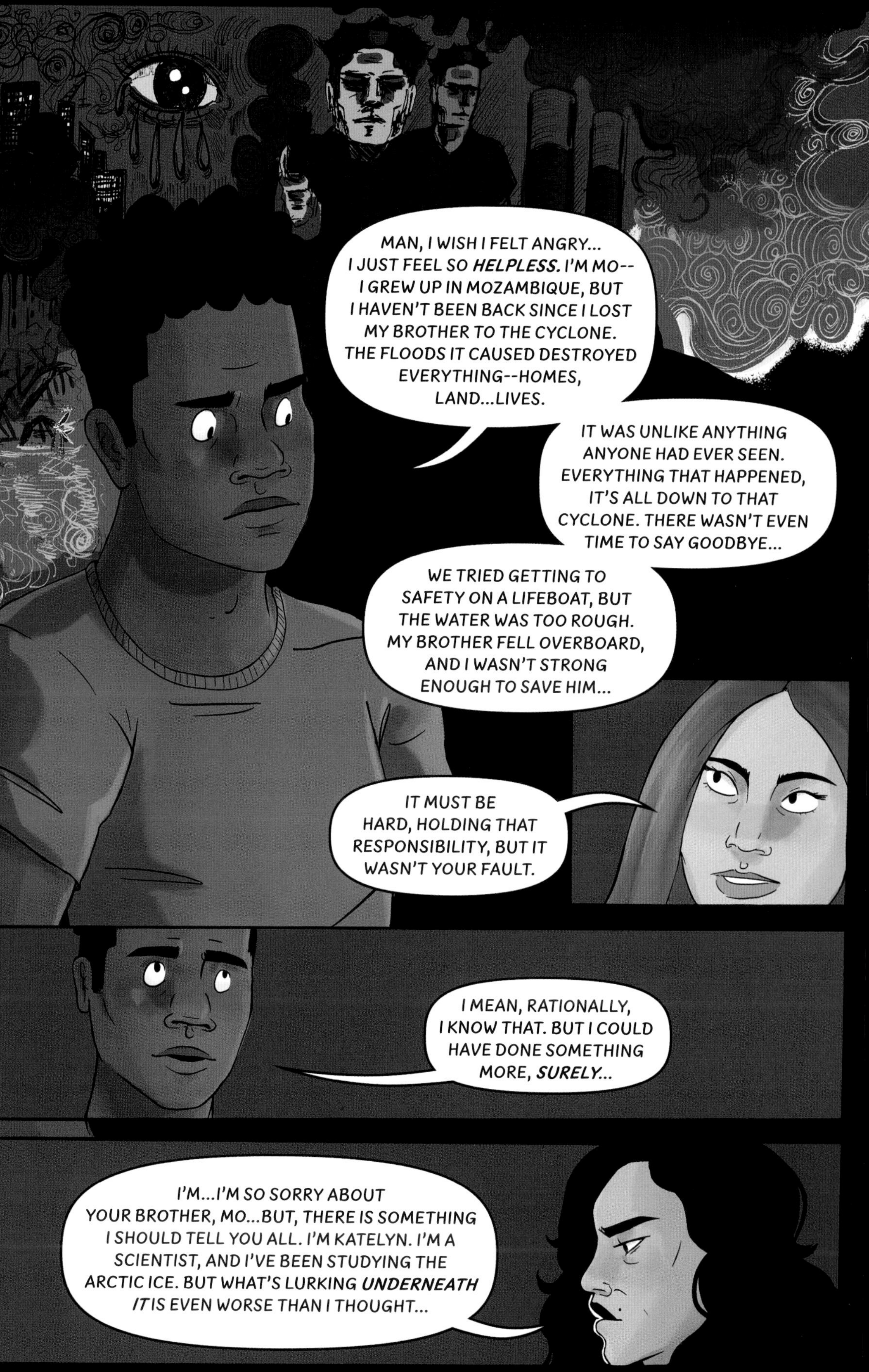
MAN, I WISH I FELT ANGRY... I JUST FEEL SO ***HELPLESS.*** I'M MO-- I GREW UP IN MOZAMBIQUE, BUT I HAVEN'T BEEN BACK SINCE I LOST MY BROTHER TO THE CYCLONE. THE FLOODS IT CAUSED DESTROYED EVERYTHING--HOMES, LAND...LIVES.
IT WAS UNLIKE ANYTHING ANYONE HAD EVER SEEN. EVERYTHING THAT HAPPENED, IT'S ALL DOWN TO THAT CYCLONE. THERE WASN'T EVEN TIME TO SAY GOODBYE...
WE TRIED GETTING TO SAFETY ON A LIFEBOAT, BUT THE WATER WAS TOO ROUGH. MY BROTHER FELL OVERBOARD, AND I WASN'T STRONG ENOUGH TO SAVE HIM...
IT MUST BE HARD, HOLDING THAT RESPONSIBILITY, BUT IT WASN'T YOUR FAULT.
I MEAN, RATIONALLY, I KNOW THAT. BUT I COULD HAVE DONE SOMETHING MORE, ***SURELY...***
I'M...I'M SO SORRY ABOUT YOUR BROTHER, MO...BUT, THERE IS SOMETHING I SHOULD TELL YOU ALL. I'M KATELYN. I'M A SCIENTIST, AND I'VE BEEN STUDYING THE ARCTIC ICE. BUT WHAT'S LURKING ***UNDERNEATH IT*** IS EVEN WORSE THAN I THOUGHT...

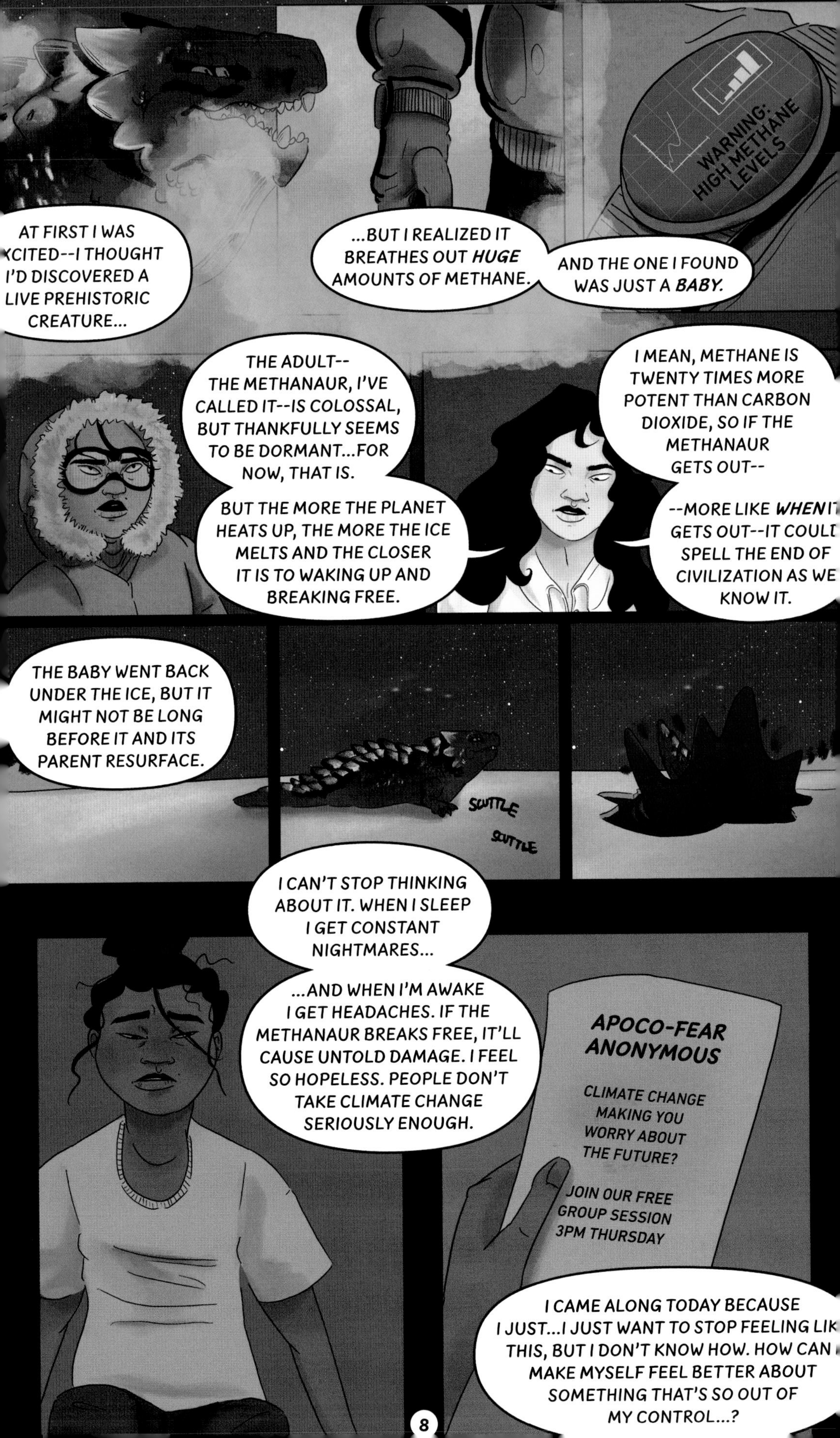
WARNING: HIGH METHANE LEVELS
AT FIRST I WAS XCITED--I THOUGHT I'D DISCOVERED A LIVE PREHISTORIC CREATURE...
...BUT I REALIZED IT BREATHES OUT *HUGE* AMOUNTS OF METHANE.
AND THE ONE I FOUND WAS JUST A *BABY.*
THE ADULT-- THE METHANAUR, I'VE CALLED IT--IS COLOSSAL, BUT THANKFULLY SEEMS TO BE DORMANT...FOR NOW, THAT IS.
BUT THE MORE THE PLANET HEATS UP, THE MORE THE ICE MELTS AND THE CLOSER IT IS TO WAKING UP AND BREAKING FREE.
I MEAN, METHANE IS TWENTY TIMES MORE POTENT THAN CARBON DIOXIDE, SO IF THE METHANAUR GETS OUT--
--MORE LIKE *WHEN* I GETS OUT--IT COUL SPELL THE END OF CIVILIZATION AS WE KNOW IT.
THE BABY WENT BACK UNDER THE ICE, BUT IT MIGHT NOT BE LONG BEFORE IT AND ITS PARENT RESURFACE.
SCUTTLE
SCUTTLE
I CAN'T STOP THINKING ABOUT IT. WHEN I SLEEP I GET CONSTANT NIGHTMARES...
...AND WHEN I'M AWAKE I GET HEADACHES. IF THE METHANAUR BREAKS FREE, IT'LL CAUSE UNTOLD DAMAGE. I FEEL SO HOPELESS. PEOPLE DON'T TAKE CLIMATE CHANGE SERIOUSLY ENOUGH.
APOCO-FEAR ANONYMOUS
CLIMATE CHANGE MAKING YOU WORRY ABOUT THE FUTURE?
JOIN OUR FREE GROUP SESSION 3PM THURSDAY
I CAME ALONG TODAY BECAUSE I JUST...I JUST WANT TO STOP FEELING LIK THIS, BUT I DON'T KNOW HOW. HOW CAN MAKE MYSELF FEEL BETTER ABOUT SOMETHING THAT'S SO OUT OF MY CONTROL...?

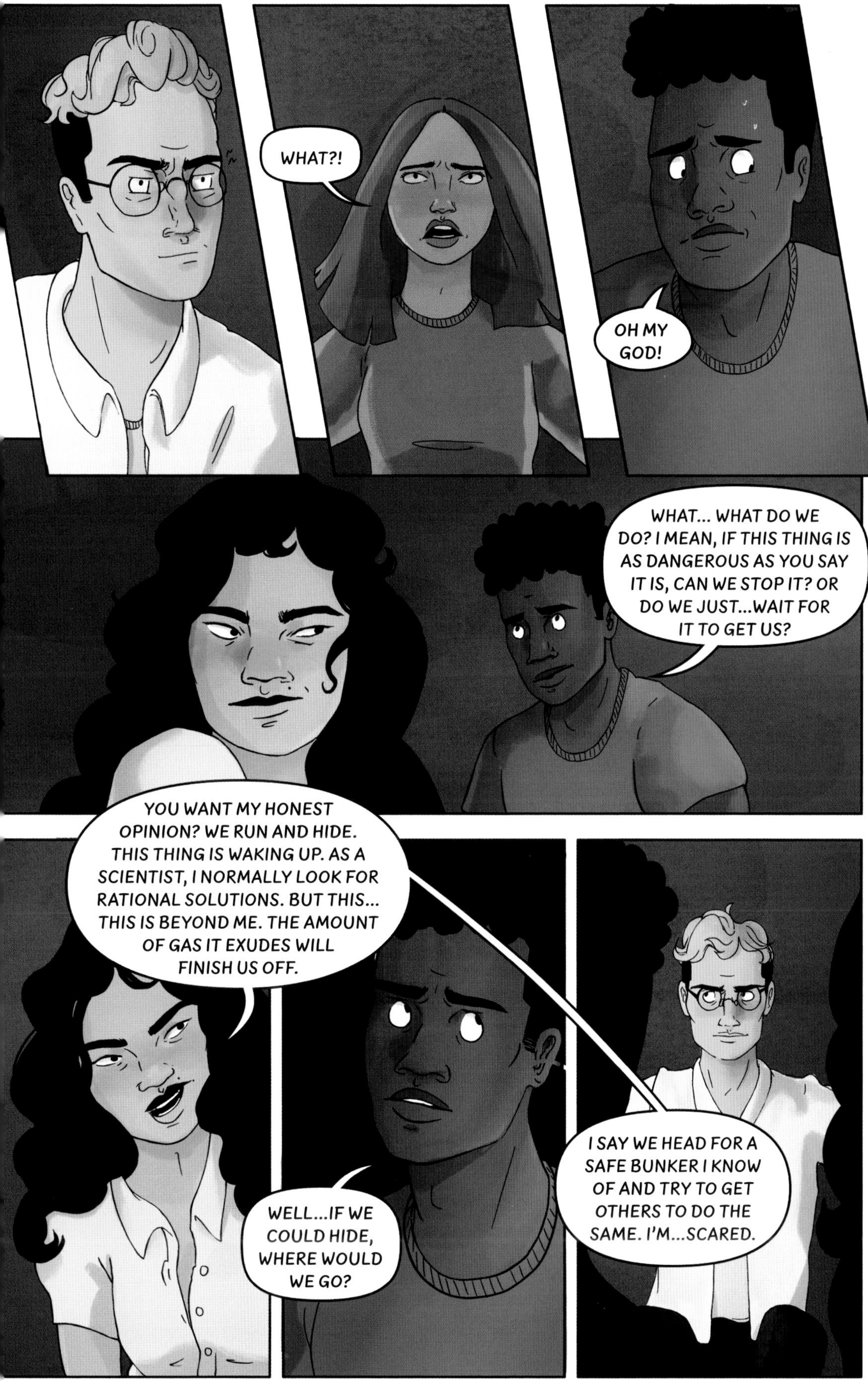
WHAT?!
OH MY GOD!
WHAT... WHAT DO WE DO? I MEAN, IF THIS THING IS AS DANGEROUS AS YOU SAY IT IS, CAN WE STOP IT? OR DO WE JUST...WAIT FOR IT TO GET US?
YOU WANT MY HONEST OPINION? WE RUN AND HIDE. THIS THING IS WAKING UP. AS A SCIENTIST, I NORMALLY LOOK FOR RATIONAL SOLUTIONS. BUT THIS... THIS IS BEYOND ME. THE AMOUNT OF GAS IT EXUDES WILL FINISH US OFF.
WELL...IF WE COULD HIDE, WHERE WOULD WE GO?
I SAY WE HEAD FOR A SAFE BUNKER I KNOW OF AND TRY TO GET OTHERS TO DO THE SAME. I'M...SCARED.

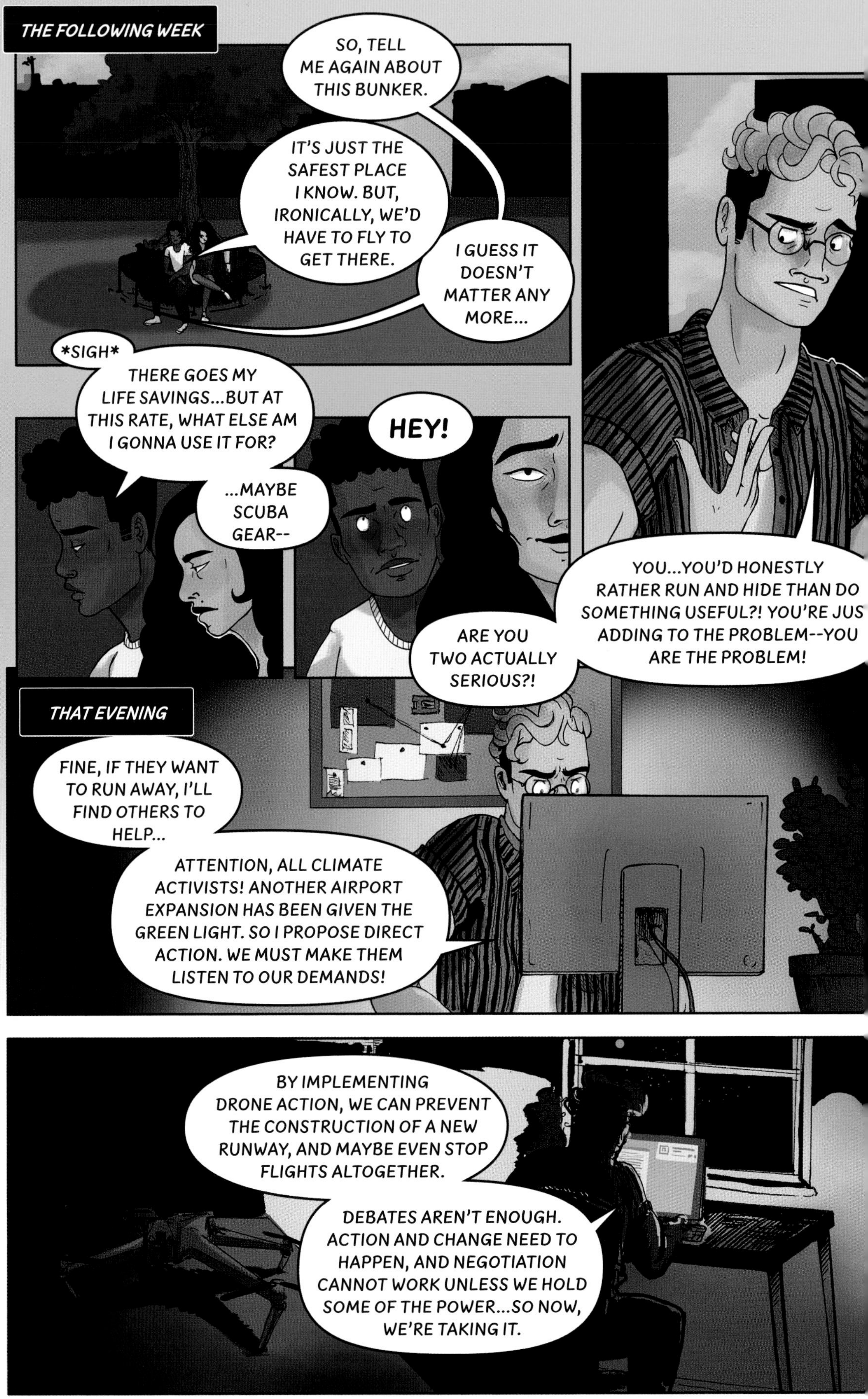
THE FOLLOWING WEEK
SO, TELL ME AGAIN ABOUT THIS BUNKER.
IT'S JUST THE SAFEST PLACE I KNOW. BUT, IRONICALLY, WE'D HAVE TO FLY TO GET THERE.
I GUESS IT DOESN'T MATTER ANY MORE...
SIGH
THERE GOES MY LIFE SAVINGS...BUT AT THIS RATE, WHAT ELSE AM I GONNA USE IT FOR?
...MAYBE SCUBA GEAR--
HEY!
ARE YOU TWO ACTUALLY SERIOUS?!
YOU...YOU'D HONESTLY RATHER RUN AND HIDE THAN DO SOMETHING USEFUL?! YOU'RE JUS ADDING TO THE PROBLEM--YOU ARE THE PROBLEM!
THAT EVENING
FINE, IF THEY WANT TO RUN AWAY, I'LL FIND OTHERS TO HELP...
ATTENTION, ALL CLIMATE ACTIVISTS! ANOTHER AIRPORT EXPANSION HAS BEEN GIVEN THE GREEN LIGHT. SO I PROPOSE DIRECT ACTION. WE MUST MAKE THEM LISTEN TO OUR DEMANDS!
BY IMPLEMENTING DRONE ACTION, WE CAN PREVENT THE CONSTRUCTION OF A NEW RUNWAY, AND MAYBE EVEN STOP FLIGHTS ALTOGETHER.
DEBATES AREN'T ENOUGH. ACTION AND CHANGE NEED TO HAPPEN, AND NEGOTIATION CANNOT WORK UNLESS WE HOLD SOME OF THE POWER...SO NOW, WE'RE TAKING IT.

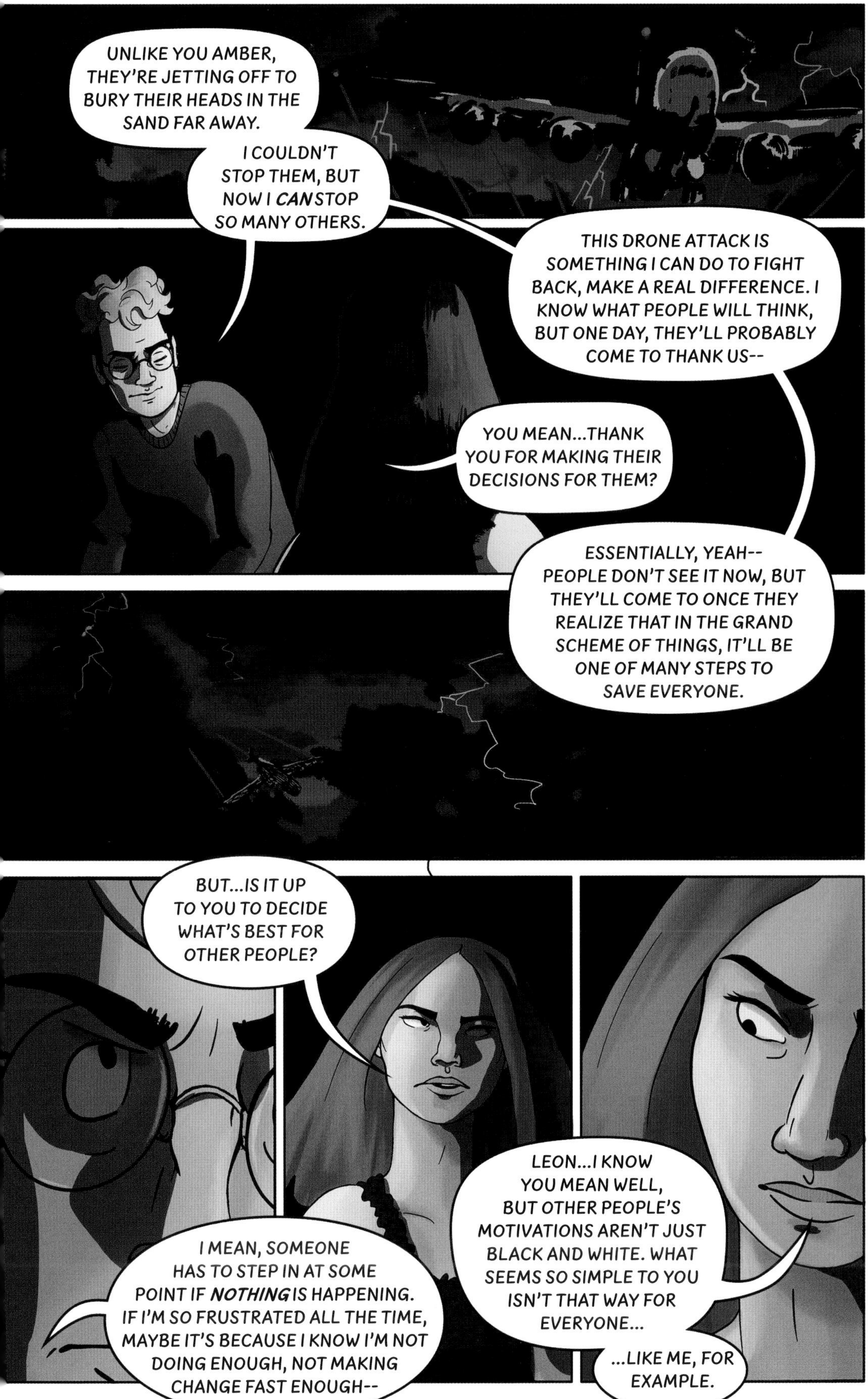
UNLIKE YOU AMBER, THEY'RE JETTING OFF TO BURY THEIR HEADS IN THE SAND FAR AWAY.
I COULDN'T STOP THEM, BUT NOW I *CAN* STOP SO MANY OTHERS.
THIS DRONE ATTACK IS SOMETHING I CAN DO TO FIGHT BACK, MAKE A REAL DIFFERENCE. I KNOW WHAT PEOPLE WILL THINK, BUT ONE DAY, THEY'LL PROBABLY COME TO THANK US--
YOU MEAN...THANK YOU FOR MAKING THEIR DECISIONS FOR THEM?
ESSENTIALLY, YEAH-- PEOPLE DON'T SEE IT NOW, BUT THEY'LL COME TO ONCE THEY REALIZE THAT IN THE GRAND SCHEME OF THINGS, IT'LL BE ONE OF MANY STEPS TO SAVE EVERYONE.
BUT...IS IT UP TO YOU TO DECIDE WHAT'S BEST FOR OTHER PEOPLE?
I MEAN, SOMEONE HAS TO STEP IN AT SOME POINT IF *NOTHING* IS HAPPENING. IF I'M SO FRUSTRATED ALL THE TIME, MAYBE IT'S BECAUSE I KNOW I'M NOT DOING ENOUGH, NOT MAKING CHANGE FAST ENOUGH--
LEON...I KNOW YOU MEAN WELL, BUT OTHER PEOPLE'S MOTIVATIONS AREN'T JUST BLACK AND WHITE. WHAT SEEMS SO SIMPLE TO YOU ISN'T THAT WAY FOR EVERYONE...
...LIKE ME, FOR EXAMPLE.

MY FIANCÉ LIVED OVERSEAS, AND I WAS GOING TO JOIN HIM, BUT...HE PASSED AWAY.

I NEED TO FLY OUT FOR THE FUNERAL, AS THERE'S NO OTHER WAY I CAN GET THERE IN TIME. AND IT'S NOT JUST ME--THERE ARE LOTS OF PEOPLE THAT COULD BE HURT BY YOUR ACTIONS--

--AND THEY AREN'T BAD--THEY'RE JUST PEOPLE, LEON.

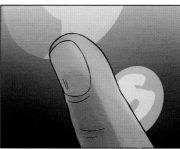

I...AMBER, I'M SORRY. I HAD NO IDEA. I DIDN'T EVEN THINK OR CONSIDER... ANYTHING LIKE THAT, HONESTLY.

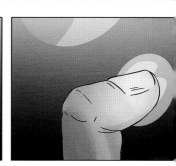

BUT YOU'RE RIGHT--MY FIGHT ISN'T AGAINST PEOPLE JUST TRYING TO LIVE AS BEST AS THEY CAN WITH WHAT THEY... WELL, WHAT WE'VE ALL BEEN DEALT.

SO WILL YOU GO THROUGH WITH IT?

NO...I THIN I'LL DO SOMETHIN DIFFERENT.

I THINK WE SHOULD SCRAP THE DRONES...YEAH, YOU HEARD ME RIGHT. I WAS THINKING A LESS...AGGRESSIVE AND MORE PEACEFUL OPTION INSTEAD...

...YES, THIS IS REALLY LEON SPEAKING.

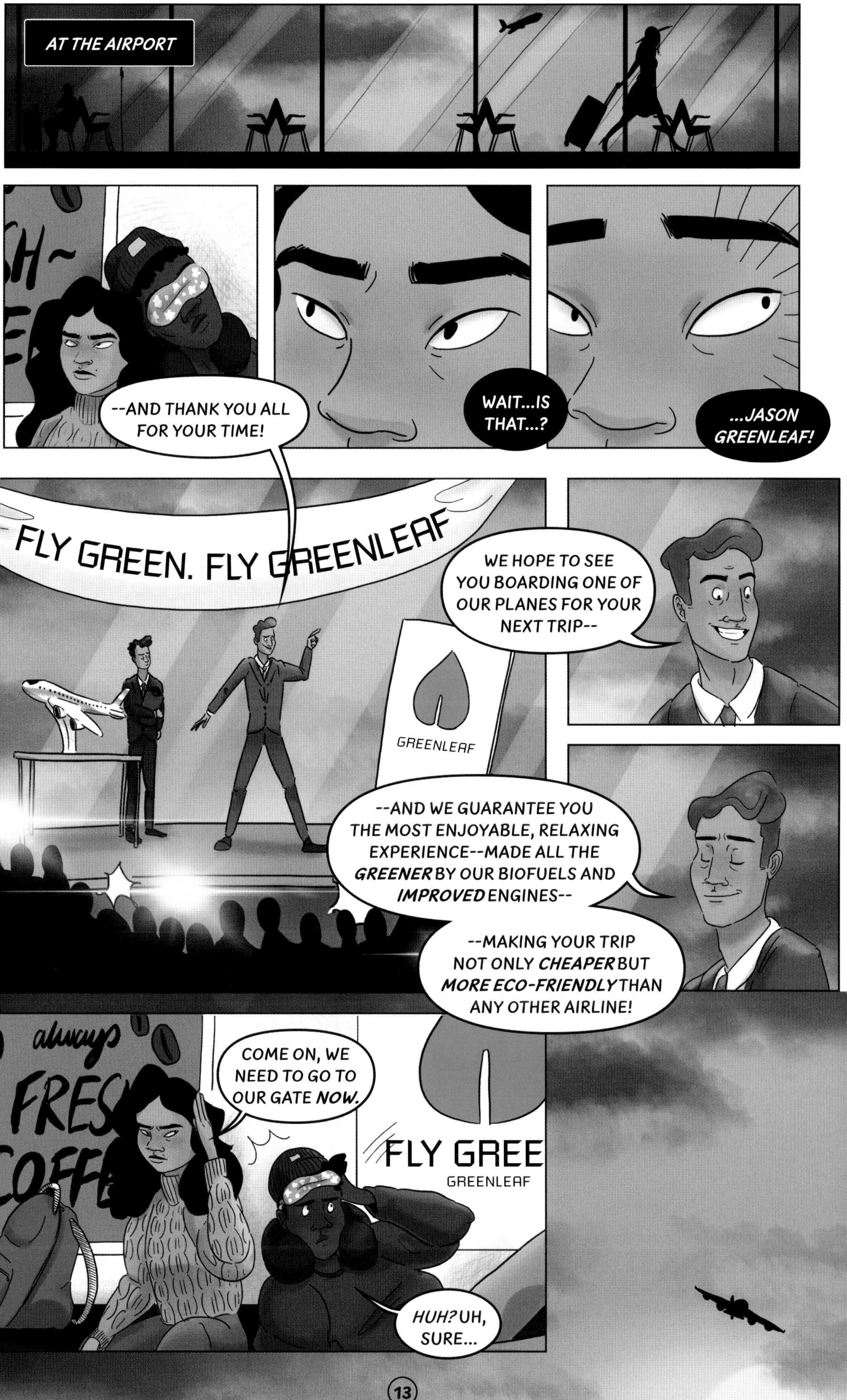

AT THE AIRPORT
--AND THANK YOU ALL FOR YOUR TIME!
WAIT...IS THAT...?
...JASON GREENLEAF!
FLY GREEN. FLY GREENLEAF
GREENLEAF
WE HOPE TO SEE YOU BOARDING ONE OF OUR PLANES FOR YOUR NEXT TRIP--
--AND WE GUARANTEE YOU THE MOST ENJOYABLE, RELAXING EXPERIENCE--MADE ALL THE *GREENER* BY OUR BIOFUELS AND *IMPROVED* ENGINES--
--MAKING YOUR TRIP NOT ONLY *CHEAPER* BUT *MORE ECO-FRIENDLY* THAN ANY OTHER AIRLINE!
always FRES COFF
COME ON, WE NEED TO GO TO OUR GATE *NOW.*
FLY GREE
GREENLEAF
HUH? UH, SURE...

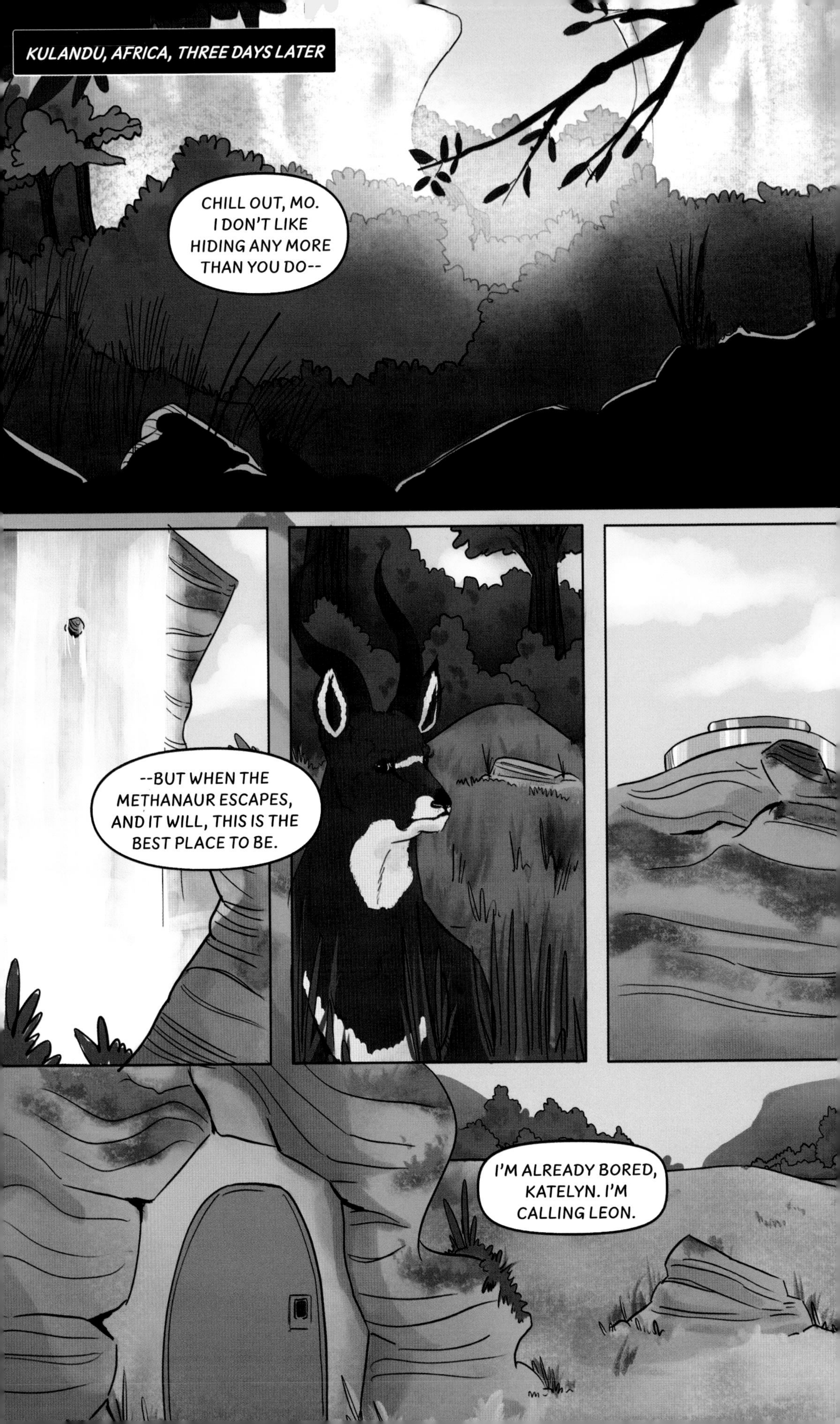

KULANDU, AFRICA, THREE DAYS LATER
CHILL OUT, MO. I DON'T LIKE HIDING ANY MORE THAN YOU DO--
--BUT WHEN THE METHANAUR ESCAPES, AND IT WILL, THIS IS THE BEST PLACE TO BE.
I'M ALREADY BORED, KATELYN. I'M CALLING LEON.

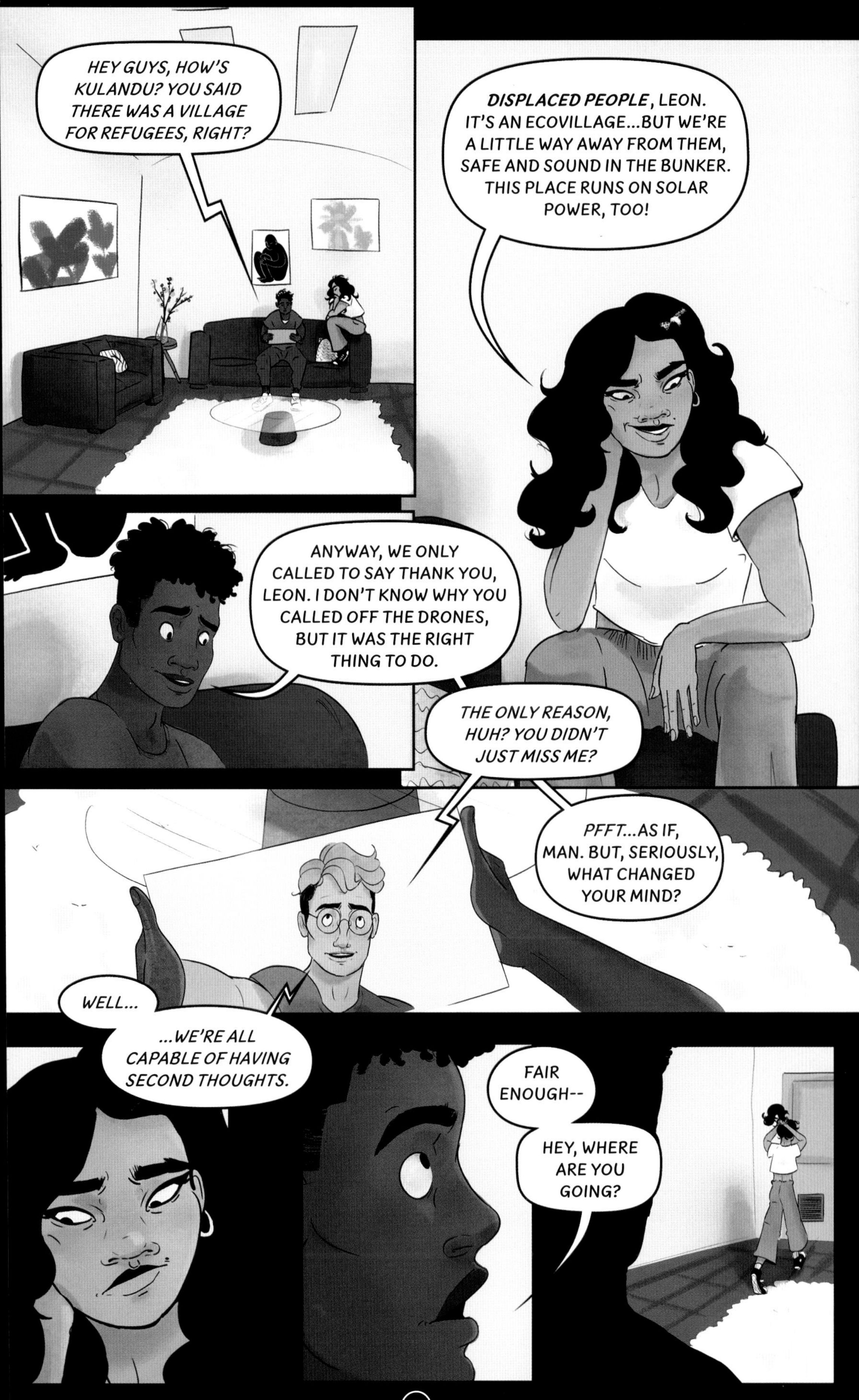
HEY GUYS, HOW'S KULANDU? YOU SAID THERE WAS A VILLAGE FOR REFUGEES, RIGHT?
DISPLACED PEOPLE, LEON. IT'S AN ECOVILLAGE...BUT WE'RE A LITTLE WAY AWAY FROM THEM, SAFE AND SOUND IN THE BUNKER. THIS PLACE RUNS ON SOLAR POWER, TOO!
ANYWAY, WE ONLY CALLED TO SAY THANK YOU, LEON. I DON'T KNOW WHY YOU CALLED OFF THE DRONES, BUT IT WAS THE RIGHT THING TO DO.
THE ONLY REASON, HUH? YOU DIDN'T JUST MISS ME?
PFFT...AS IF, MAN. BUT, SERIOUSLY, WHAT CHANGED YOUR MIND?
WELL...
...WE'RE ALL CAPABLE OF HAVING SECOND THOUGHTS.
FAIR ENOUGH--
HEY, WHERE ARE YOU GOING?

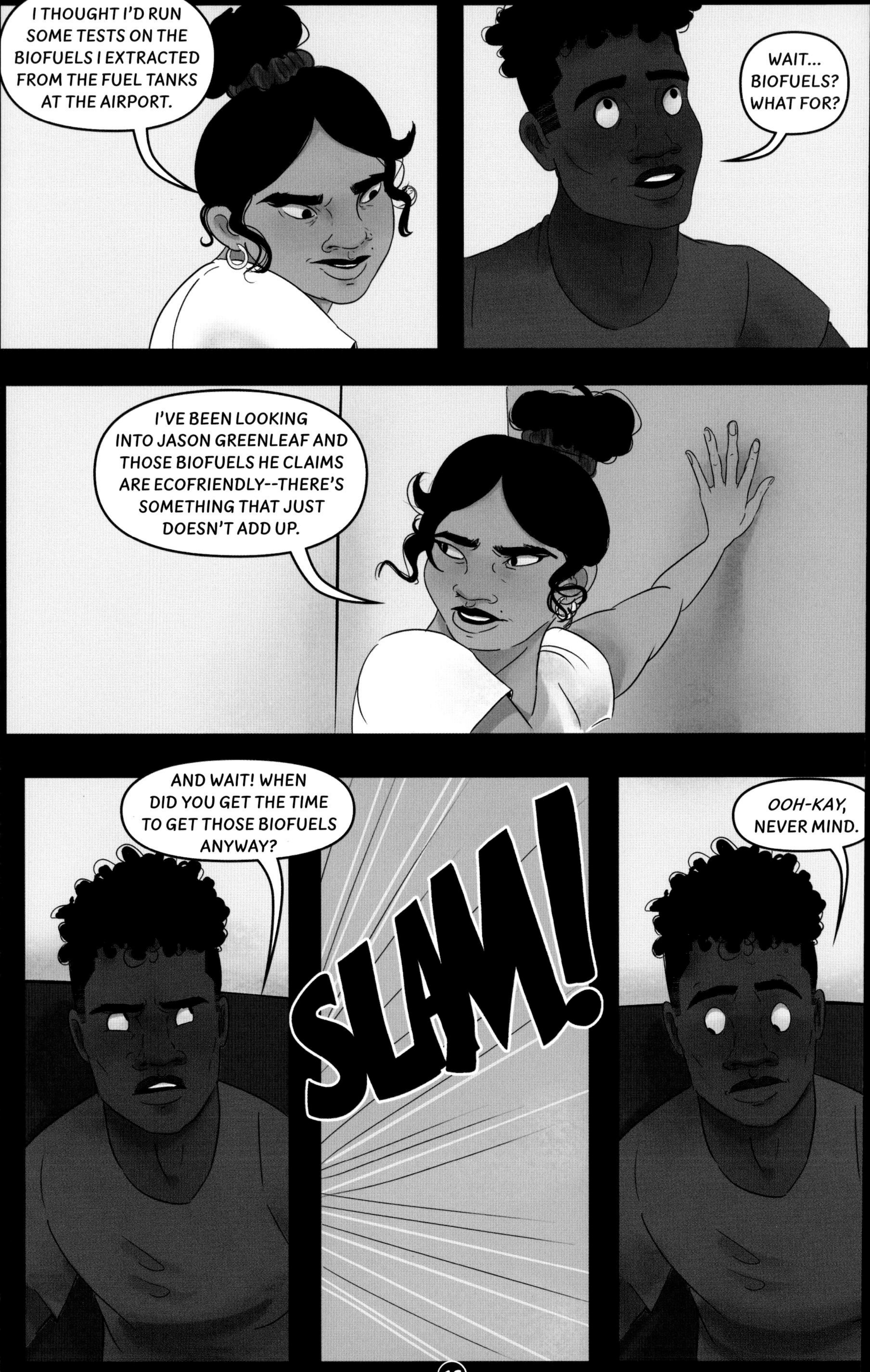
I THOUGHT I'D RUN SOME TESTS ON THE BIOFUELS I EXTRACTED FROM THE FUEL TANKS AT THE AIRPORT.
WAIT... BIOFUELS? WHAT FOR?
I'VE BEEN LOOKING INTO JASON GREENLEAF AND THOSE BIOFUELS HE CLAIMS ARE ECOFRIENDLY--THERE'S SOMETHING THAT JUST DOESN'T ADD UP.
AND WAIT! WHEN DID YOU GET THE TIME TO GET THOSE BIOFUELS ANYWAY?
SLAM!
OOH-KAY, NEVER MIND.

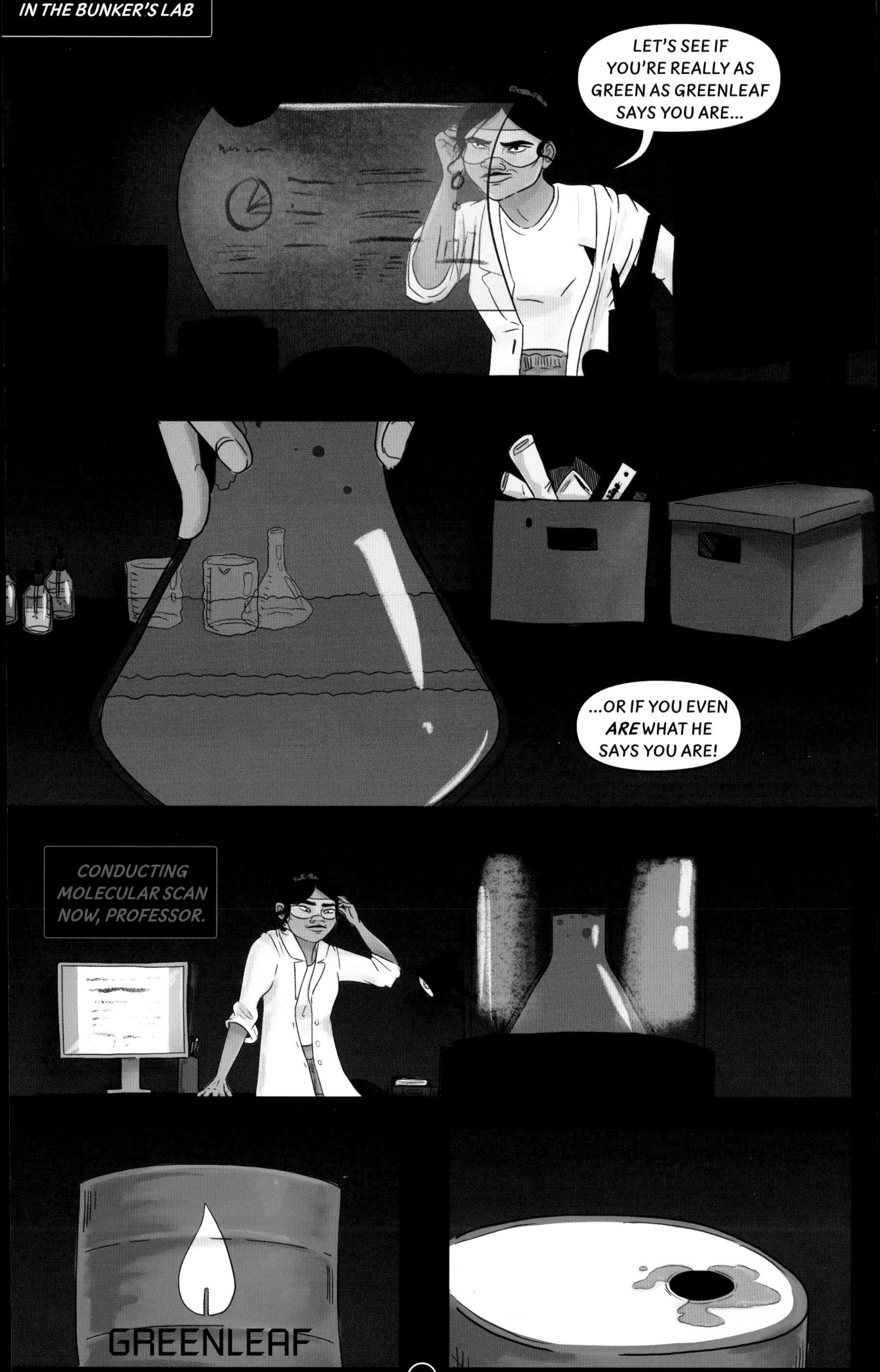
IN THE BUNKER'S LAB
LET'S SEE IF YOU'RE REALLY AS GREEN AS GREENLEAF SAYS YOU ARE...
...OR IF YOU EVEN *ARE* WHAT HE SAYS YOU ARE!
CONDUCTING MOLECULAR SCAN NOW, PROFESSOR.
GREENLEAF

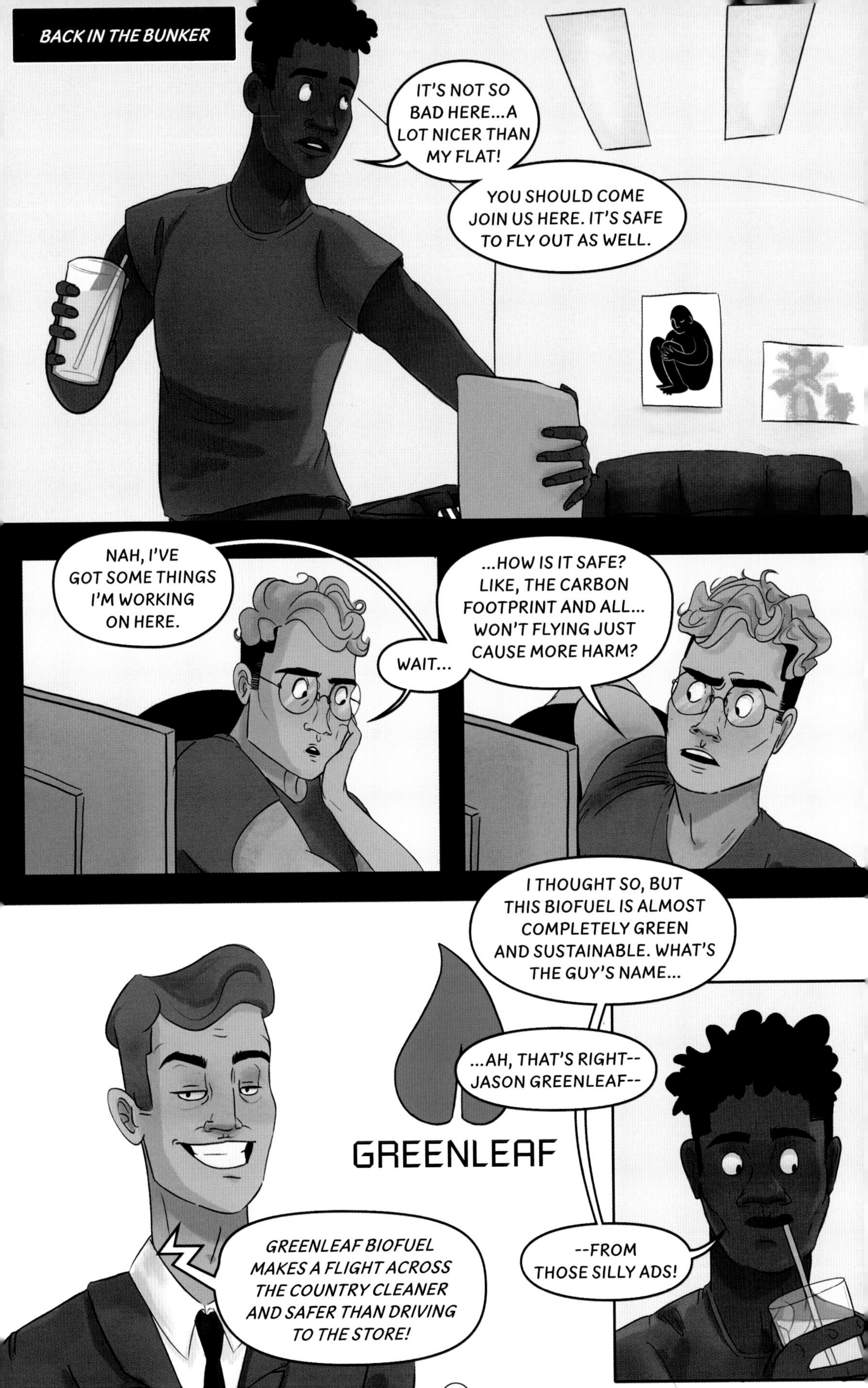
BACK IN THE BUNKER
IT'S NOT SO BAD HERE...A LOT NICER THAN MY FLAT!
YOU SHOULD COME JOIN US HERE. IT'S SAFE TO FLY OUT AS WELL.
NAH, I'VE GOT SOME THINGS I'M WORKING ON HERE.
WAIT...
...HOW IS IT SAFE? LIKE, THE CARBON FOOTPRINT AND ALL... WON'T FLYING JUST CAUSE MORE HARM?
I THOUGHT SO, BUT THIS BIOFUEL IS ALMOST COMPLETELY GREEN AND SUSTAINABLE. WHAT'S THE GUY'S NAME...
...AH, THAT'S RIGHT-- JASON GREENLEAF--
GREENLEAF
GREENLEAF BIOFUEL MAKES A FLIGHT ACROSS THE COUNTRY CLEANER AND SAFER THAN DRIVING TO THE STORE!
--FROM THOSE SILLY ADS!

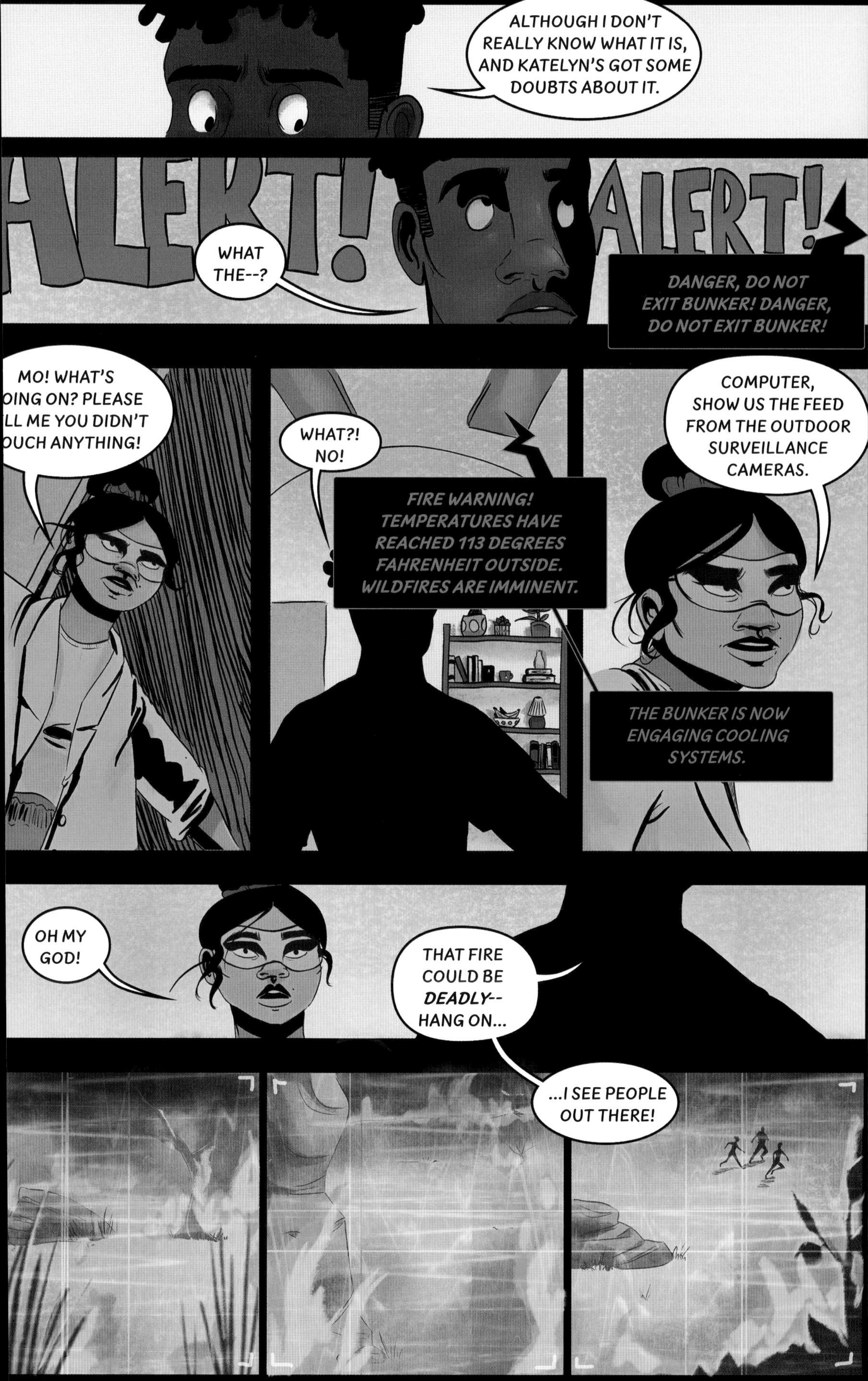
ALTHOUGH I DON'T REALLY KNOW WHAT IT IS, AND KATELYN'S GOT SOME DOUBTS ABOUT IT.
ALERT! ALERT!
WHAT THE--?
DANGER, DO NOT EXIT BUNKER! DANGER, DO NOT EXIT BUNKER!
MO! WHAT'S GOING ON? PLEASE TELL ME YOU DIDN'T TOUCH ANYTHING!
WHAT?! NO!
FIRE WARNING! TEMPERATURES HAVE REACHED 113 DEGREES FAHRENHEIT OUTSIDE. WILDFIRES ARE IMMINENT.
COMPUTER, SHOW US THE FEED FROM THE OUTDOOR SURVEILLANCE CAMERAS.
THE BUNKER IS NOW ENGAGING COOLING SYSTEMS.
OH MY GOD!
THAT FIRE COULD BE *DEADLY*-- HANG ON...
...I SEE PEOPLE OUT THERE!

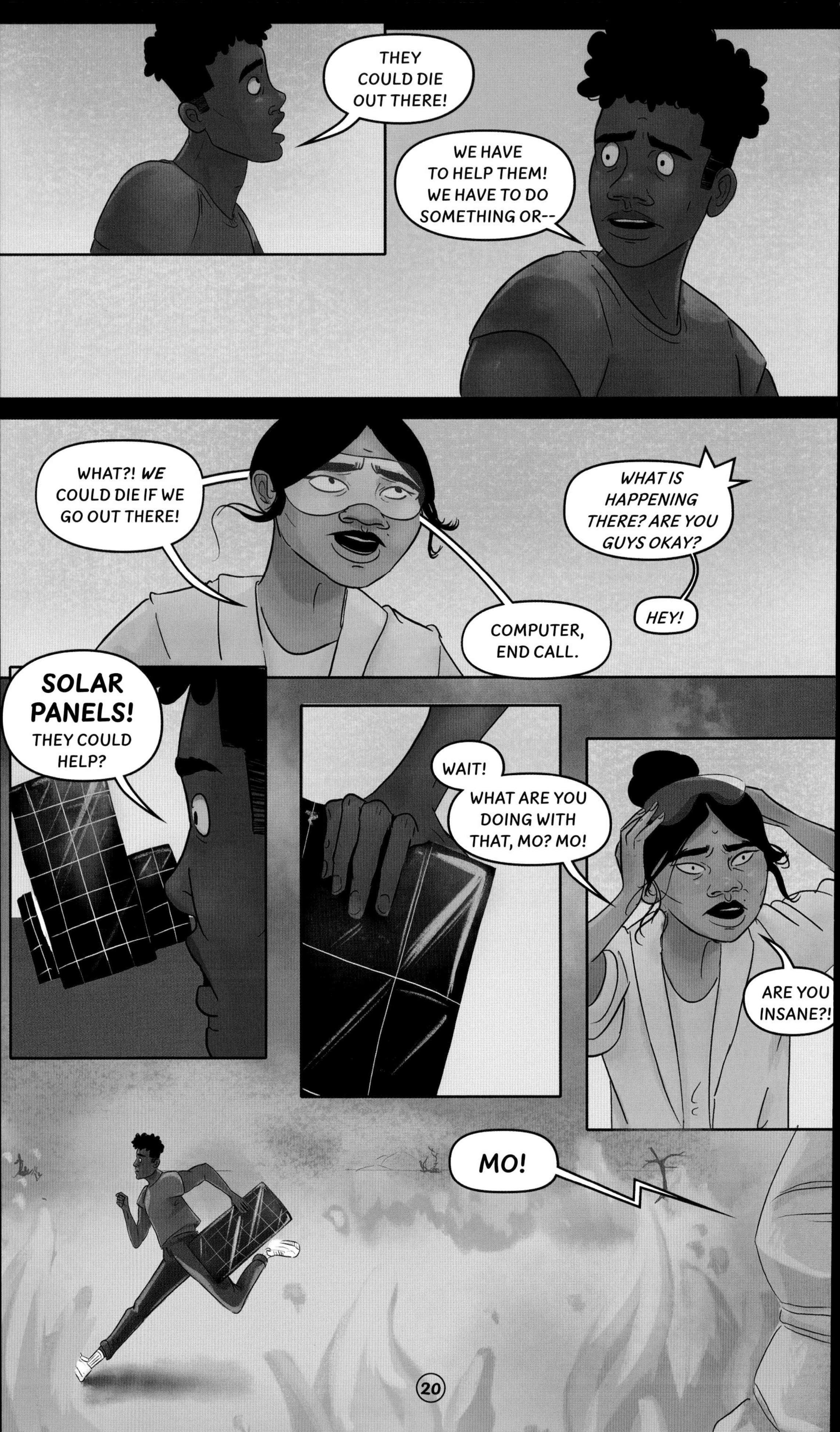

THEY COULD DIE OUT THERE!
WE HAVE TO HELP THEM! WE HAVE TO DO SOMETHING OR--
WHAT?! *WE* COULD DIE IF WE GO OUT THERE!
WHAT IS HAPPENING THERE? ARE YOU GUYS OKAY?
HEY!
COMPUTER, END CALL.
SOLAR PANELS! THEY COULD HELP?
WAIT!
WHAT ARE YOU DOING WITH THAT, MO? MO!
ARE YOU INSANE?!
MO!

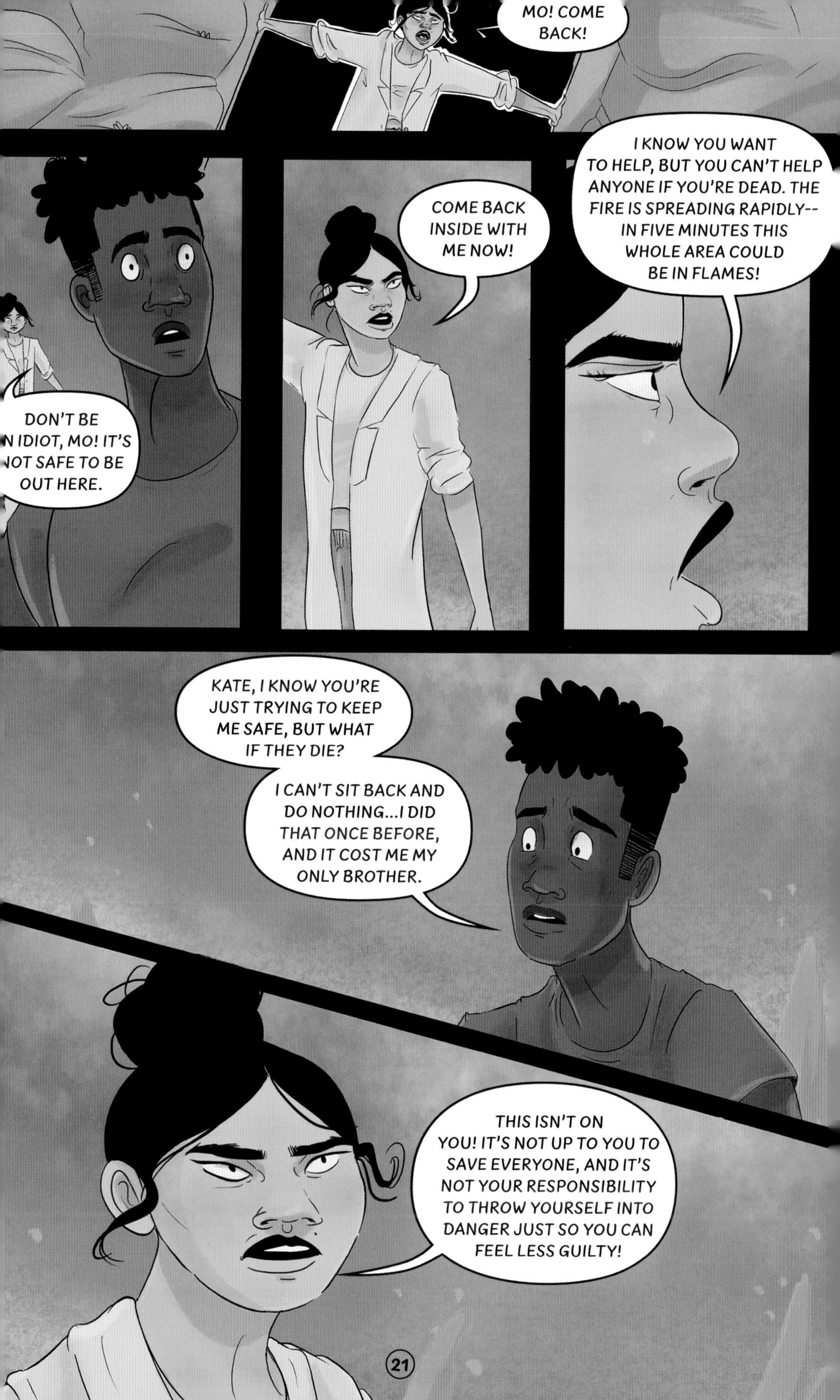
MO! COME BACK!
DON'T BE N IDIOT, MO! IT'S IOT SAFE TO BE OUT HERE.
COME BACK INSIDE WITH ME NOW!
I KNOW YOU WANT TO HELP, BUT YOU CAN'T HELP ANYONE IF YOU'RE DEAD. THE FIRE IS SPREADING RAPIDLY-- IN FIVE MINUTES THIS WHOLE AREA COULD BE IN FLAMES!
KATE, I KNOW YOU'RE JUST TRYING TO KEEP ME SAFE, BUT WHAT IF THEY DIE?
I CAN'T SIT BACK AND DO NOTHING...I DID THAT ONCE BEFORE, AND IT COST ME MY ONLY BROTHER.
THIS ISN'T ON YOU! IT'S NOT UP TO YOU TO SAVE EVERYONE, AND IT'S NOT YOUR RESPONSIBILITY TO THROW YOURSELF INTO DANGER JUST SO YOU CAN FEEL LESS GUILTY!

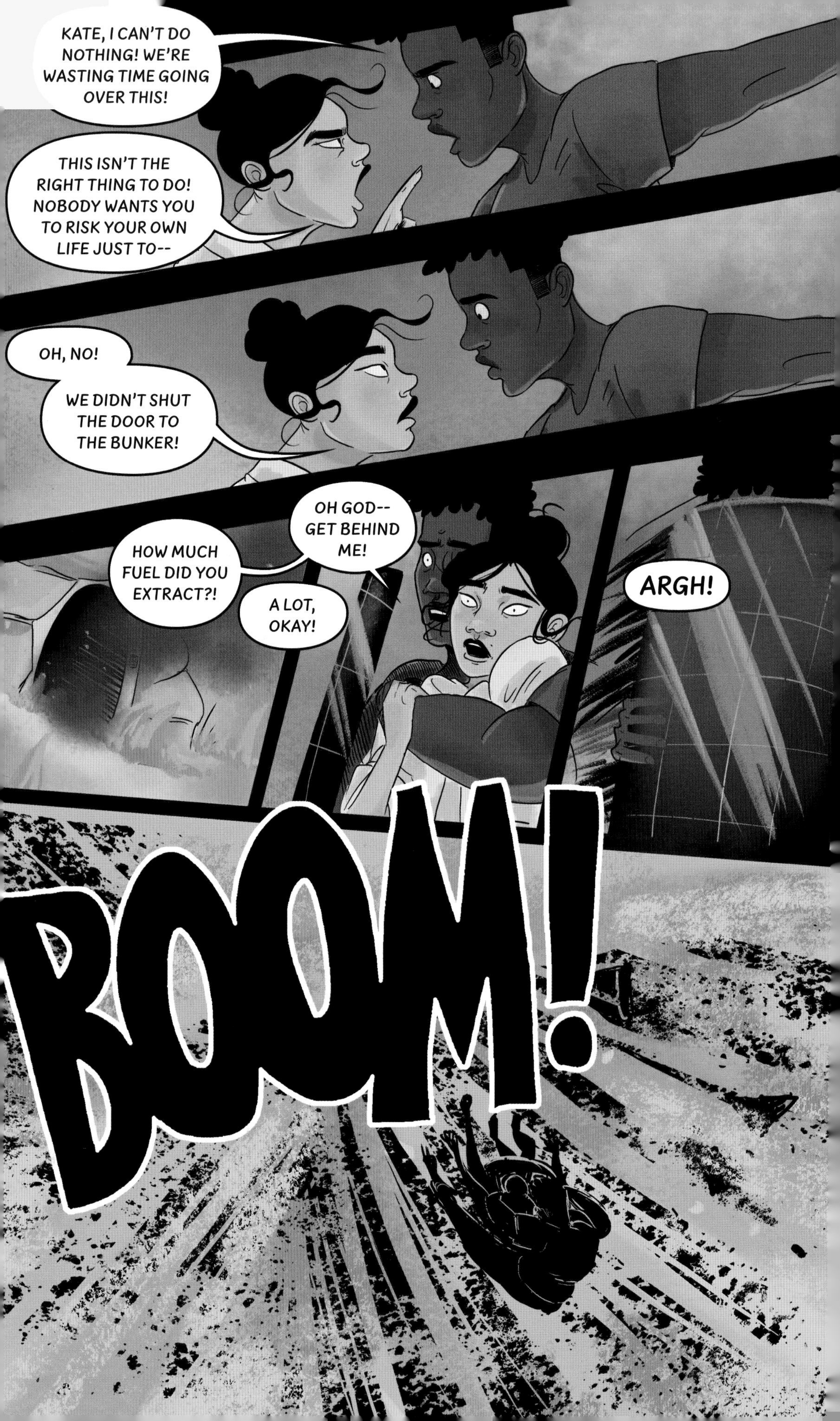
KATE, I CAN'T DO NOTHING! WE'RE WASTING TIME GOING OVER THIS!
THIS ISN'T THE RIGHT THING TO DO! NOBODY WANTS YOU TO RISK YOUR OWN LIFE JUST TO--
OH, NO!
WE DIDN'T SHUT THE DOOR TO THE BUNKER!
HOW MUCH FUEL DID YOU EXTRACT?!
OH GOD-- GET BEHIND ME!
A LOT, OKAY!
ARGH!
BOOM!

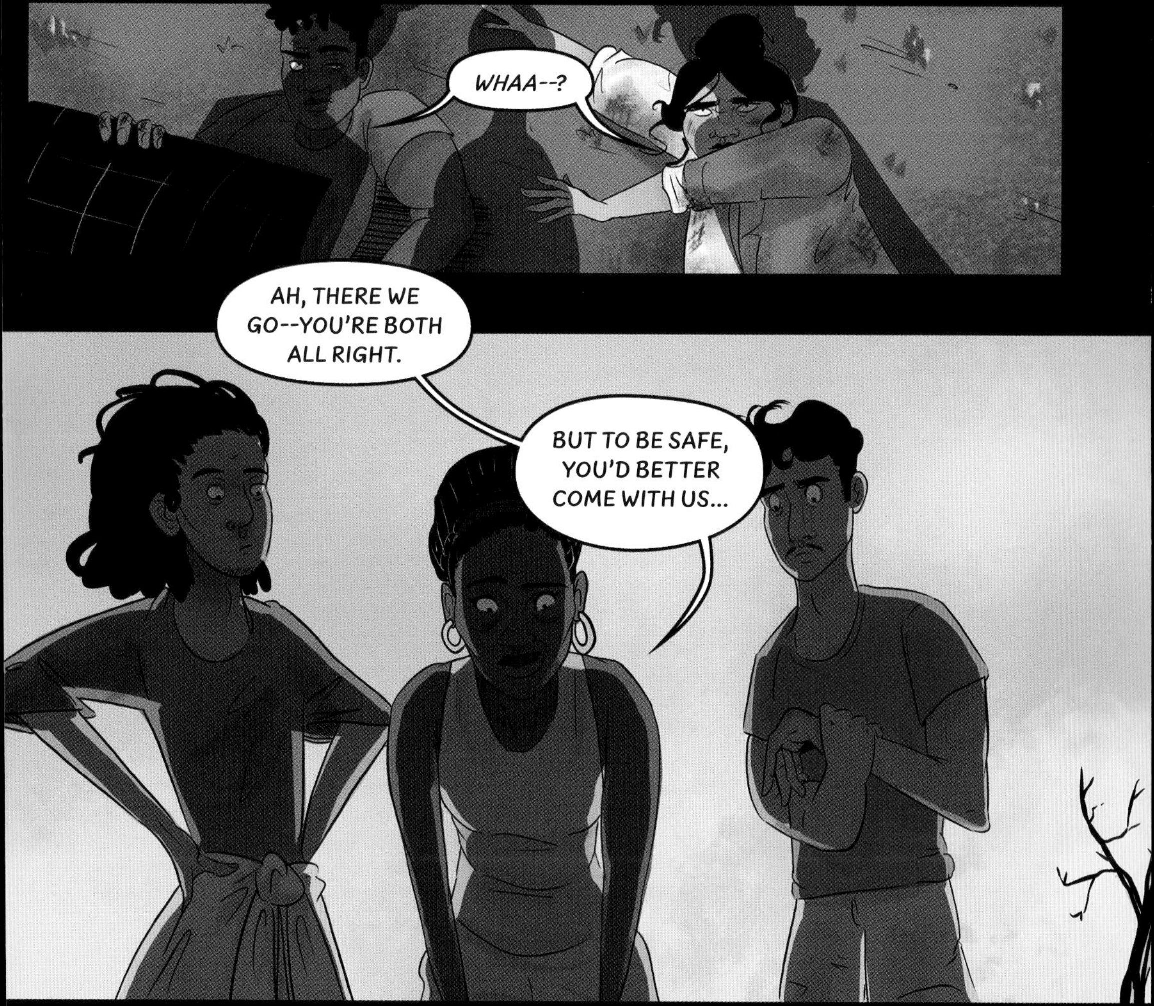
WHAA--?
AH, THERE WE GO--YOU'RE BOTH ALL RIGHT.
BUT TO BE SAFE, YOU'D BETTER COME WITH US...

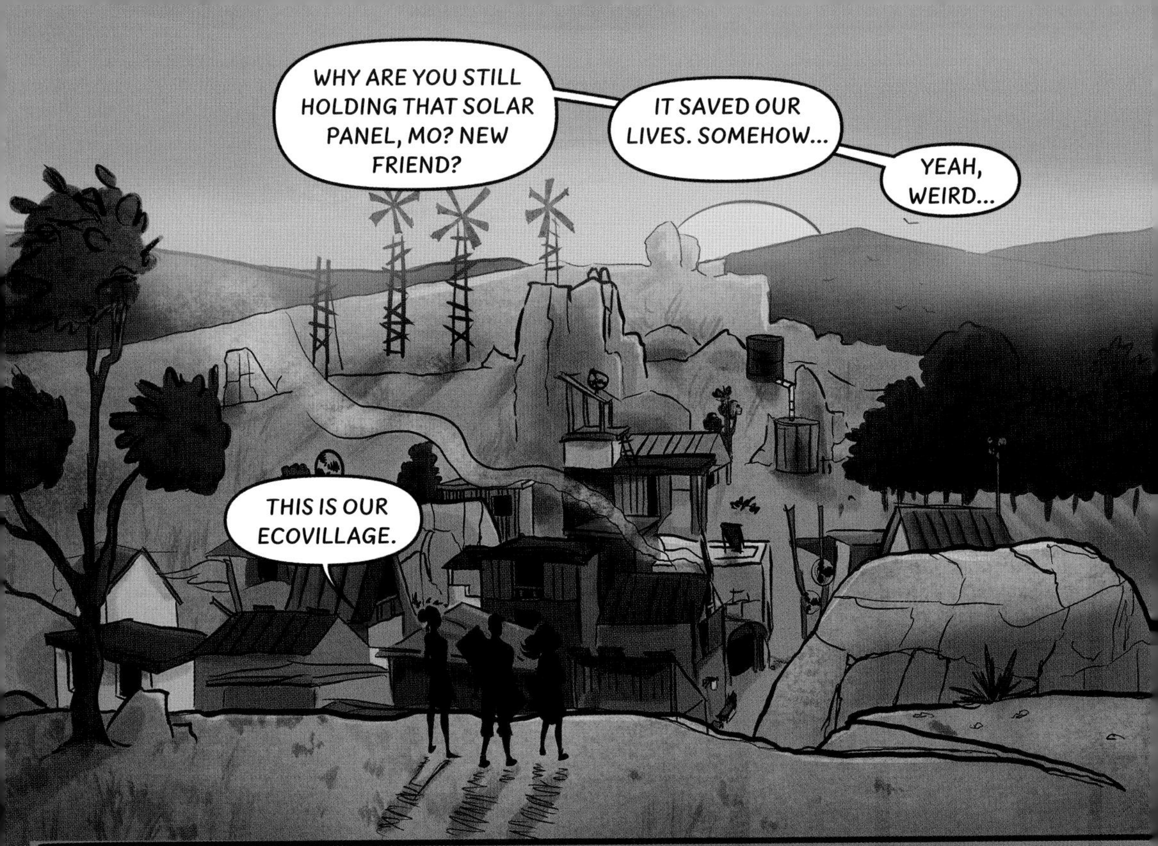
WHY ARE YOU STILL HOLDING THAT SOLAR PANEL, MO? NEW FRIEND?
IT SAVED OUR LIVES. SOMEHOW...
YEAH, WEIRD...
THIS IS OUR ECOVILLAGE.

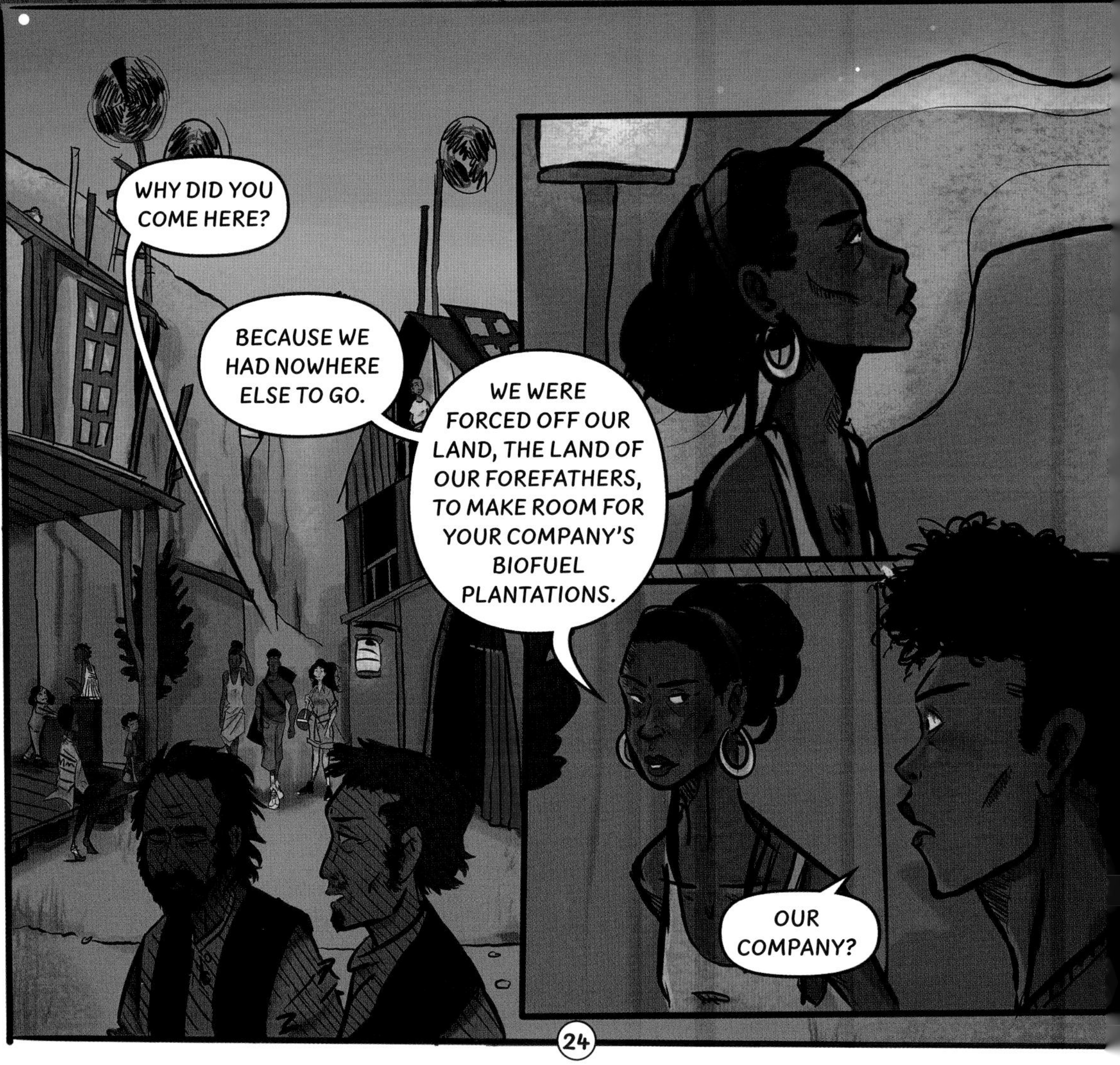
WHY DID YOU COME HERE?
BECAUSE WE HAD NOWHERE ELSE TO GO.
WE WERE FORCED OFF OUR LAND, THE LAND OF OUR FOREFATHERS, TO MAKE ROOM FOR YOUR COMPANY'S BIOFUEL PLANTATIONS.
OUR COMPANY?

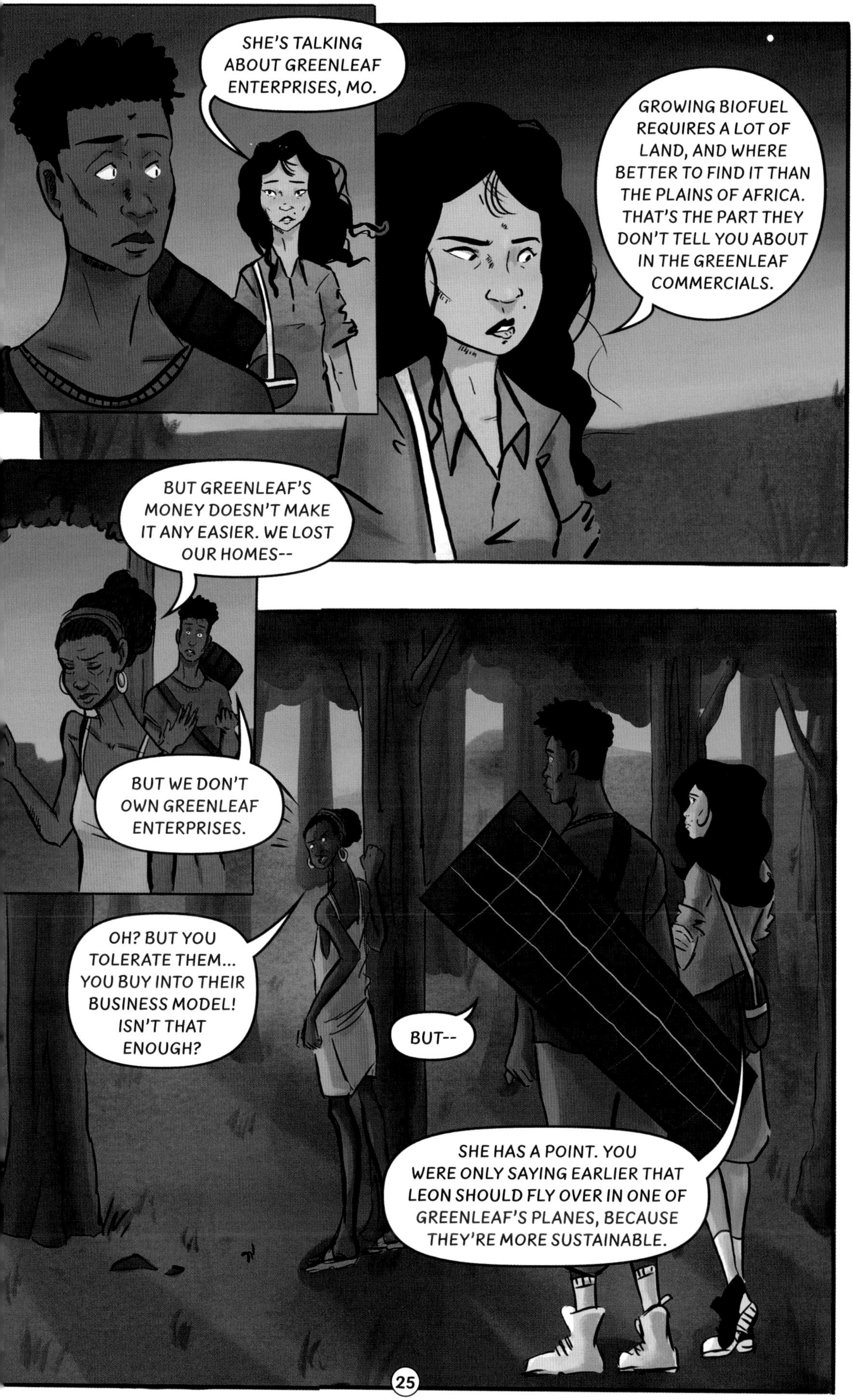

SHE'S TALKING ABOUT GREENLEAF ENTERPRISES, MO.
GROWING BIOFUEL REQUIRES A LOT OF LAND, AND WHERE BETTER TO FIND IT THAN THE PLAINS OF AFRICA. THAT'S THE PART THEY DON'T TELL YOU ABOUT IN THE GREENLEAF COMMERCIALS.
BUT GREENLEAF'S MONEY DOESN'T MAKE IT ANY EASIER. WE LOST OUR HOMES--
BUT WE DON'T OWN GREENLEAF ENTERPRISES.
OH? BUT YOU TOLERATE THEM... YOU BUY INTO THEIR BUSINESS MODEL! ISN'T THAT ENOUGH?
BUT--
SHE HAS A POINT. YOU WERE ONLY SAYING EARLIER THAT LEON SHOULD FLY OVER IN ONE OF GREENLEAF'S PLANES, BECAUSE THEY'RE MORE SUSTAINABLE.

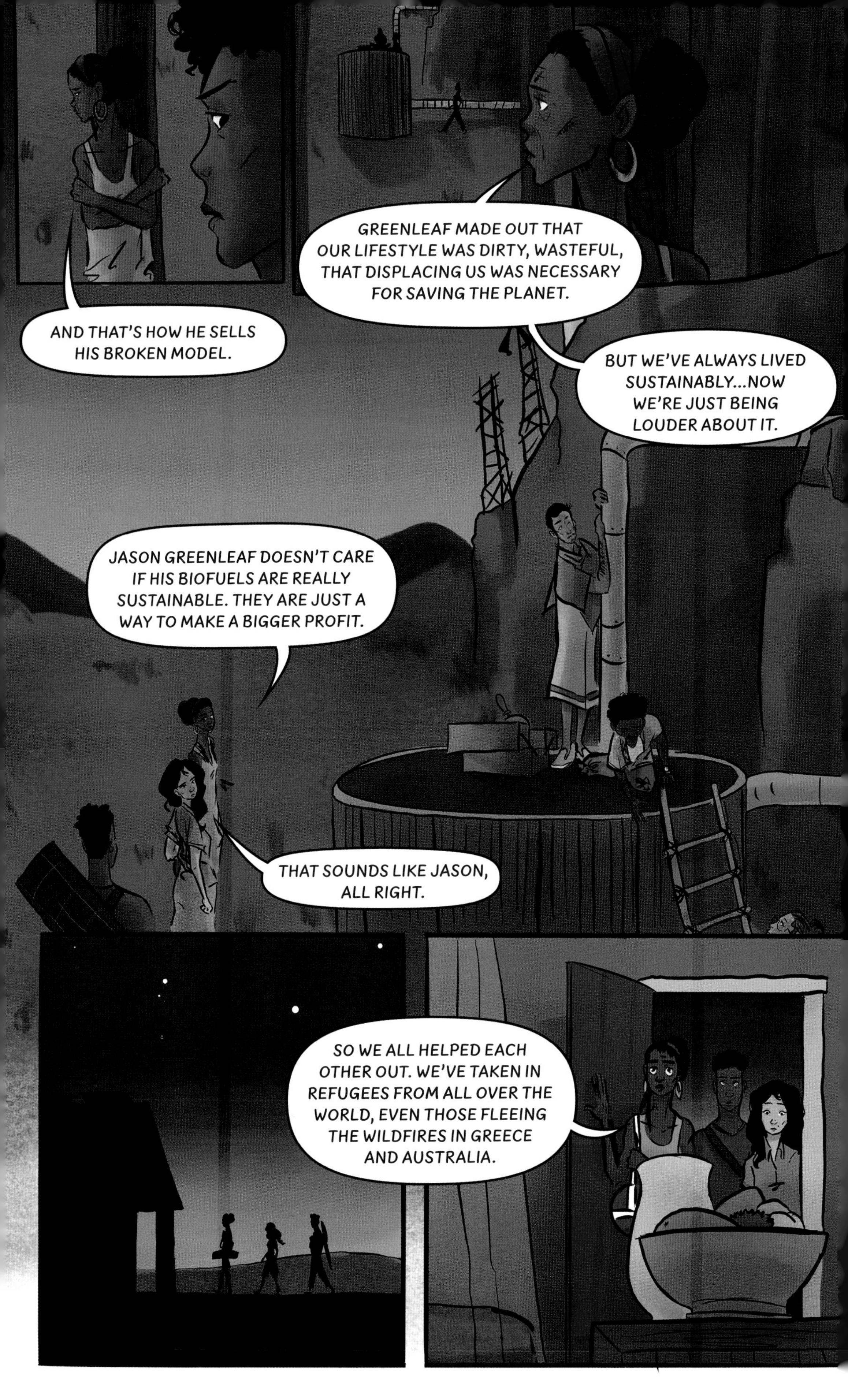
AND THAT'S HOW HE SELLS HIS BROKEN MODEL.
GREENLEAF MADE OUT THAT OUR LIFESTYLE WAS DIRTY, WASTEFUL, THAT DISPLACING US WAS NECESSARY FOR SAVING THE PLANET.
BUT WE'VE ALWAYS LIVED SUSTAINABLY...NOW WE'RE JUST BEING LOUDER ABOUT IT.
JASON GREENLEAF DOESN'T CARE IF HIS BIOFUELS ARE REALLY SUSTAINABLE. THEY ARE JUST A WAY TO MAKE A BIGGER PROFIT.
THAT SOUNDS LIKE JASON, ALL RIGHT.
SO WE ALL HELPED EACH OTHER OUT. WE'VE TAKEN IN REFUGEES FROM ALL OVER THE WORLD, EVEN THOSE FLEEING THE WILDFIRES IN GREECE AND AUSTRALIA.

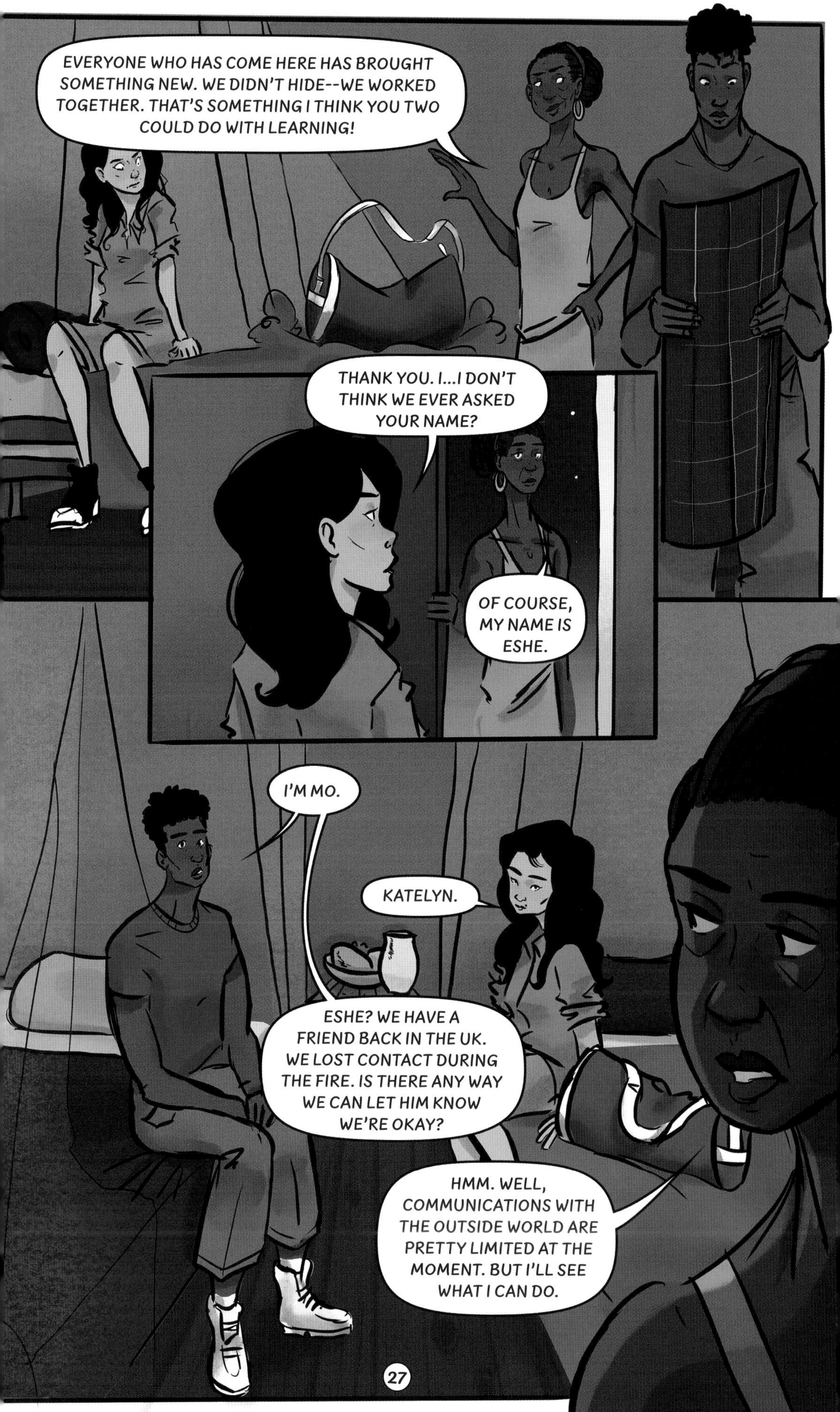
EVERYONE WHO HAS COME HERE HAS BROUGHT SOMETHING NEW. WE DIDN'T HIDE--WE WORKED TOGETHER. THAT'S SOMETHING I THINK YOU TWO COULD DO WITH LEARNING!
THANK YOU. I...I DON'T THINK WE EVER ASKED YOUR NAME?
OF COURSE, MY NAME IS ESHE.
I'M MO.
KATELYN.
ESHE? WE HAVE A FRIEND BACK IN THE UK. WE LOST CONTACT DURING THE FIRE. IS THERE ANY WAY WE CAN LET HIM KNOW WE'RE OKAY?
HMM. WELL, COMMUNICATIONS WITH THE OUTSIDE WORLD ARE PRETTY LIMITED AT THE MOMENT. BUT I'LL SEE WHAT I CAN DO.

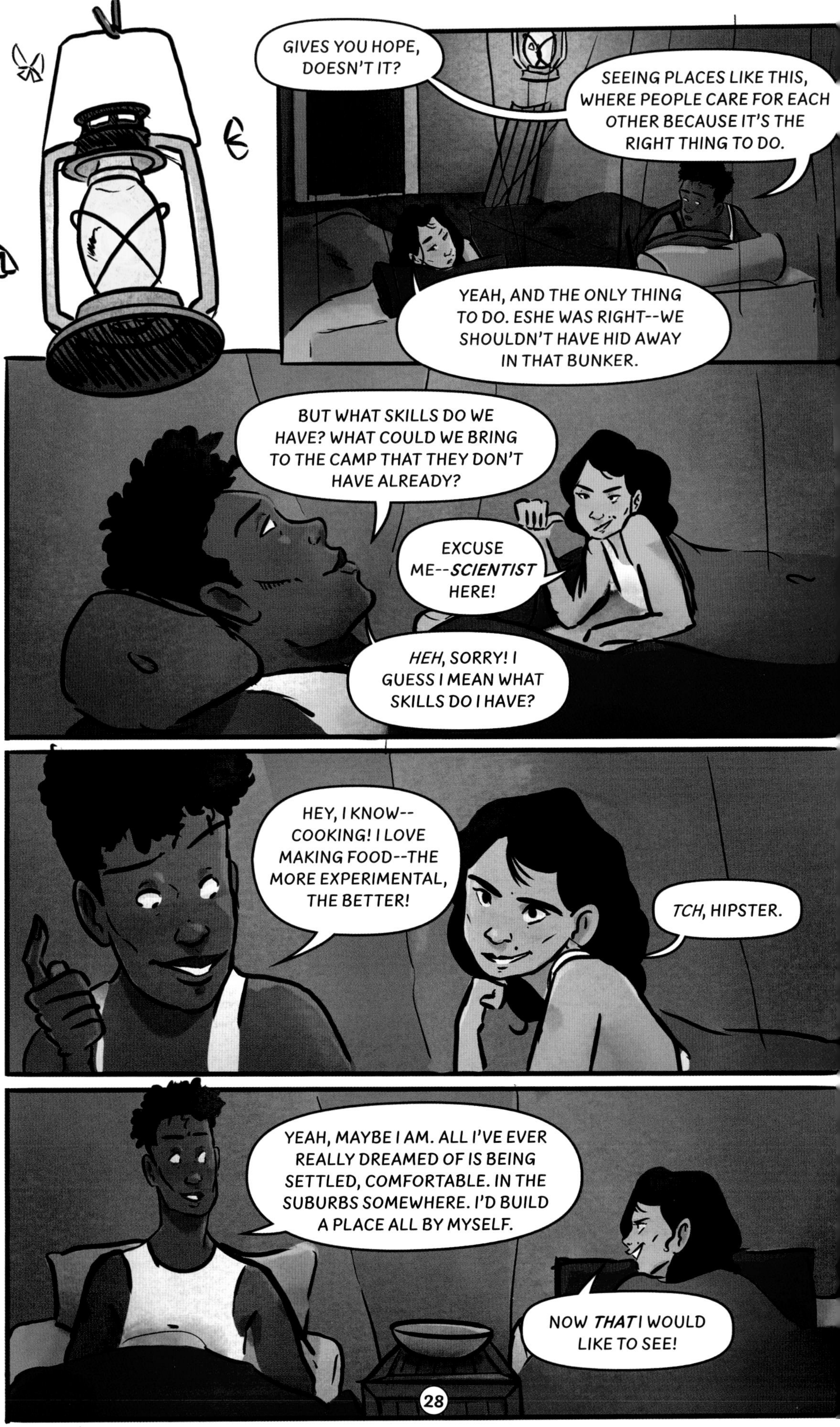
GIVES YOU HOPE, DOESN'T IT?
SEEING PLACES LIKE THIS, WHERE PEOPLE CARE FOR EACH OTHER BECAUSE IT'S THE RIGHT THING TO DO.
YEAH, AND THE ONLY THING TO DO. ESHE WAS RIGHT--WE SHOULDN'T HAVE HID AWAY IN THAT BUNKER.
BUT WHAT SKILLS DO WE HAVE? WHAT COULD WE BRING TO THE CAMP THAT THEY DON'T HAVE ALREADY?
EXCUSE ME--*SCIENTIST* HERE!
HEH, SORRY! I GUESS I MEAN WHAT SKILLS DO I HAVE?
HEY, I KNOW--COOKING! I LOVE MAKING FOOD--THE MORE EXPERIMENTAL, THE BETTER!
TCH, HIPSTER.
YEAH, MAYBE I AM. ALL I'VE EVER REALLY DREAMED OF IS BEING SETTLED, COMFORTABLE. IN THE SUBURBS SOMEWHERE. I'D BUILD A PLACE ALL BY MYSELF.
NOW *THAT* I WOULD LIKE TO SEE!

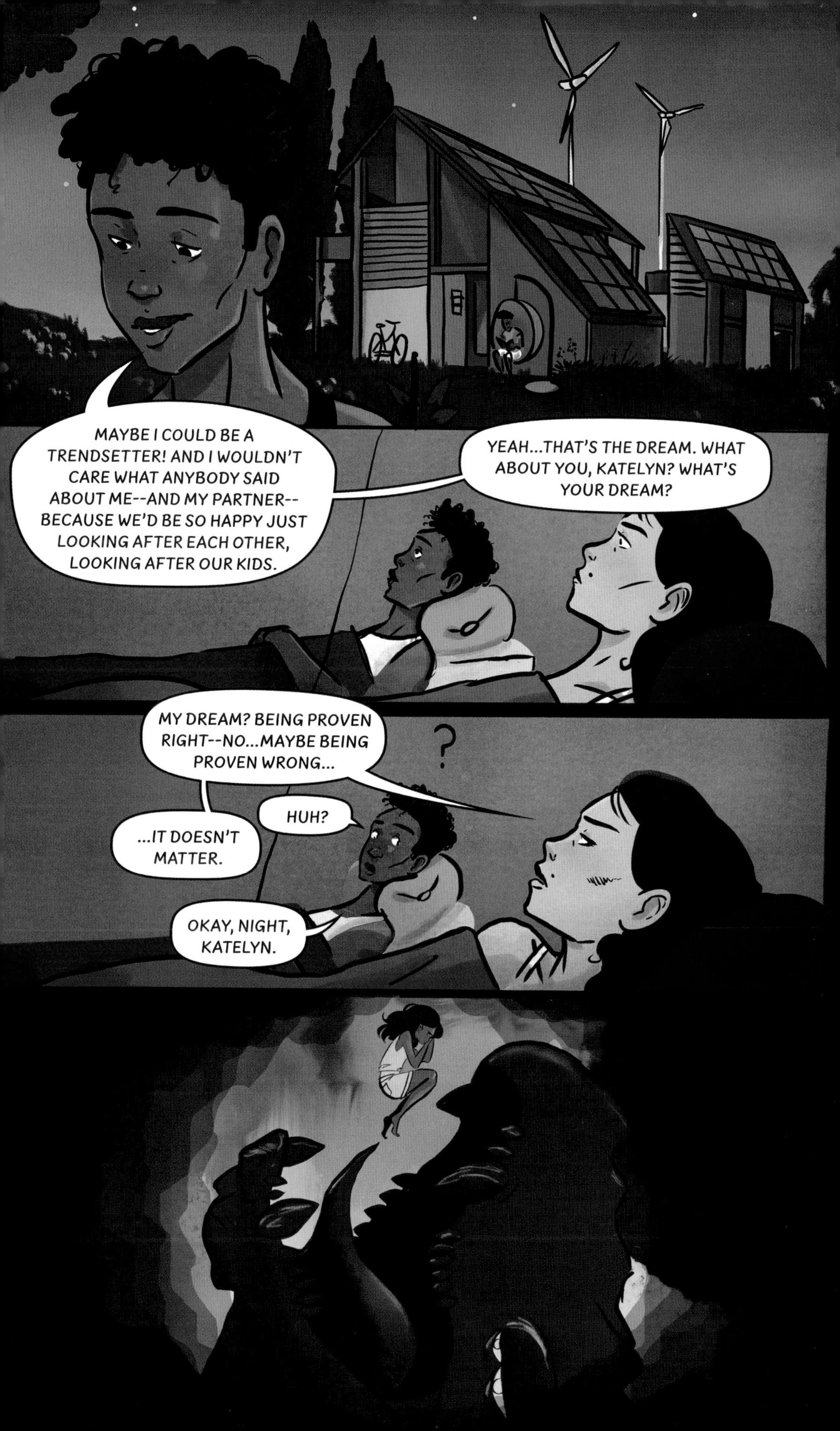

MAYBE I COULD BE A TRENDSETTER! AND I WOULDN'T CARE WHAT ANYBODY SAID ABOUT ME--AND MY PARTNER--BECAUSE WE'D BE SO HAPPY JUST LOOKING AFTER EACH OTHER, LOOKING AFTER OUR KIDS.
YEAH...THAT'S THE DREAM. WHAT ABOUT YOU, KATELYN? WHAT'S YOUR DREAM?
MY DREAM? BEING PROVEN RIGHT--NO...MAYBE BEING PROVEN WRONG...
?
...IT DOESN'T MATTER.
HUH?
OKAY, NIGHT, KATELYN.

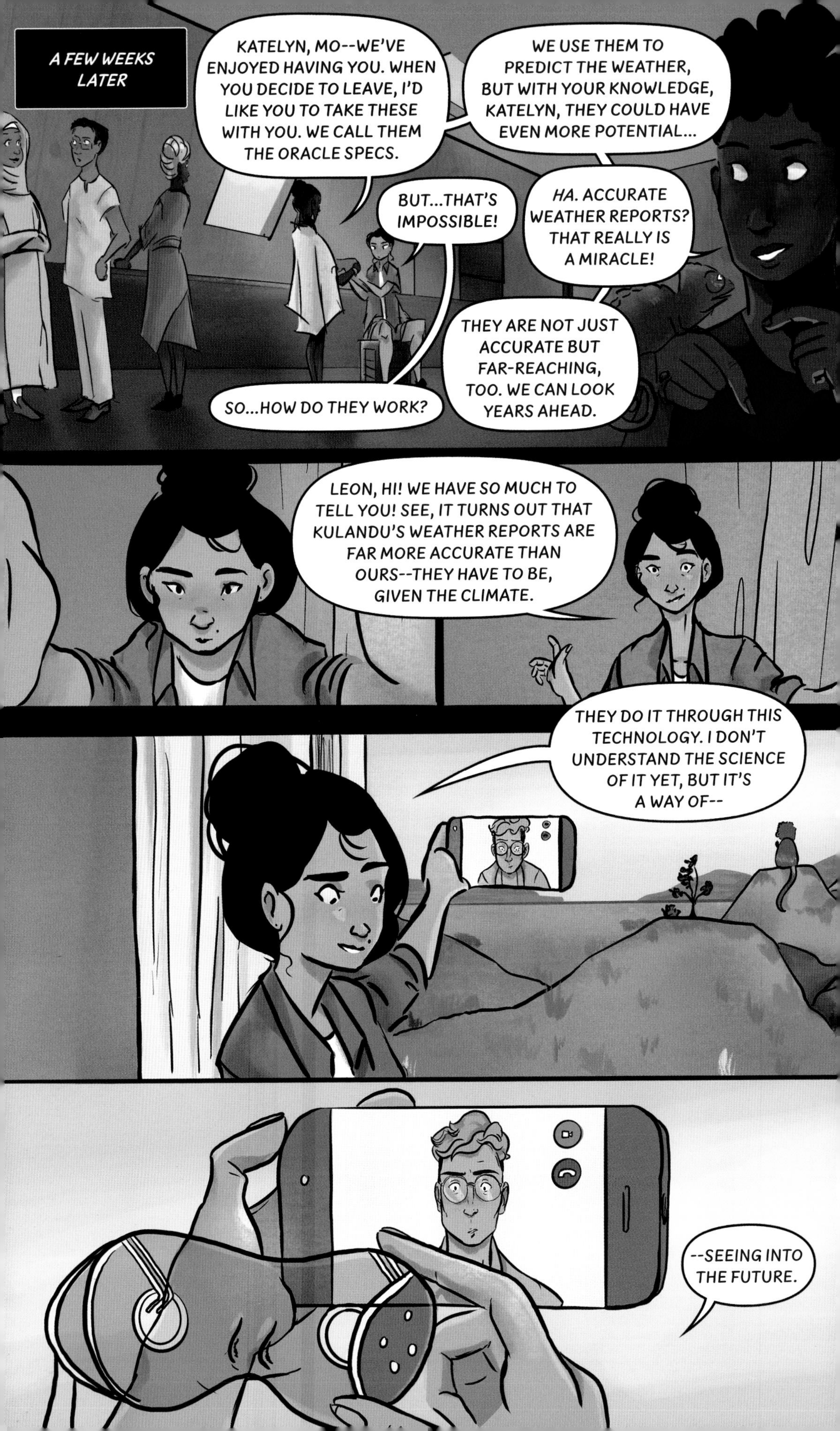
A FEW WEEKS LATER
KATELYN, MO--WE'VE ENJOYED HAVING YOU. WHEN YOU DECIDE TO LEAVE, I'D LIKE YOU TO TAKE THESE WITH YOU. WE CALL THEM THE ORACLE SPECS.
WE USE THEM TO PREDICT THE WEATHER, BUT WITH YOUR KNOWLEDGE, KATELYN, THEY COULD HAVE EVEN MORE POTENTIAL...
BUT...THAT'S IMPOSSIBLE!
HA. ACCURATE WEATHER REPORTS? THAT REALLY IS A MIRACLE!
THEY ARE NOT JUST ACCURATE BUT FAR-REACHING, TOO. WE CAN LOOK YEARS AHEAD.
SO...HOW DO THEY WORK?
LEON, HI! WE HAVE SO MUCH TO TELL YOU! SEE, IT TURNS OUT THAT KULANDU'S WEATHER REPORTS ARE FAR MORE ACCURATE THAN OURS--THEY HAVE TO BE, GIVEN THE CLIMATE.
THEY DO IT THROUGH THIS TECHNOLOGY. I DON'T UNDERSTAND THE SCIENCE OF IT YET, BUT IT'S A WAY OF--
--SEEING INTO THE FUTURE.

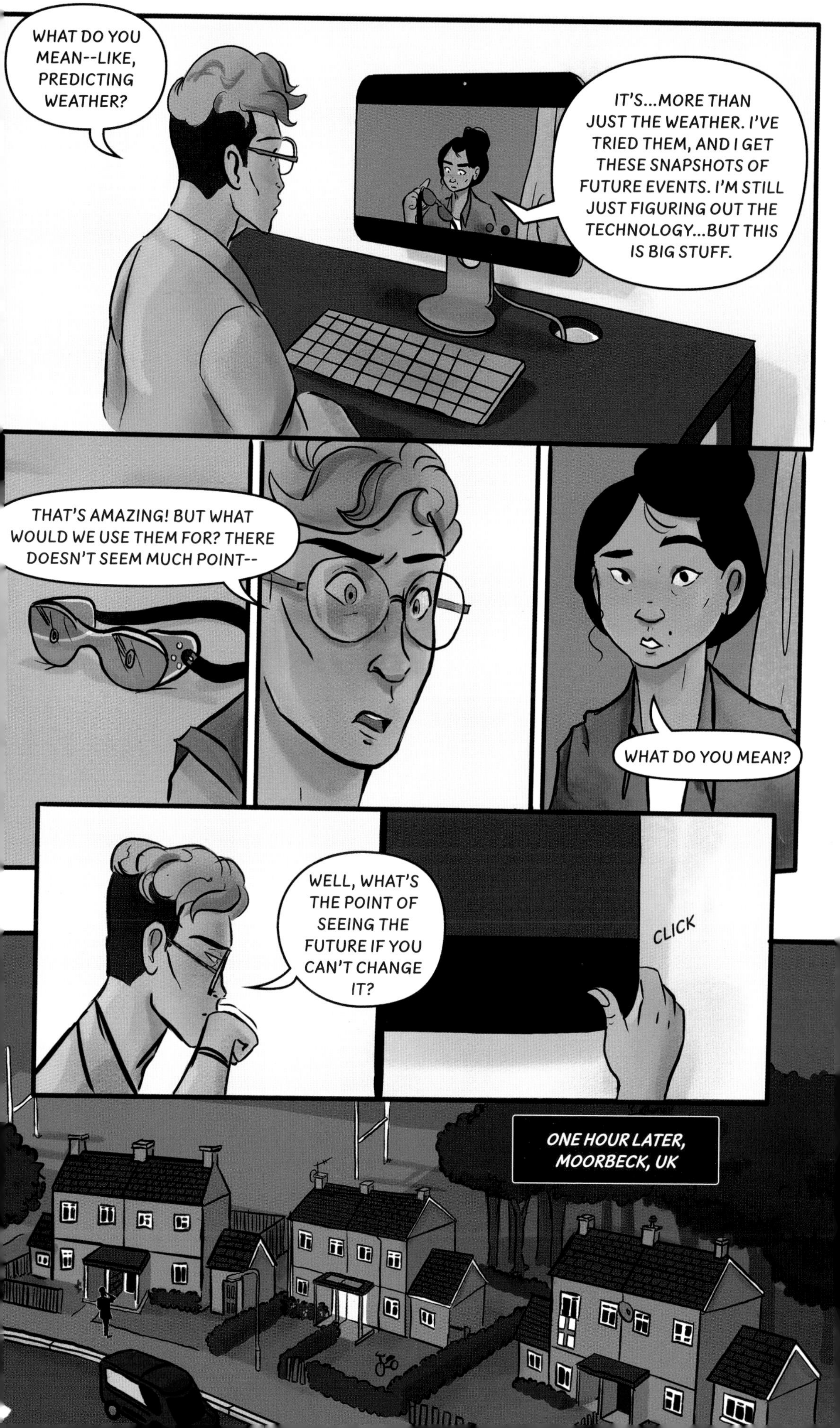
WHAT DO YOU MEAN--LIKE, PREDICTING WEATHER?
IT'S...MORE THAN JUST THE WEATHER. I'VE TRIED THEM, AND I GET THESE SNAPSHOTS OF FUTURE EVENTS. I'M STILL JUST FIGURING OUT THE TECHNOLOGY...BUT THIS IS BIG STUFF.
THAT'S AMAZING! BUT WHAT WOULD WE USE THEM FOR? THERE DOESN'T SEEM MUCH POINT--
WHAT DO YOU MEAN?
WELL, WHAT'S THE POINT OF SEEING THE FUTURE IF YOU CAN'T CHANGE IT?
CLICK
ONE HOUR LATER, MOORBECK, UK

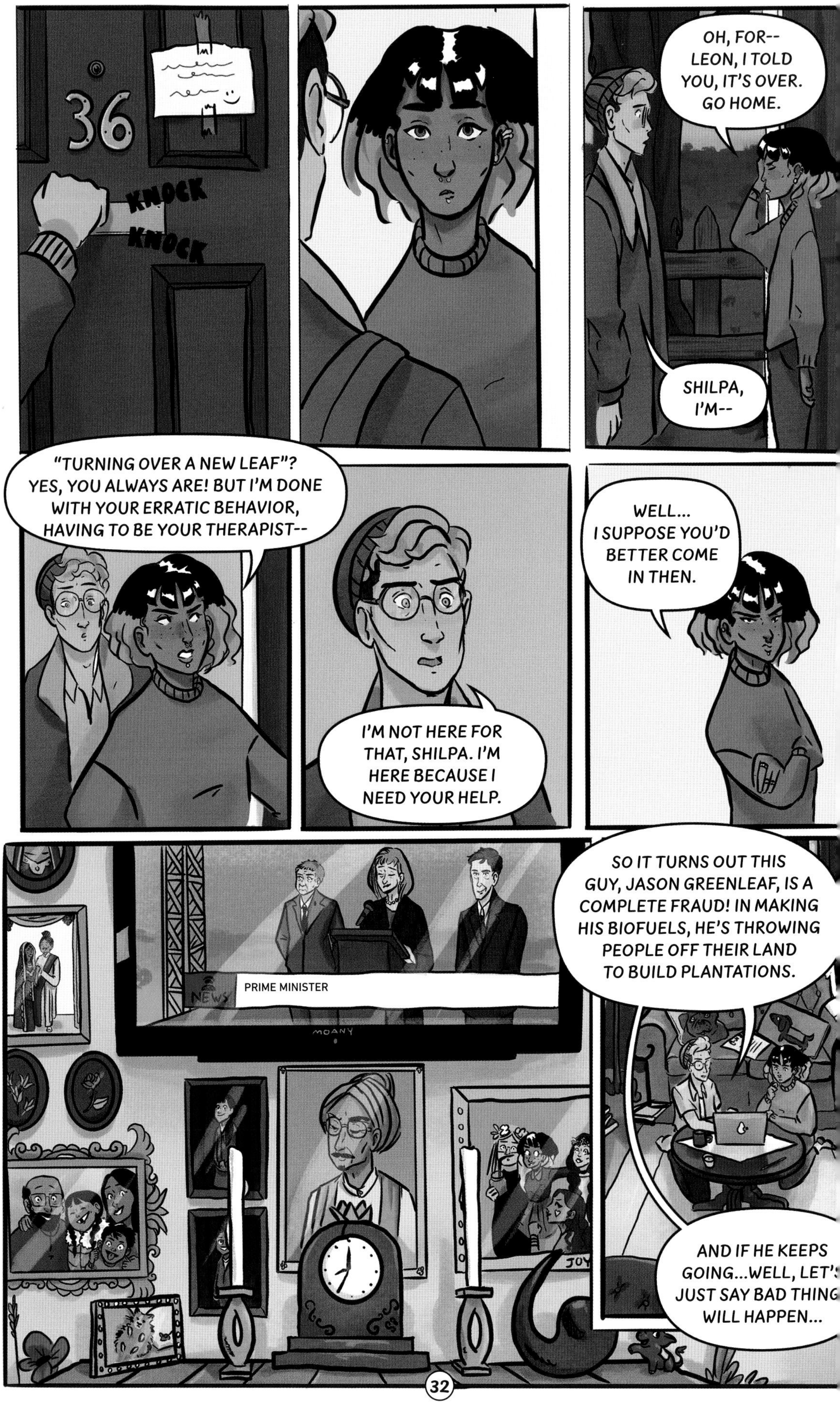
36
KNOCK
KNOCK
OH, FOR-- LEON, I TOLD YOU, IT'S OVER. GO HOME.
SHILPA, I'M--
"TURNING OVER A NEW LEAF"? YES, YOU ALWAYS ARE! BUT I'M DONE WITH YOUR ERRATIC BEHAVIOR, HAVING TO BE YOUR THERAPIST--
I'M NOT HERE FOR THAT, SHILPA. I'M HERE BECAUSE I NEED YOUR HELP.
WELL... I SUPPOSE YOU'D BETTER COME IN THEN.
NEWS
PRIME MINISTER
MOANY
SO IT TURNS OUT THIS GUY, JASON GREENLEAF, IS A COMPLETE FRAUD! IN MAKING HIS BIOFUELS, HE'S THROWING PEOPLE OFF THEIR LAND TO BUILD PLANTATIONS.
AND IF HE KEEPS GOING...WELL, LET'S JUST SAY BAD THINGS WILL HAPPEN...
JOY

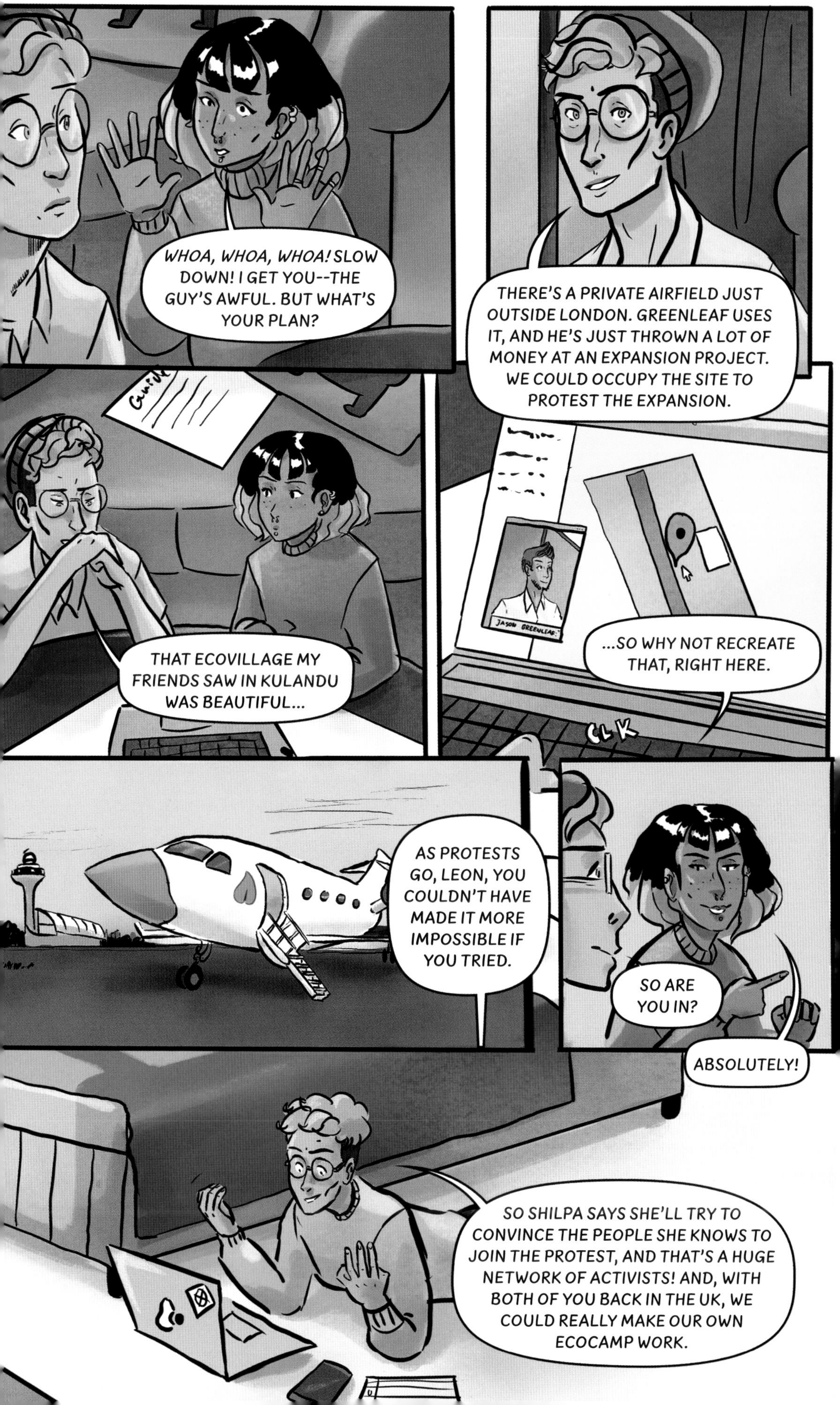
WHOA, WHOA, WHOA! SLOW DOWN! I GET YOU--THE GUY'S AWFUL. BUT WHAT'S YOUR PLAN?
THERE'S A PRIVATE AIRFIELD JUST OUTSIDE LONDON. GREENLEAF USES IT, AND HE'S JUST THROWN A LOT OF MONEY AT AN EXPANSION PROJECT. WE COULD OCCUPY THE SITE TO PROTEST THE EXPANSION.
THAT ECOVILLAGE MY FRIENDS SAW IN KULANDU WAS BEAUTIFUL...
JASON GREENLEAF
...SO WHY NOT RECREATE THAT, RIGHT HERE.
CLK
AS PROTESTS GO, LEON, YOU COULDN'T HAVE MADE IT MORE IMPOSSIBLE IF YOU TRIED.
SO ARE YOU IN?
ABSOLUTELY!
SO SHILPA SAYS SHE'LL TRY TO CONVINCE THE PEOPLE SHE KNOWS TO JOIN THE PROTEST, AND THAT'S A HUGE NETWORK OF ACTIVISTS! AND, WITH BOTH OF YOU BACK IN THE UK, WE COULD REALLY MAKE OUR OWN ECOCAMP WORK.

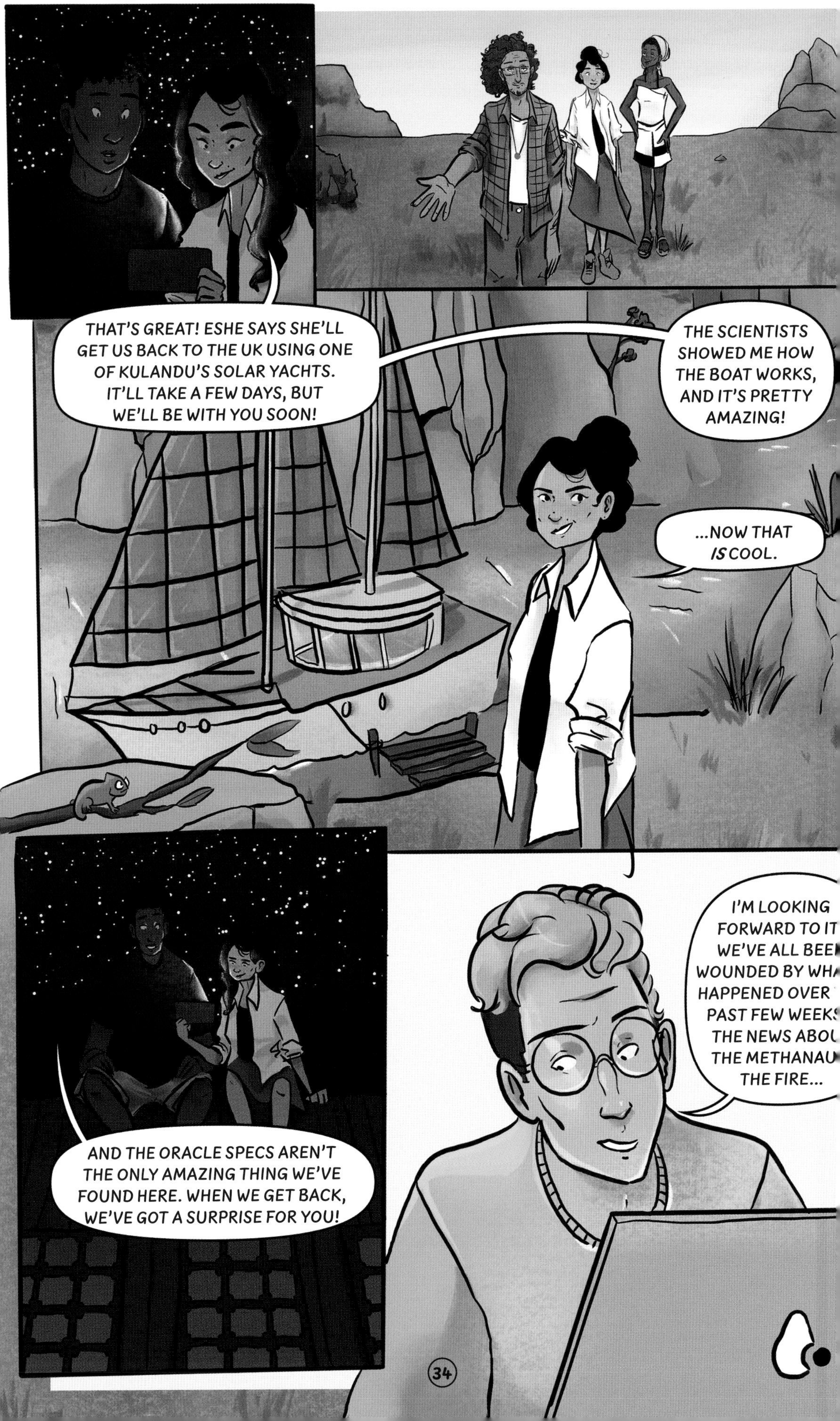
THAT'S GREAT! ESHE SAYS SHE'LL GET US BACK TO THE UK USING ONE OF KULANDU'S SOLAR YACHTS. IT'LL TAKE A FEW DAYS, BUT WE'LL BE WITH YOU SOON!
THE SCIENTISTS SHOWED ME HOW THE BOAT WORKS, AND IT'S PRETTY AMAZING!
...NOW THAT *IS* COOL.
AND THE ORACLE SPECS AREN'T THE ONLY AMAZING THING WE'VE FOUND HERE. WHEN WE GET BACK, WE'VE GOT A SURPRISE FOR YOU!
I'M LOOKING FORWARD TO IT WE'VE ALL BEE WOUNDED BY WHA HAPPENED OVER PAST FEW WEEK THE NEWS ABO THE METHANAU THE FIRE...

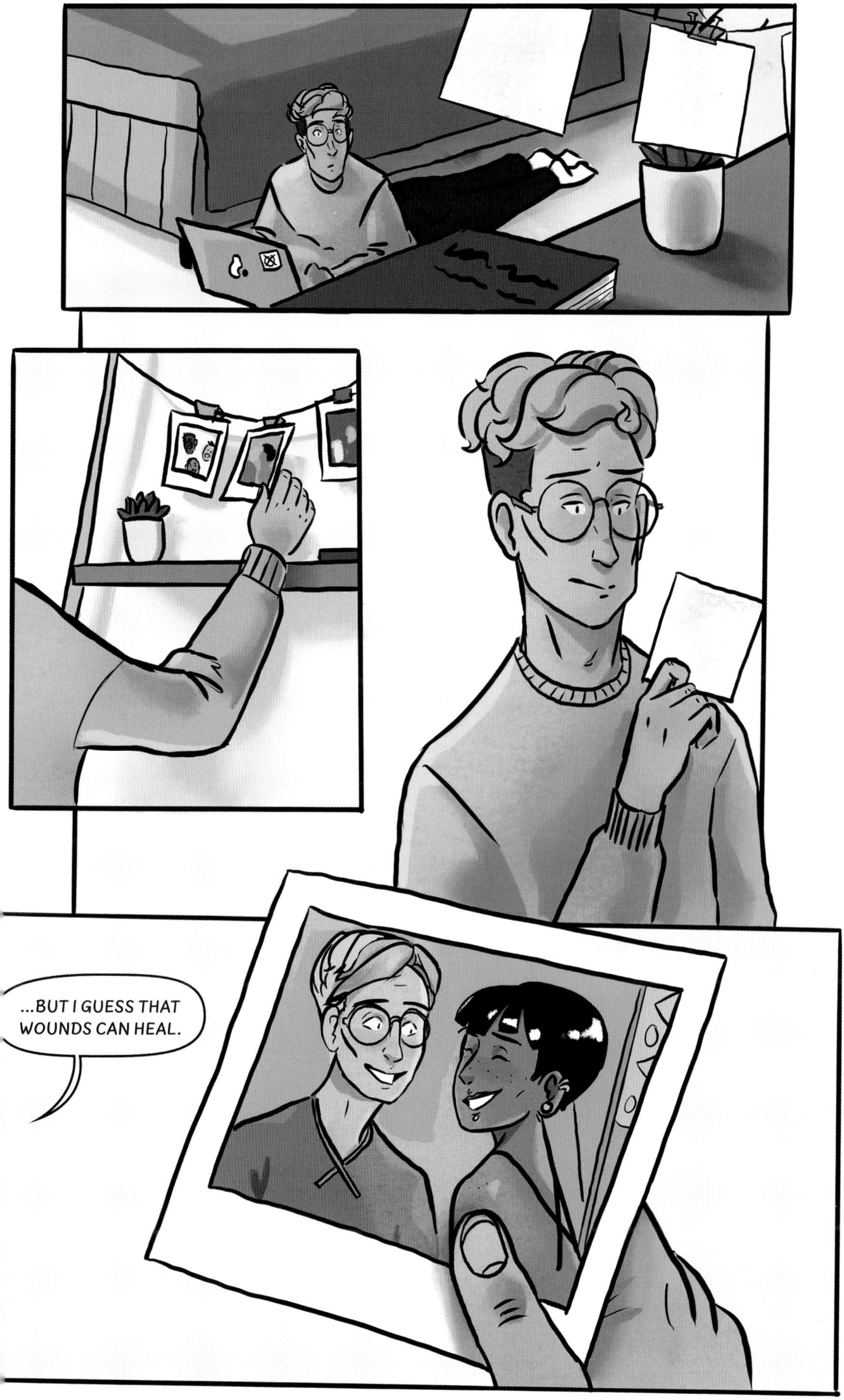
...BUT I GUESS THAT WOUNDS CAN HEAL.

EXCITED TO GET BACK HOME, MO?

OH, SURE. I'VE BEEN GETTING BORED OF ALL THE HOT WEATHER AND STUNNING WILDLIFE ANYWAY...

LONDON, UNOFFICIAL APOCO-FEAR ANONYMOUS MEETING

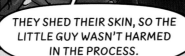

SO WHILE WE WERE IN KULANDU, WE EXTRACTED THE DNA OF A NATIVE SPECIES OF CHAMELEON.

THEY SHED THEIR SKIN, SO THE LITTLE GUY WASN'T HARMED IN THE PROCESS.

HAVE YOU EVER LOOKED AT A CHAMELEON AND THOUGHT, "THAT WOULD BE AWESOME"-- BLENDING IN TO YOUR ENVIRONMENT AT WILL?

WEIRDLY, NO.

WELL, NOW YOU CAN--CATCH!

OF ALL THE SUPERPOWERS I COULD CHOOSE...INVISIBILITY ISN'T THE ONE I'D GO FOR.

YOU ALWAYS WERE VERY STUCK IN YOU WAYS.

AND THIS ISN'T ABOUT YOU LIVING YOUR FANTASY. IT'S ABOUT YOU--WELL, ALL OF US--LEARNING SOMETHING, TRYING TO DO WHAT WE CAN... MAYBE NOT BEING SO STUBBORN.

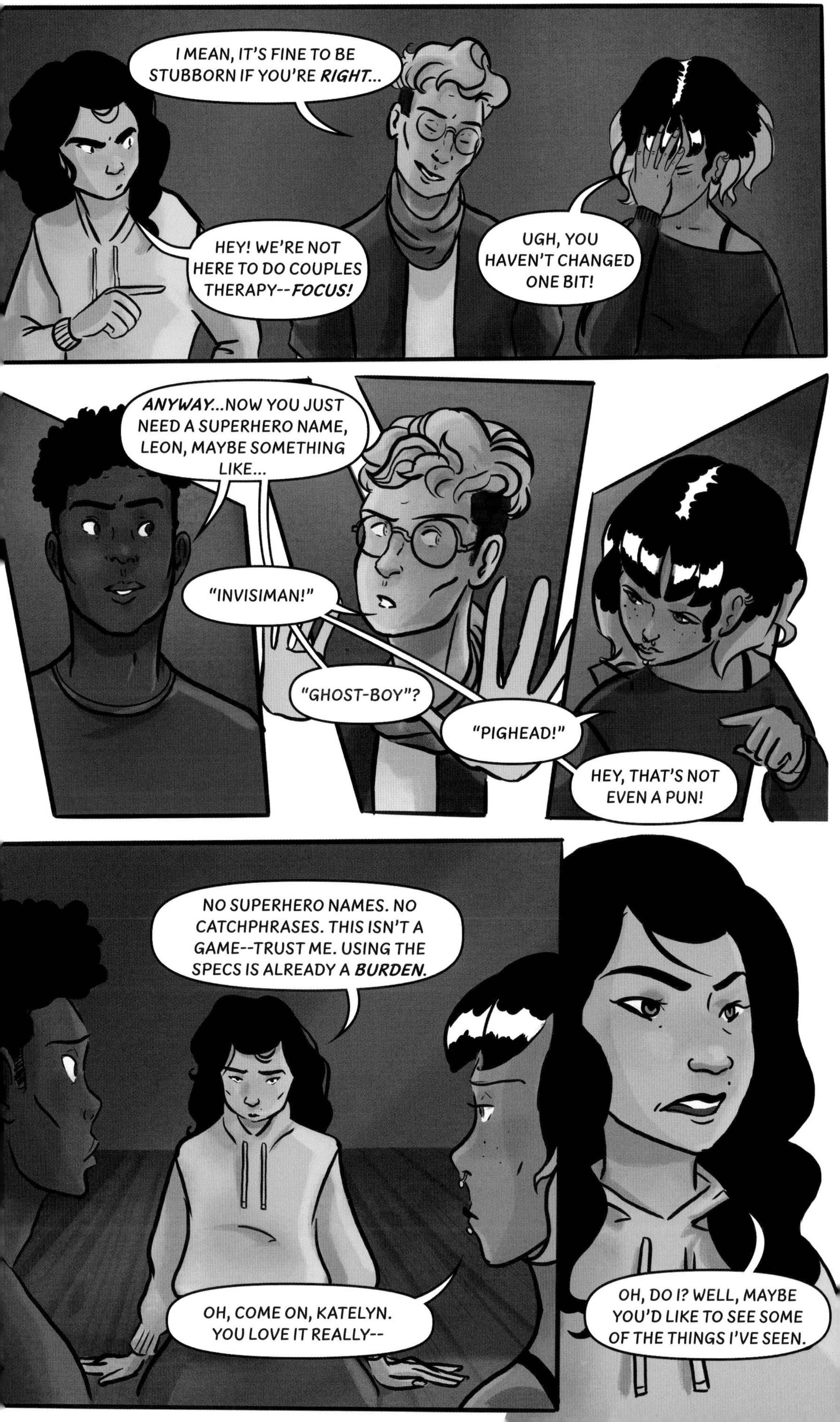
I MEAN, IT'S FINE TO BE STUBBORN IF YOU'RE *RIGHT*...
HEY! WE'RE NOT HERE TO DO COUPLES THERAPY--*FOCUS!*
UGH, YOU HAVEN'T CHANGED ONE BIT!
ANYWAY...NOW YOU JUST NEED A SUPERHERO NAME, LEON, MAYBE SOMETHING LIKE...
"INVISIMAN!"
"GHOST-BOY"?
"PIGHEAD!"
HEY, THAT'S NOT EVEN A PUN!
NO SUPERHERO NAMES. NO CATCHPHRASES. THIS ISN'T A GAME--TRUST ME. USING THE SPECS IS ALREADY A *BURDEN*.
OH, COME ON, KATELYN. YOU LOVE IT REALLY--
OH, DO I? WELL, MAYBE YOU'D LIKE TO SEE SOME OF THE THINGS I'VE SEEN.

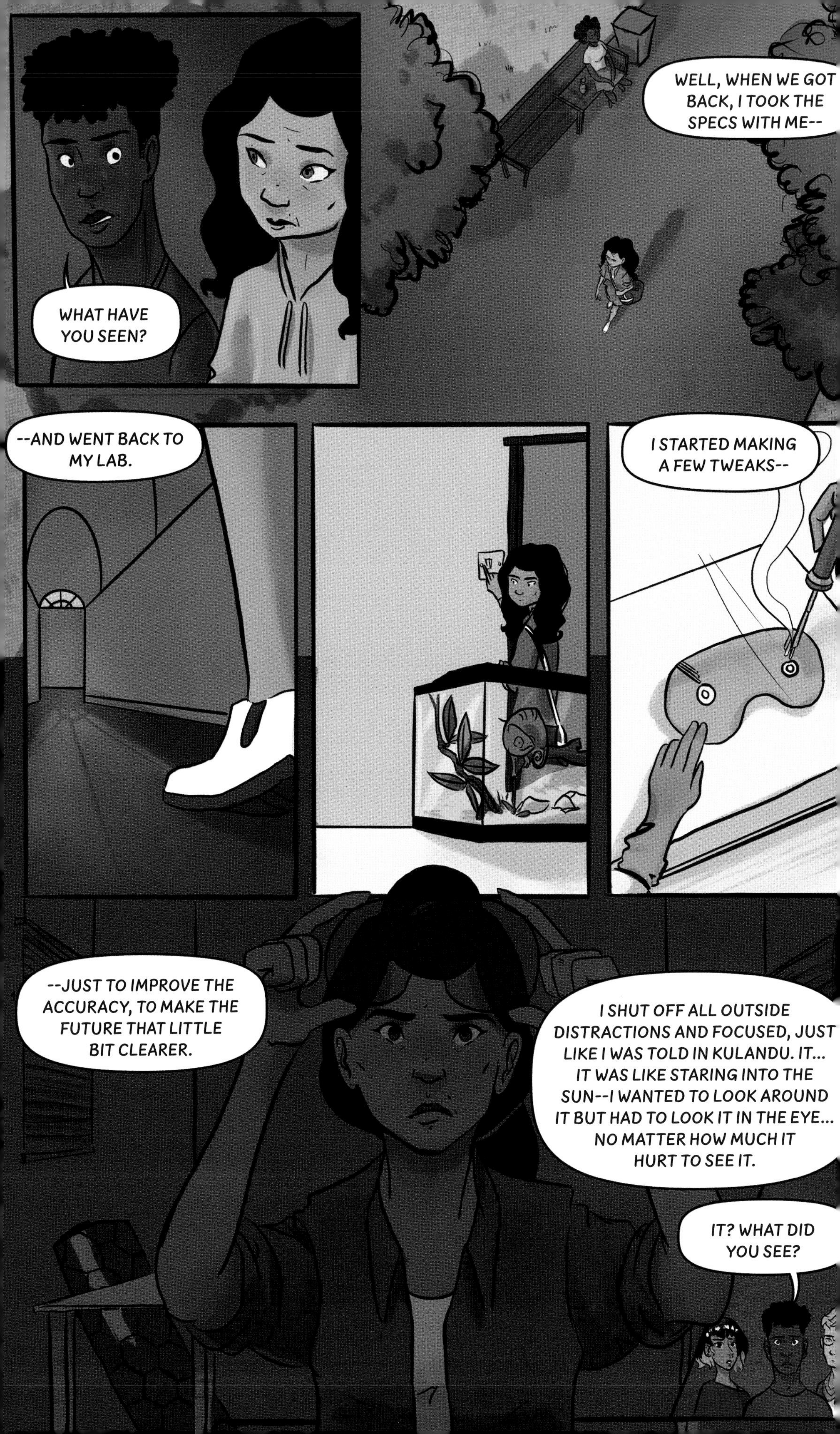
WHAT HAVE YOU SEEN?
WELL, WHEN WE GOT BACK, I TOOK THE SPECS WITH ME--
--AND WENT BACK TO MY LAB.
I STARTED MAKING A FEW TWEAKS--
--JUST TO IMPROVE THE ACCURACY, TO MAKE THE FUTURE THAT LITTLE BIT CLEARER.
I SHUT OFF ALL OUTSIDE DISTRACTIONS AND FOCUSED, JUST LIKE I WAS TOLD IN KULANDU. IT... IT WAS LIKE STARING INTO THE SUN--I WANTED TO LOOK AROUND IT BUT HAD TO LOOK IT IN THE EYE... NO MATTER HOW MUCH IT HURT TO SEE IT.
IT? WHAT DID YOU SEE?

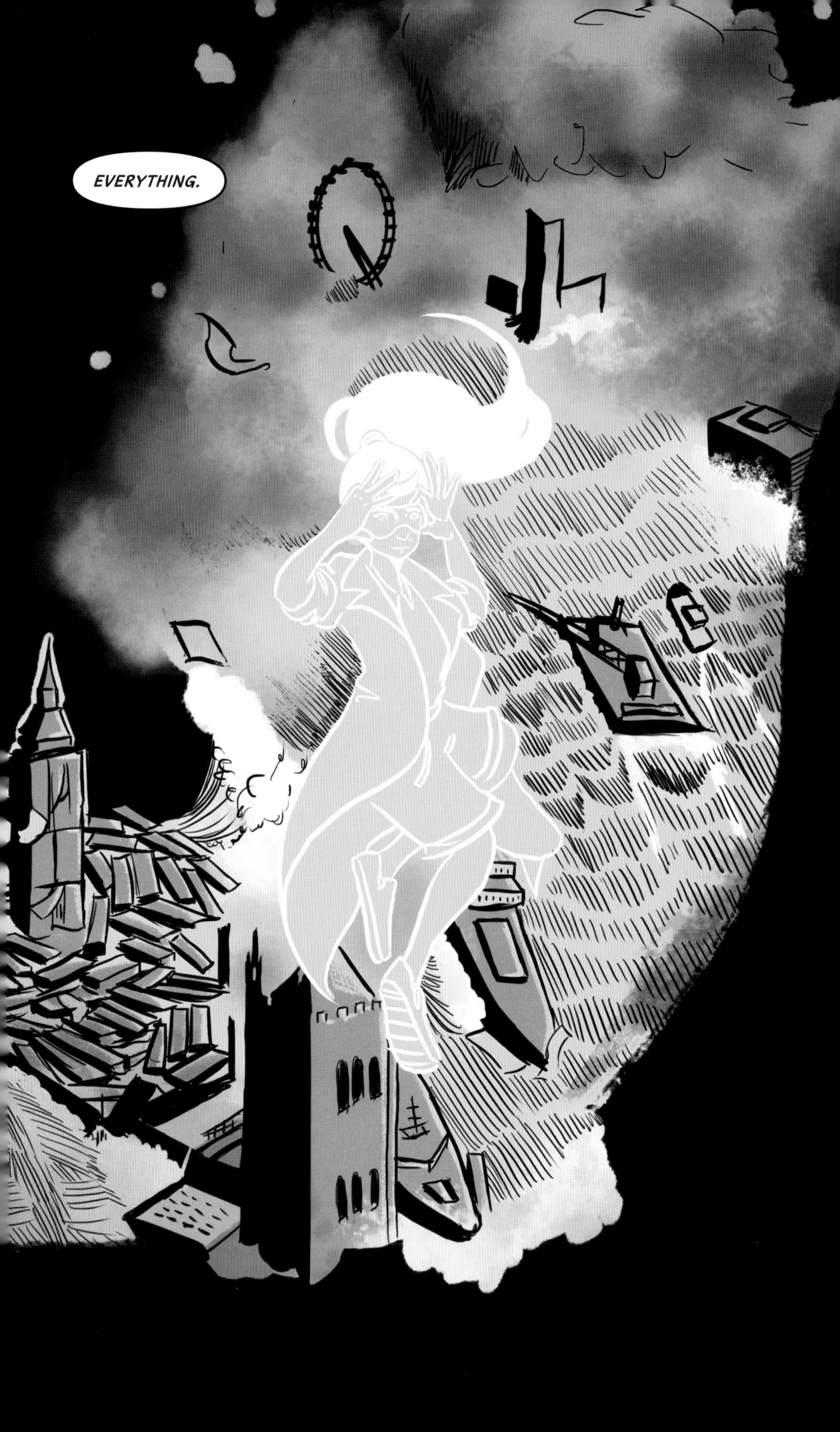
EVERYTHING.

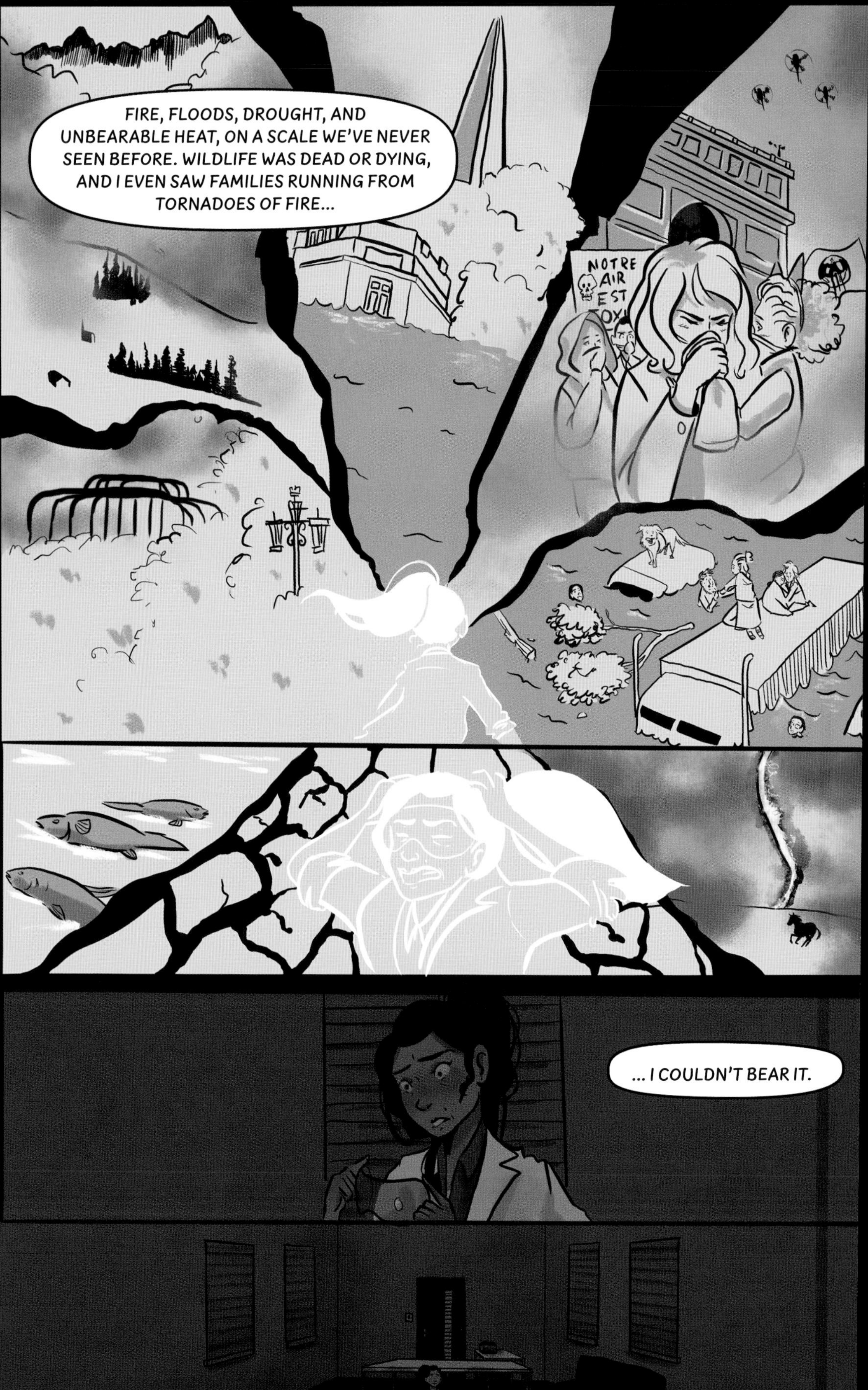
FIRE, FLOODS, DROUGHT, AND UNBEARABLE HEAT, ON A SCALE WE'VE NEVER SEEN BEFORE. WILDLIFE WAS DEAD OR DYING, AND I EVEN SAW FAMILIES RUNNING FROM TORNADOES OF FIRE...
NOTRE AIR EST TOX
... I COULDN'T BEAR IT.

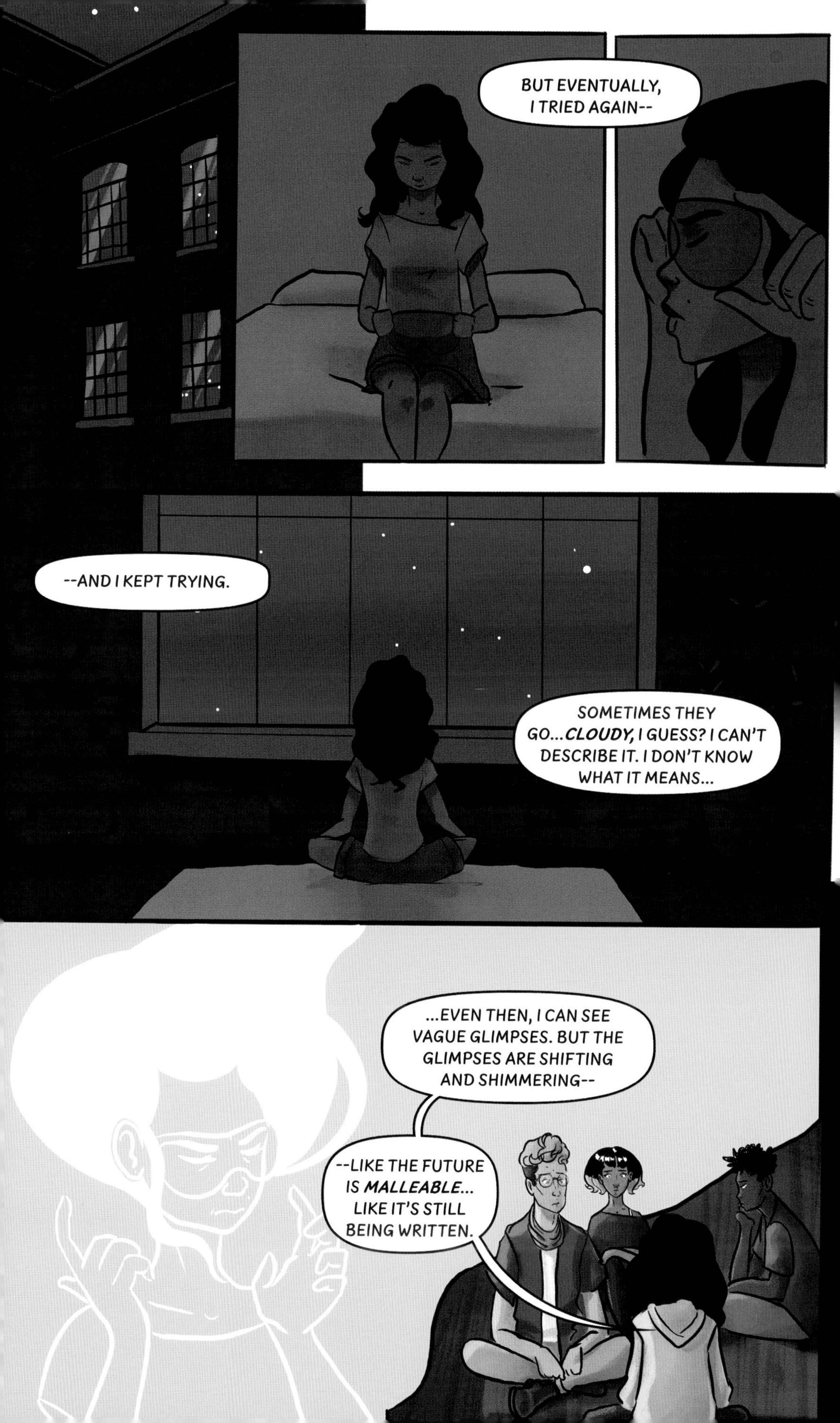
BUT EVENTUALLY, I TRIED AGAIN--
--AND I KEPT TRYING.
SOMETIMES THEY GO...*CLOUDY,* I GUESS? I CAN'T DESCRIBE IT. I DON'T KNOW WHAT IT MEANS...
...EVEN THEN, I CAN SEE VAGUE GLIMPSES. BUT THE GLIMPSES ARE SHIFTING AND SHIMMERING--
--LIKE THE FUTURE IS *MALLEABLE*... LIKE IT'S STILL BEING WRITTEN.

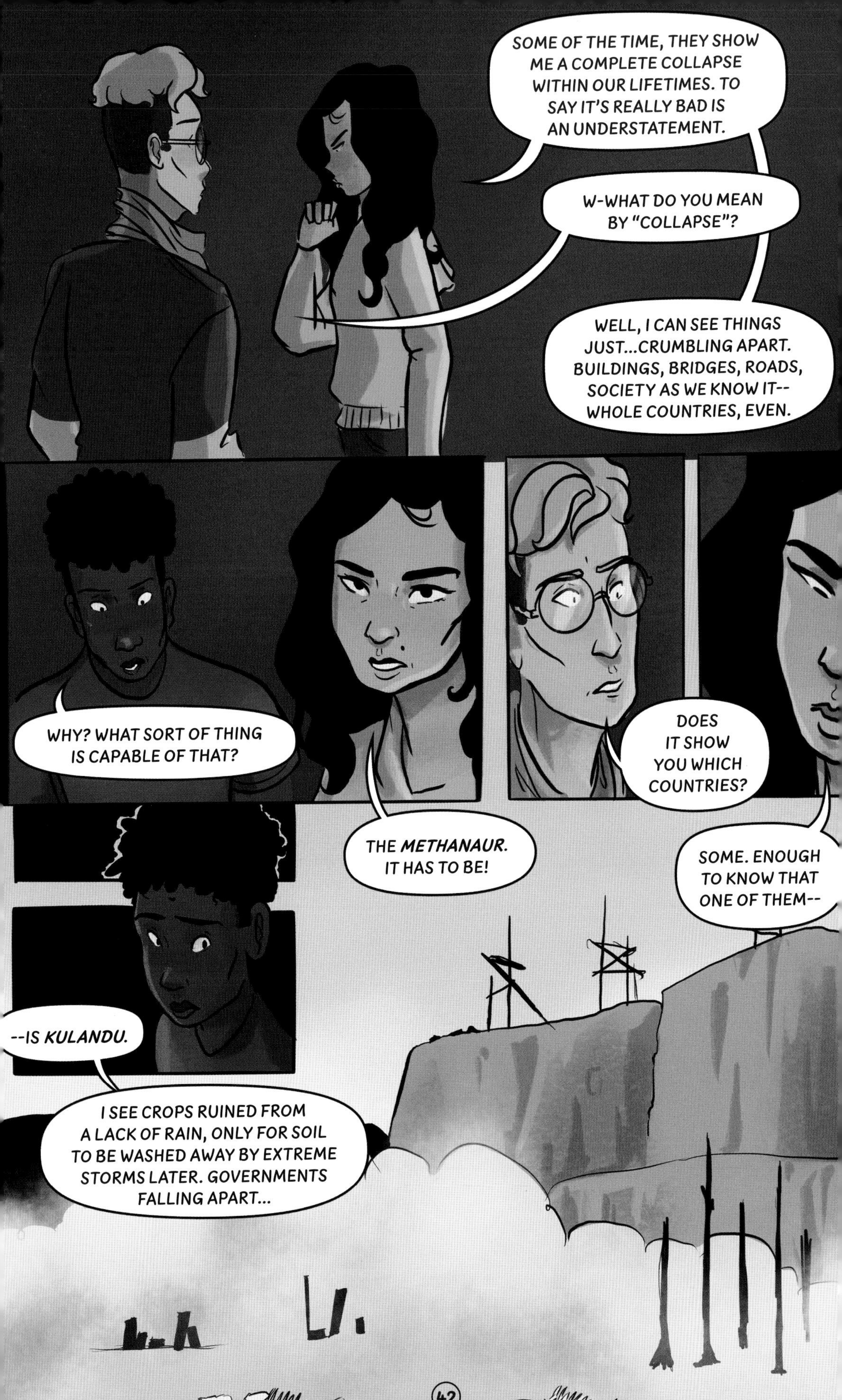

SOME OF THE TIME, THEY SHOW ME A COMPLETE COLLAPSE WITHIN OUR LIFETIMES. TO SAY IT'S REALLY BAD IS AN UNDERSTATEMENT.
W-WHAT DO YOU MEAN BY "COLLAPSE"?
WELL, I CAN SEE THINGS JUST...CRUMBLING APART. BUILDINGS, BRIDGES, ROADS, SOCIETY AS WE KNOW IT--WHOLE COUNTRIES, EVEN.
WHY? WHAT SORT OF THING IS CAPABLE OF THAT?
THE *METHANAUR*. IT HAS TO BE!
DOES IT SHOW YOU WHICH COUNTRIES?
SOME. ENOUGH TO KNOW THAT ONE OF THEM--
--IS *KULANDU*.
I SEE CROPS RUINED FROM A LACK OF RAIN, ONLY FOR SOIL TO BE WASHED AWAY BY EXTREME STORMS LATER. GOVERNMENTS FALLING APART...

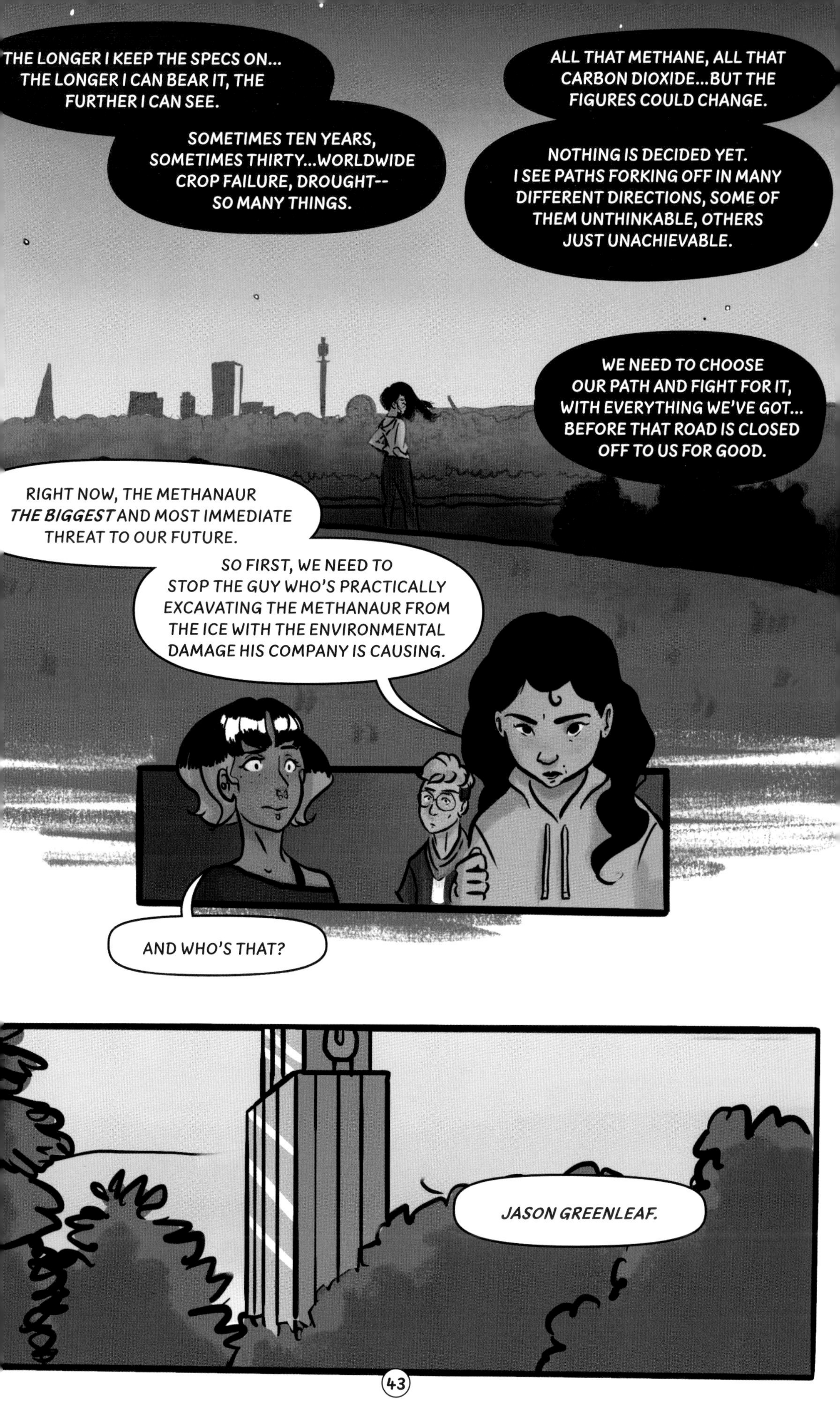
THE LONGER I KEEP THE SPECS ON... THE LONGER I CAN BEAR IT, THE FURTHER I CAN SEE.
SOMETIMES TEN YEARS, SOMETIMES THIRTY...WORLDWIDE CROP FAILURE, DROUGHT-- SO MANY THINGS.
ALL THAT METHANE, ALL THAT CARBON DIOXIDE...BUT THE FIGURES COULD CHANGE.
NOTHING IS DECIDED YET. I SEE PATHS FORKING OFF IN MANY DIFFERENT DIRECTIONS, SOME OF THEM UNTHINKABLE, OTHERS JUST UNACHIEVABLE.
WE NEED TO CHOOSE OUR PATH AND FIGHT FOR IT, WITH EVERYTHING WE'VE GOT... BEFORE THAT ROAD IS CLOSED OFF TO US FOR GOOD.
RIGHT NOW, THE METHANAUR *THE BIGGEST* AND MOST IMMEDIATE THREAT TO OUR FUTURE.
SO FIRST, WE NEED TO STOP THE GUY WHO'S PRACTICALLY EXCAVATING THE METHANAUR FROM THE ICE WITH THE ENVIRONMENTAL DAMAGE HIS COMPANY IS CAUSING.
AND WHO'S THAT?
JASON GREENLEAF.

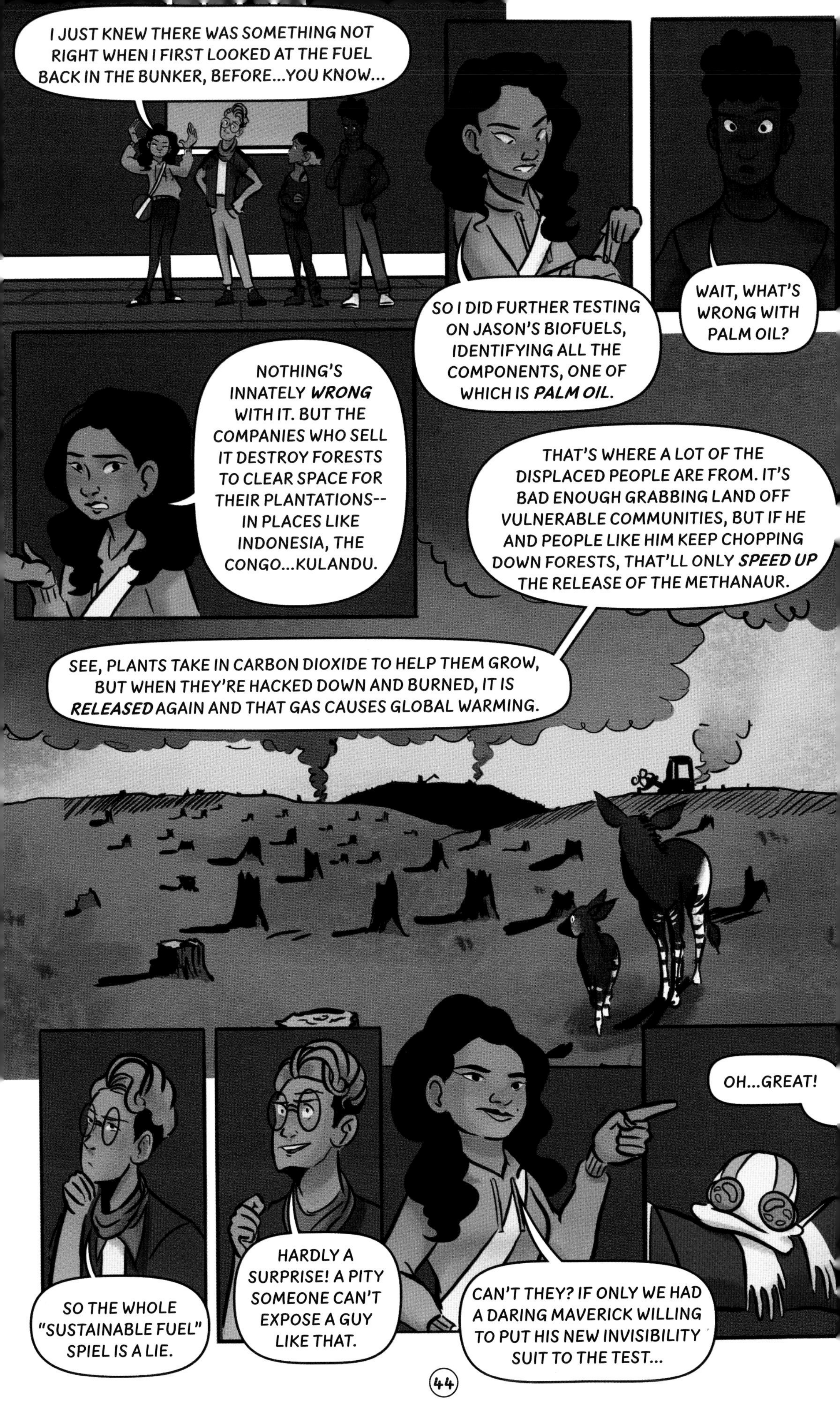
I JUST KNEW THERE WAS SOMETHING NOT RIGHT WHEN I FIRST LOOKED AT THE FUEL BACK IN THE BUNKER, BEFORE...YOU KNOW...
SO I DID FURTHER TESTING ON JASON'S BIOFUELS, IDENTIFYING ALL THE COMPONENTS, ONE OF WHICH IS *PALM OIL*.
WAIT, WHAT'S WRONG WITH PALM OIL?
NOTHING'S INNATELY *WRONG* WITH IT. BUT THE COMPANIES WHO SELL IT DESTROY FORESTS TO CLEAR SPACE FOR THEIR PLANTATIONS--IN PLACES LIKE INDONESIA, THE CONGO...KULANDU.
THAT'S WHERE A LOT OF THE DISPLACED PEOPLE ARE FROM. IT'S BAD ENOUGH GRABBING LAND OFF VULNERABLE COMMUNITIES, BUT IF HE AND PEOPLE LIKE HIM KEEP CHOPPING DOWN FORESTS, THAT'LL ONLY *SPEED UP* THE RELEASE OF THE METHANAUR.
SEE, PLANTS TAKE IN CARBON DIOXIDE TO HELP THEM GROW, BUT WHEN THEY'RE HACKED DOWN AND BURNED, IT IS *RELEASED* AGAIN AND THAT GAS CAUSES GLOBAL WARMING.
SO THE WHOLE "SUSTAINABLE FUEL" SPIEL IS A LIE.
HARDLY A SURPRISE! A PITY SOMEONE CAN'T EXPOSE A GUY LIKE THAT.
CAN'T THEY? IF ONLY WE HAD A DARING MAVERICK WILLING TO PUT HIS NEW INVISIBILITY SUIT TO THE TEST...
OH...GREAT!

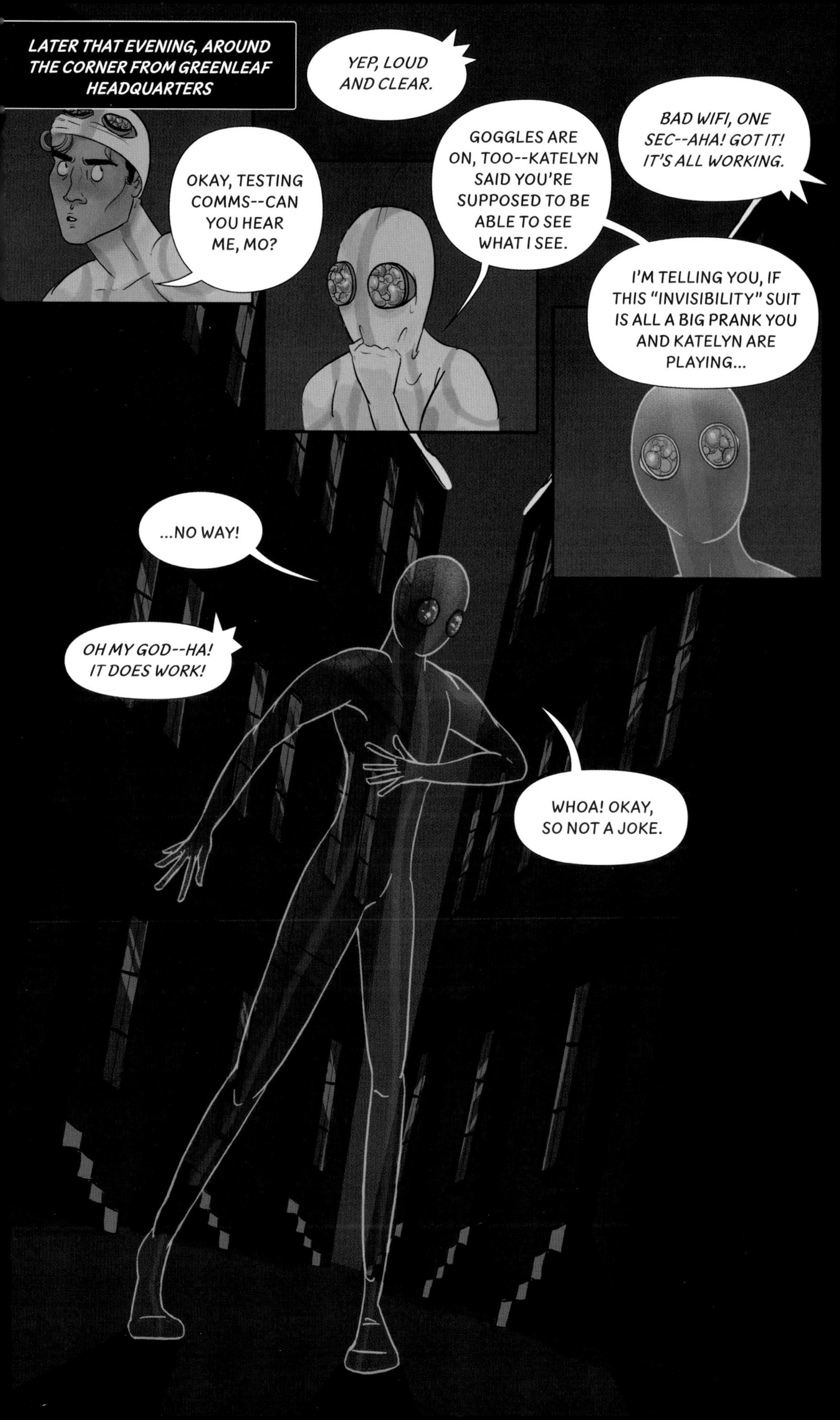
LATER THAT EVENING, AROUND THE CORNER FROM GREENLEAF HEADQUARTERS
OKAY, TESTING COMMS--CAN YOU HEAR ME, MO?
YEP, LOUD AND CLEAR.
GOGGLES ARE ON, TOO--KATELYN SAID YOU'RE SUPPOSED TO BE ABLE TO SEE WHAT I SEE.
BAD WIFI, ONE SEC--AHA! GOT IT! IT'S ALL WORKING.
I'M TELLING YOU, IF THIS "INVISIBILITY" SUIT IS ALL A BIG PRANK YOU AND KATELYN ARE PLAYING...
...NO WAY!
OH MY GOD--HA! IT DOES WORK!
WHOA! OKAY, SO NOT A JOKE.

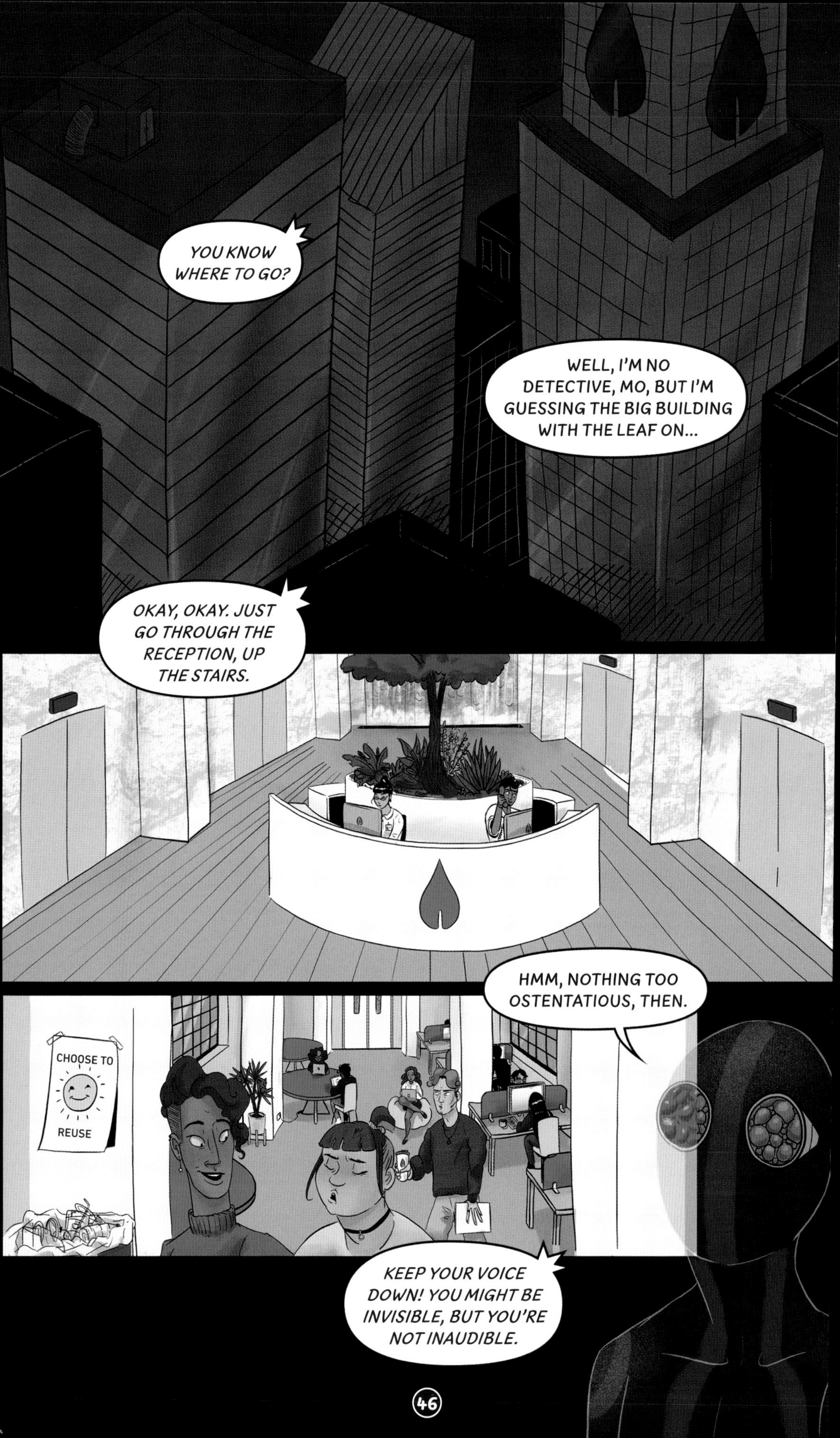
YOU KNOW WHERE TO GO?
WELL, I'M NO DETECTIVE, MO, BUT I'M GUESSING THE BIG BUILDING WITH THE LEAF ON...
OKAY, OKAY. JUST GO THROUGH THE RECEPTION, UP THE STAIRS.
CHOOSE TO REUSE
HMM, NOTHING TOO OSTENTATIOUS, THEN.
KEEP YOUR VOICE DOWN! YOU MIGHT BE INVISIBLE, BUT YOU'RE NOT INAUDIBLE.

YOU NEED O GO TO THE SOUTHEAST WING--GO RIGHT.
NO, *LEFT!*
WAIT...NO, IT *IS* RIGHT-- GO RIGHT.
YOU INSPIRE CONFIDENCE, MATE.
NOW LEFT UP THE STAIRS--WAIT! WHAT ARE YOU DOING?
DO YOU REALIZE HOW HARD IT IS WALKING UP STAIRS WHEN YOU CAN'T SEE YOUR FEET?
UGH, GOD, I NEED TO GO OUT WALKING MORE.
OKAY, SOUTHEAST WING IS JUST HERE.
COME ON!
I CAN'T GET IN. I THINK I NEED A PASS.

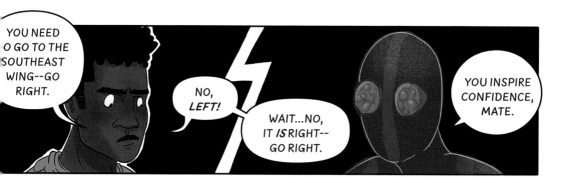

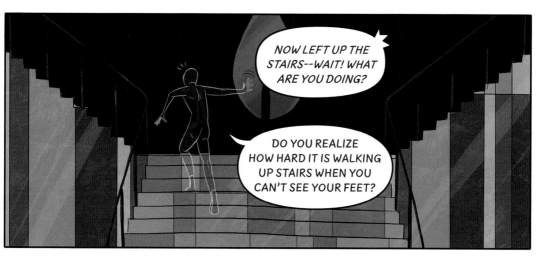

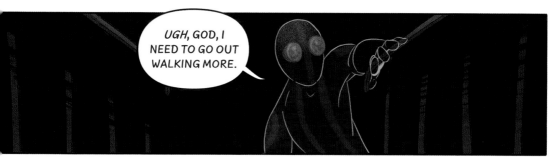

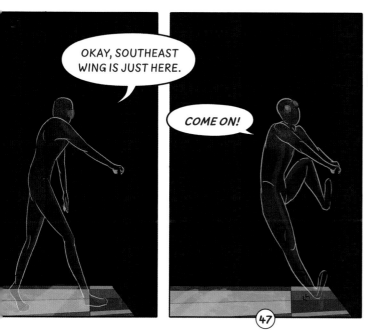

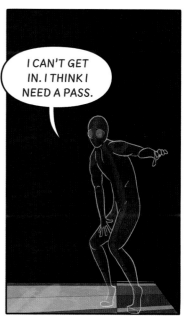

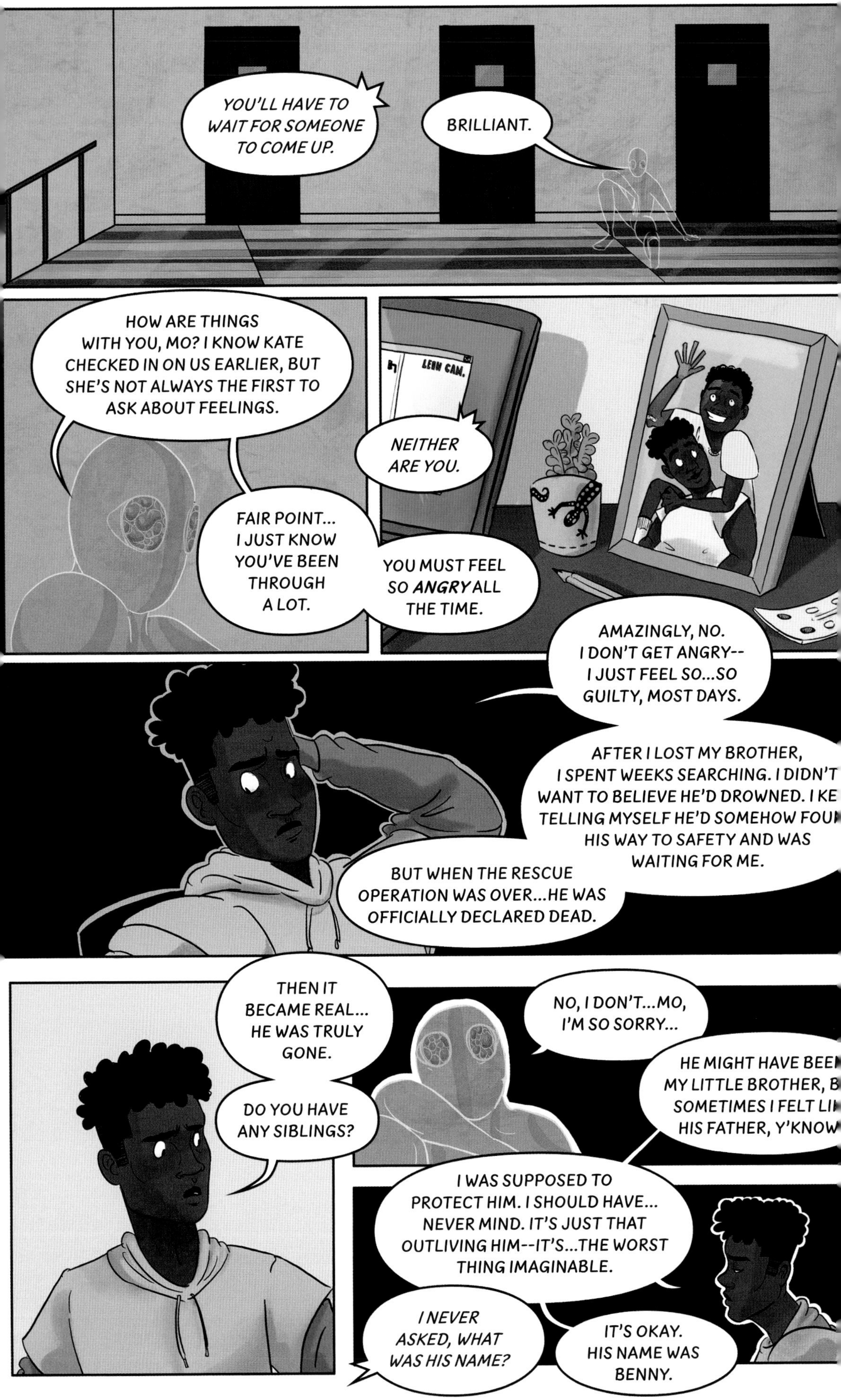
YOU'LL HAVE TO WAIT FOR SOMEONE TO COME UP.
BRILLIANT.
HOW ARE THINGS WITH YOU, MO? I KNOW KATE CHECKED IN ON US EARLIER, BUT SHE'S NOT ALWAYS THE FIRST TO ASK ABOUT FEELINGS.
NEITHER ARE YOU.
FAIR POINT... I JUST KNOW YOU'VE BEEN THROUGH A LOT.
YOU MUST FEEL SO ANGRY ALL THE TIME.
AMAZINGLY, NO. I DON'T GET ANGRY-- I JUST FEEL SO...SO GUILTY, MOST DAYS.
AFTER I LOST MY BROTHER, I SPENT WEEKS SEARCHING. I DIDN'T WANT TO BELIEVE HE'D DROWNED. I KE TELLING MYSELF HE'D SOMEHOW FOU HIS WAY TO SAFETY AND WAS WAITING FOR ME.
BUT WHEN THE RESCUE OPERATION WAS OVER...HE WAS OFFICIALLY DECLARED DEAD.
THEN IT BECAME REAL... HE WAS TRULY GONE.
DO YOU HAVE ANY SIBLINGS?
NO, I DON'T...MO, I'M SO SORRY...
HE MIGHT HAVE BEE MY LITTLE BROTHER, B SOMETIMES I FELT LI HIS FATHER, Y'KNOW
I WAS SUPPOSED TO PROTECT HIM. I SHOULD HAVE... NEVER MIND. IT'S JUST THAT OUTLIVING HIM--IT'S...THE WORST THING IMAGINABLE.
I NEVER ASKED, WHAT WAS HIS NAME?
IT'S OKAY. HIS NAME WAS BENNY.

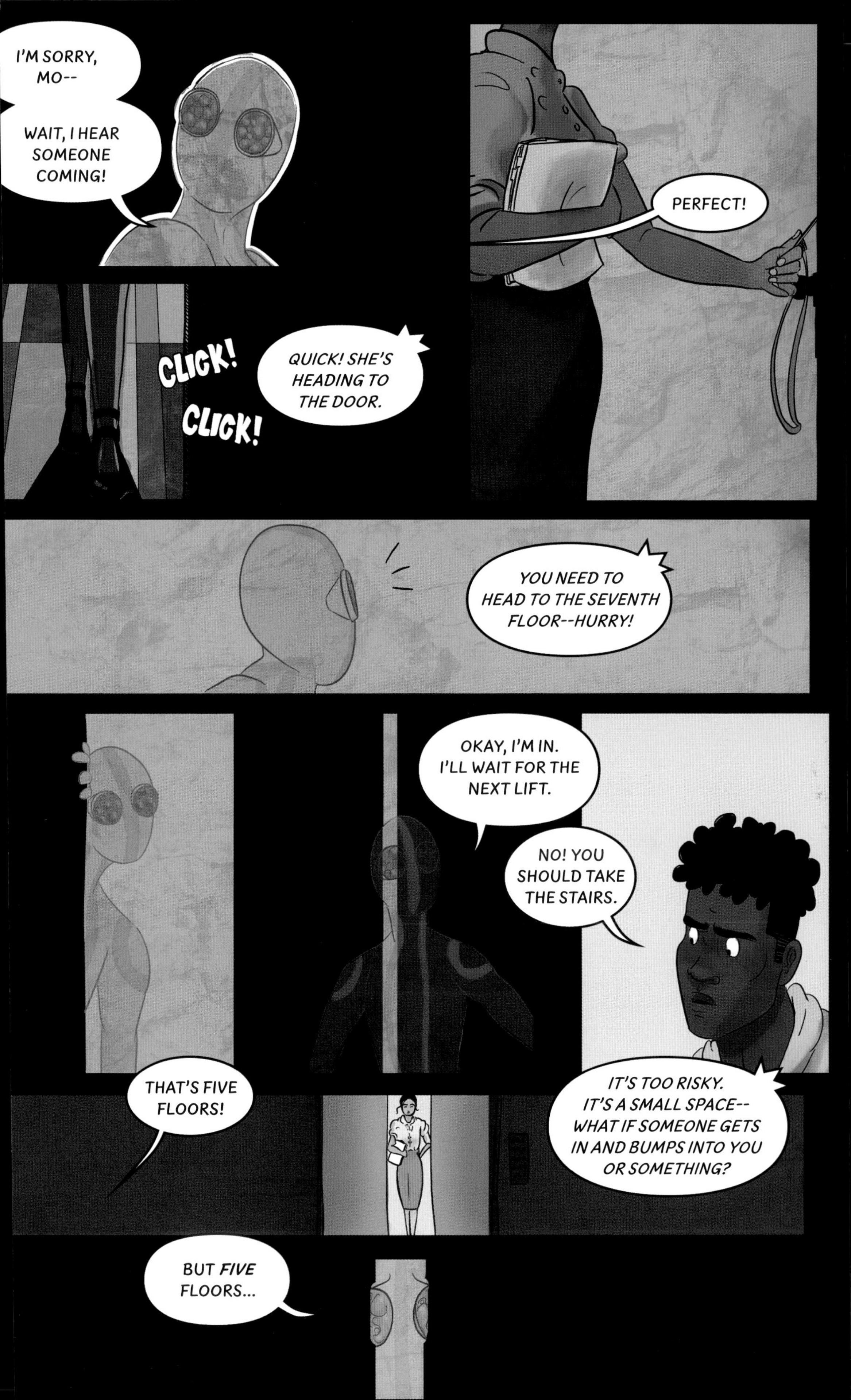

I'M SORRY, MO--
WAIT, I HEAR SOMEONE COMING!
PERFECT!
CLICK!
CLICK!
QUICK! SHE'S HEADING TO THE DOOR.
YOU NEED TO HEAD TO THE SEVENTH FLOOR--HURRY!
OKAY, I'M IN. I'LL WAIT FOR THE NEXT LIFT.
NO! YOU SHOULD TAKE THE STAIRS.
THAT'S FIVE FLOORS!
IT'S TOO RISKY. IT'S A SMALL SPACE-- WHAT IF SOMEONE GETS IN AND BUMPS INTO YOU OR SOMETHING?
BUT *FIVE* FLOORS...

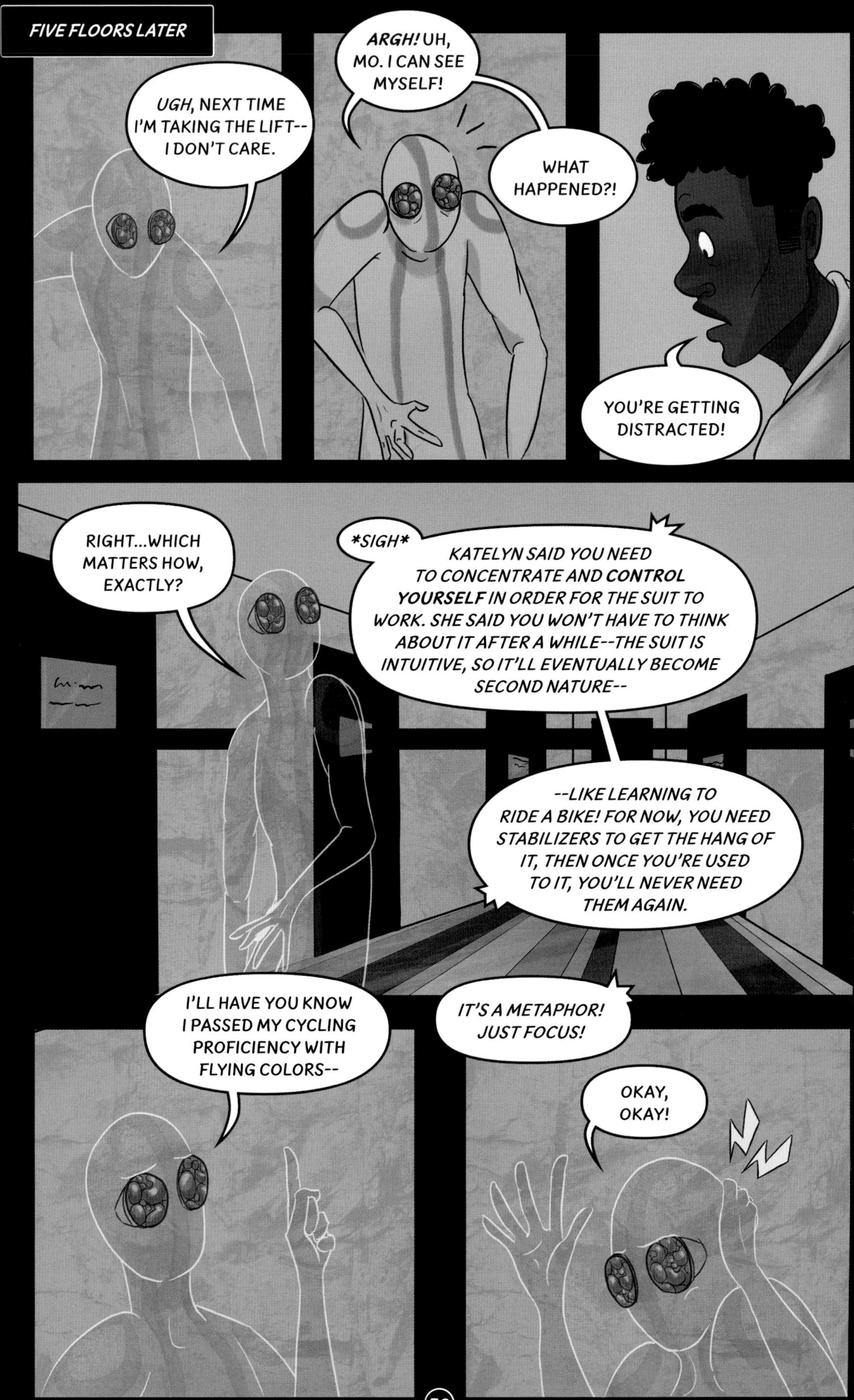
FIVE FLOORS LATER
UGH, NEXT TIME I'M TAKING THE LIFT-- I DON'T CARE.
ARGH! UH, MO. I CAN SEE MYSELF!
WHAT HAPPENED?!
YOU'RE GETTING DISTRACTED!
RIGHT...WHICH MATTERS HOW, EXACTLY?
SIGH
KATELYN SAID YOU NEED TO CONCENTRATE AND CONTROL YOURSELF IN ORDER FOR THE SUIT TO WORK. SHE SAID YOU WON'T HAVE TO THINK ABOUT IT AFTER A WHILE--THE SUIT IS INTUITIVE, SO IT'LL EVENTUALLY BECOME SECOND NATURE--
--LIKE LEARNING TO RIDE A BIKE! FOR NOW, YOU NEED STABILIZERS TO GET THE HANG OF IT, THEN ONCE YOU'RE USED TO IT, YOU'LL NEVER NEED THEM AGAIN.
I'LL HAVE YOU KNOW I PASSED MY CYCLING PROFICIENCY WITH FLYING COLORS--
IT'S A METAPHOR! JUST FOCUS!
OKAY, OKAY!

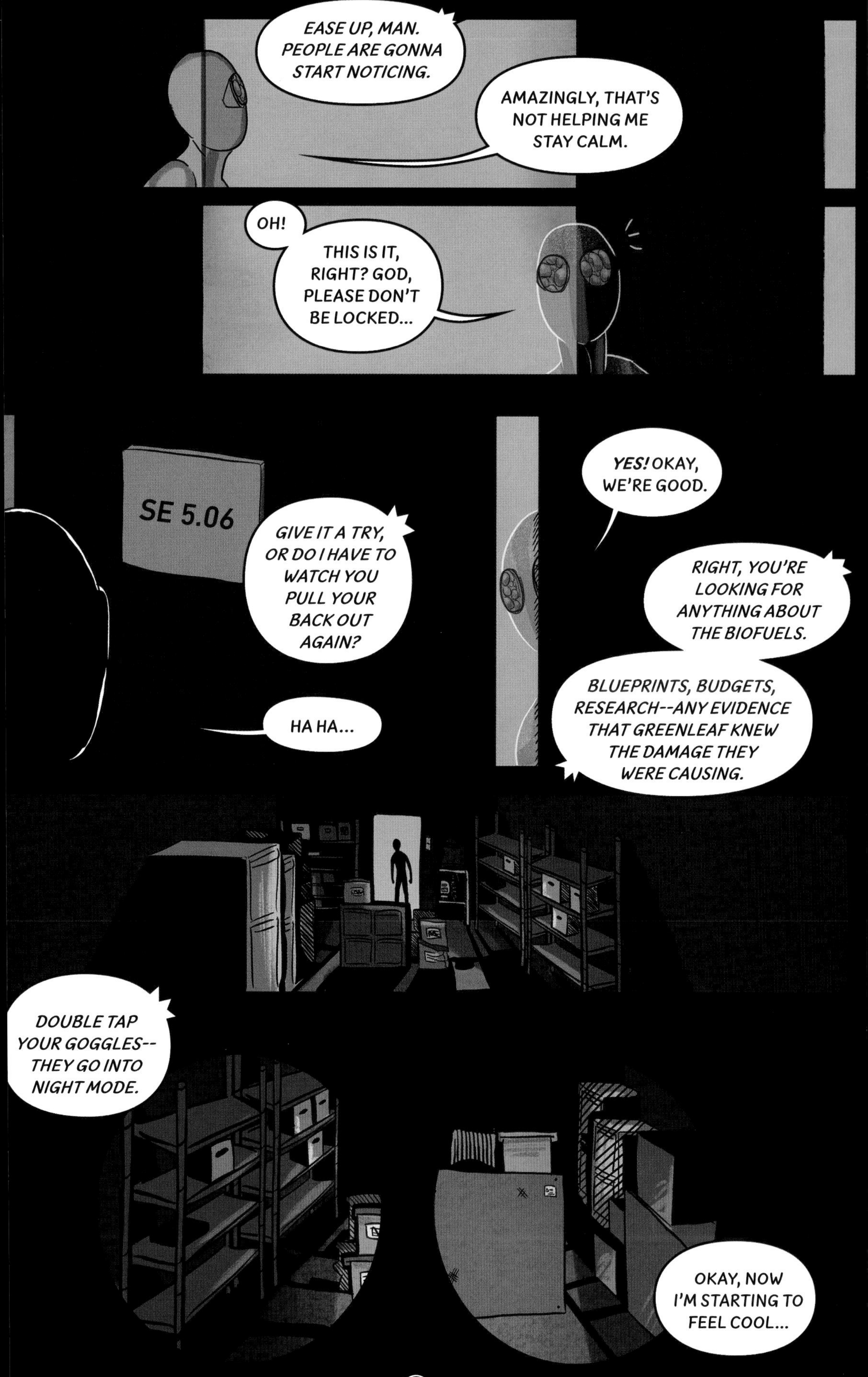
EASE UP, MAN. PEOPLE ARE GONNA START NOTICING.
AMAZINGLY, THAT'S NOT HELPING ME STAY CALM.
OH!
THIS IS IT, RIGHT? GOD, PLEASE DON'T BE LOCKED...
SE 5.06
GIVE IT A TRY, OR DO I HAVE TO WATCH YOU PULL YOUR BACK OUT AGAIN?
HA HA...
YES! OKAY, WE'RE GOOD.
RIGHT, YOU'RE LOOKING FOR ANYTHING ABOUT THE BIOFUELS.
BLUEPRINTS, BUDGETS, RESEARCH--ANY EVIDENCE THAT GREENLEAF KNEW THE DAMAGE THEY WERE CAUSING.
DOUBLE TAP YOUR GOGGLES--THEY GO INTO NIGHT MODE.
OKAY, NOW I'M STARTING TO FEEL COOL...

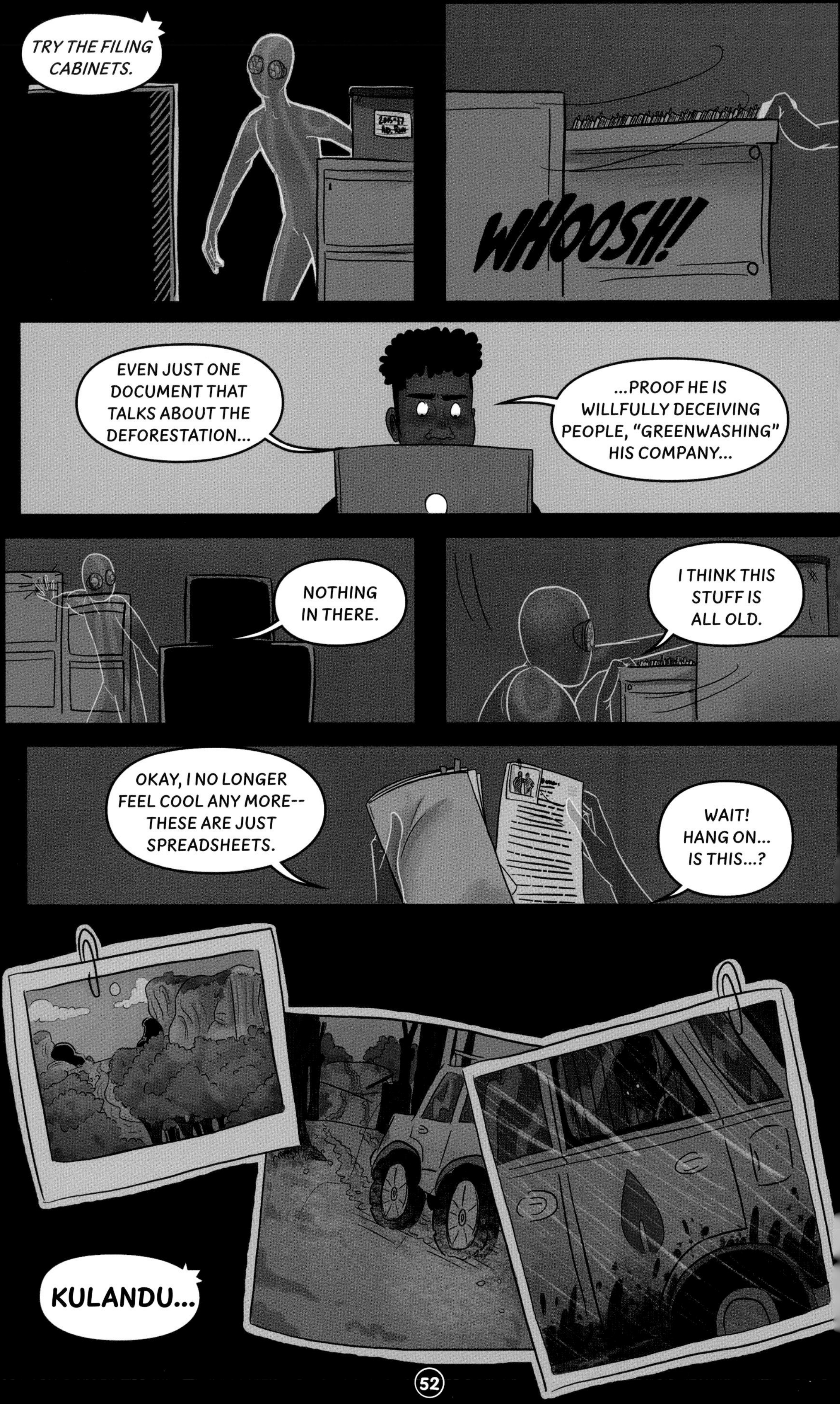
TRY THE FILING CABINETS.
WHOOSH!
EVEN JUST ONE DOCUMENT THAT TALKS ABOUT THE DEFORESTATION...
...PROOF HE IS WILLFULLY DECEIVING PEOPLE, "GREENWASHING" HIS COMPANY...
NOTHING IN THERE.
I THINK THIS STUFF IS ALL OLD.
OKAY, I NO LONGER FEEL COOL ANY MORE-- THESE ARE JUST SPREADSHEETS.
WAIT! HANG ON... IS THIS...?
KULANDU...

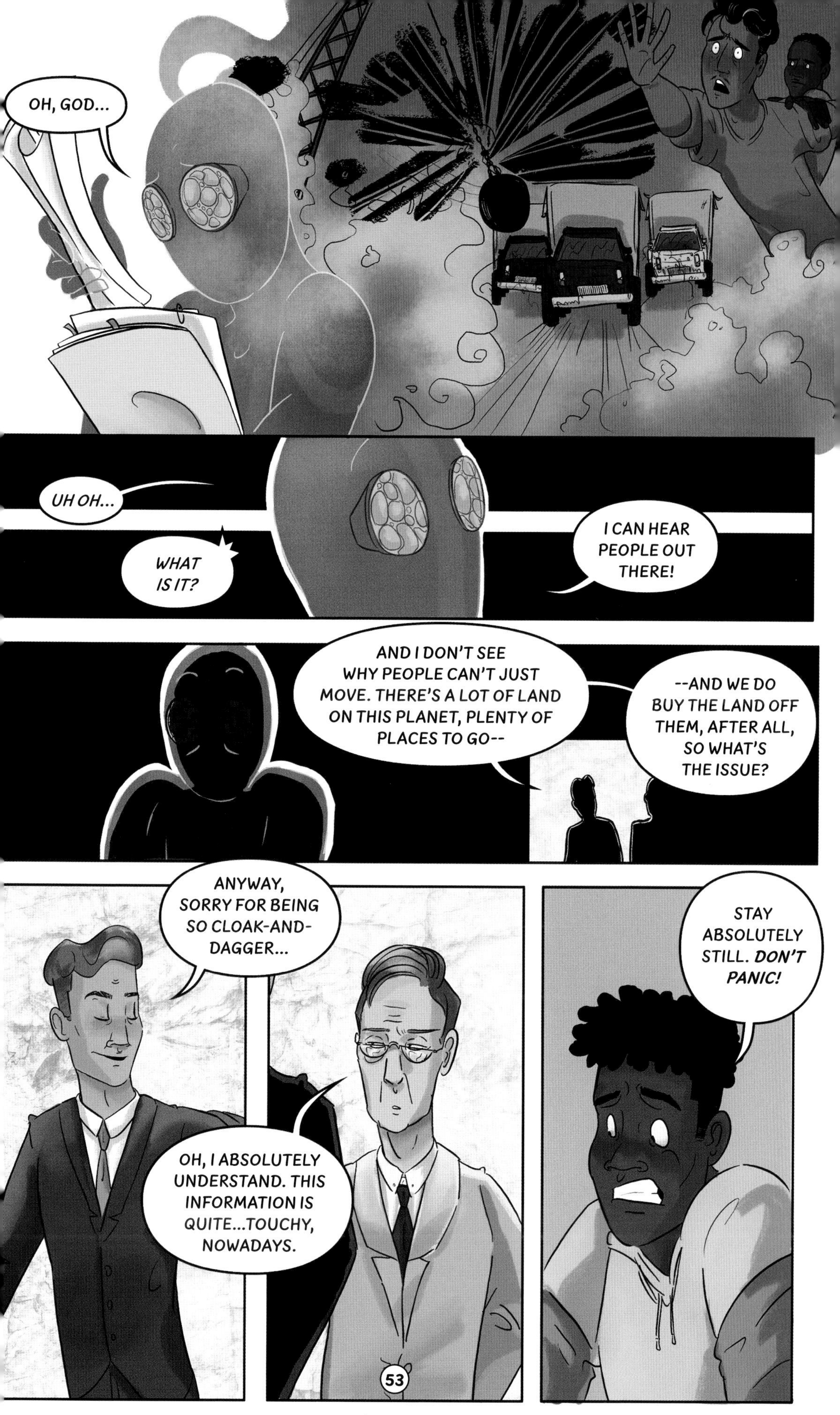
OH, GOD...
UH OH...
WHAT IS IT?
I CAN HEAR PEOPLE OUT THERE!
AND I DON'T SEE WHY PEOPLE CAN'T JUST MOVE. THERE'S A LOT OF LAND ON THIS PLANET, PLENTY OF PLACES TO GO--
--AND WE DO BUY THE LAND OFF THEM, AFTER ALL, SO WHAT'S THE ISSUE?
ANYWAY, SORRY FOR BEING SO CLOAK-AND-DAGGER...
OH, I ABSOLUTELY UNDERSTAND. THIS INFORMATION IS QUITE...TOUCHY, NOWADAYS.
STAY ABSOLUTELY STILL. DON'T PANIC!

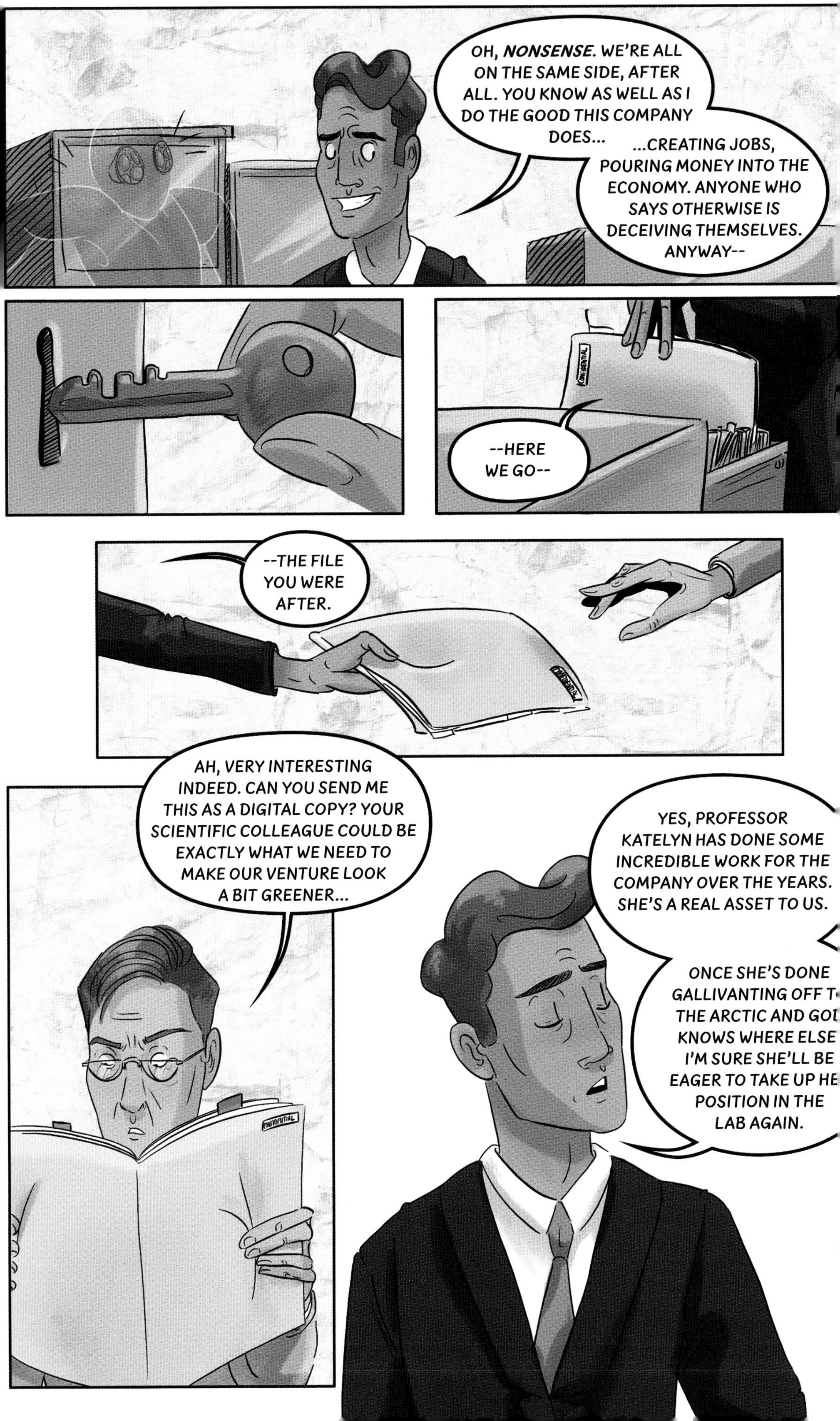
OH, NONSENSE. WE'RE ALL ON THE SAME SIDE, AFTER ALL. YOU KNOW AS WELL AS I DO THE GOOD THIS COMPANY DOES...
...CREATING JOBS, POURING MONEY INTO THE ECONOMY. ANYONE WHO SAYS OTHERWISE IS DECEIVING THEMSELVES. ANYWAY--
--HERE WE GO--
CONFIDENTIAL
--THE FILE YOU WERE AFTER.
CONFIDENTIAL
AH, VERY INTERESTING INDEED. CAN YOU SEND ME THIS AS A DIGITAL COPY? YOUR SCIENTIFIC COLLEAGUE COULD BE EXACTLY WHAT WE NEED TO MAKE OUR VENTURE LOOK A BIT GREENER...
CONFIDENTIAL
YES, PROFESSOR KATELYN HAS DONE SOME INCREDIBLE WORK FOR THE COMPANY OVER THE YEARS. SHE'S A REAL ASSET TO US.
ONCE SHE'S DONE GALLIVANTING OFF T THE ARCTIC AND GOI KNOWS WHERE ELSE I'M SURE SHE'LL BE EAGER TO TAKE UP HE POSITION IN THE LAB AGAIN.

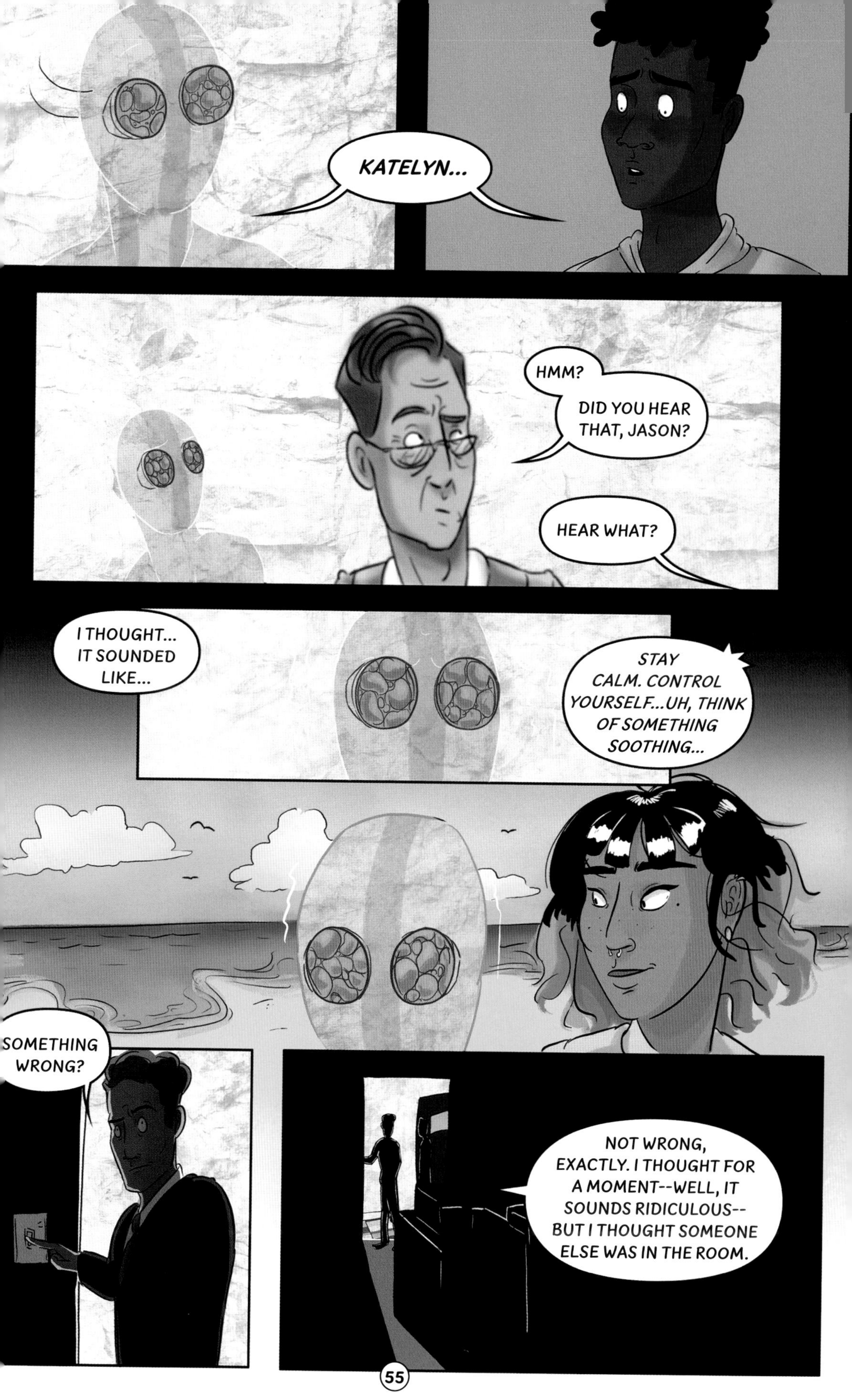
KATELYN...
HMM?
DID YOU HEAR THAT, JASON?
HEAR WHAT?
I THOUGHT... IT SOUNDED LIKE...
STAY CALM. CONTROL YOURSELF...UH, THINK OF SOMETHING SOOTHING...
SOMETHING WRONG?
NOT WRONG, EXACTLY. I THOUGHT FOR A MOMENT--WELL, IT SOUNDS RIDICULOUS--BUT I THOUGHT SOMEONE ELSE WAS IN THE ROOM.

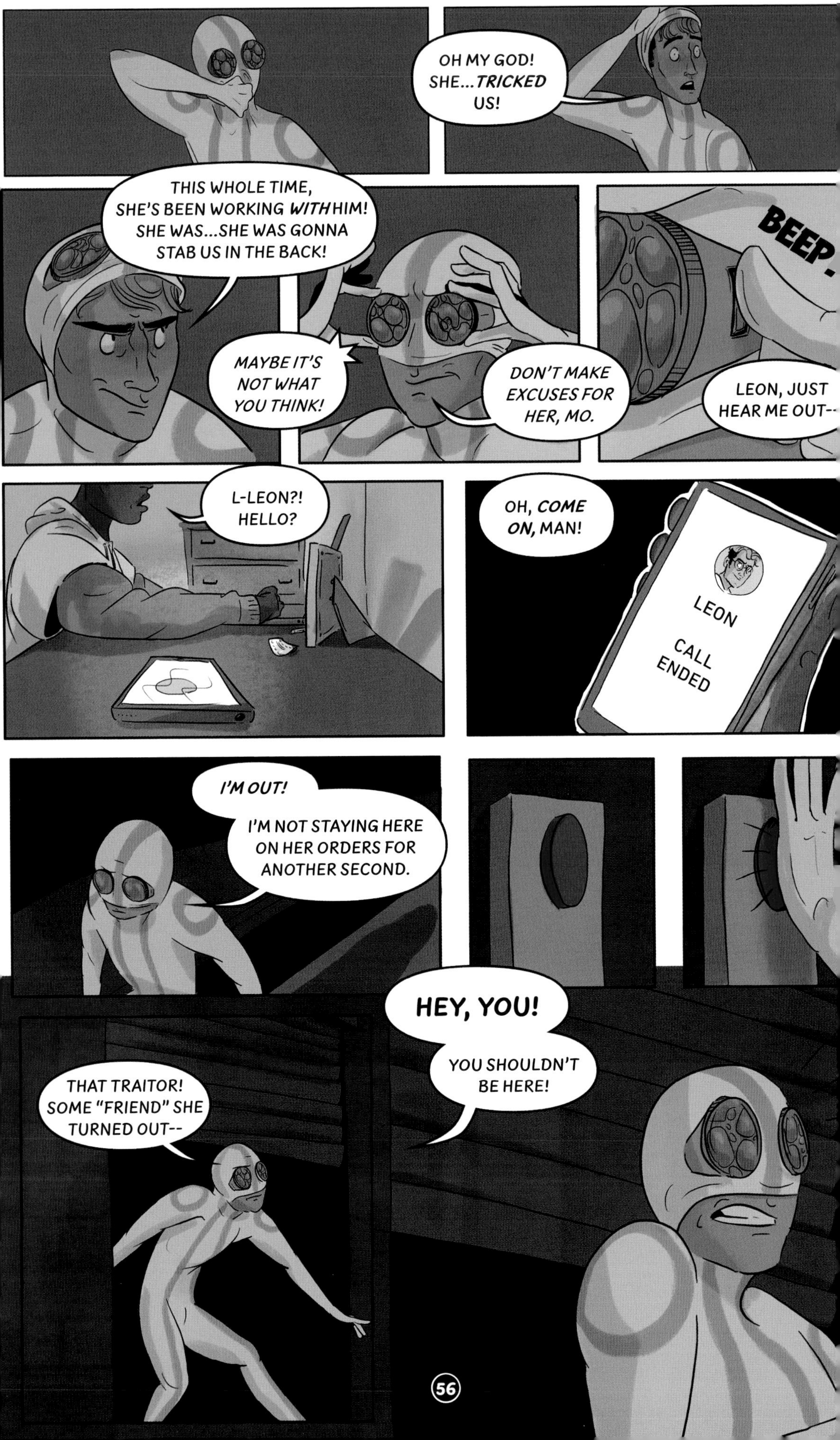
OH MY GOD! SHE...TRICKED US!
THIS WHOLE TIME, SHE'S BEEN WORKING WITH HIM! SHE WAS...SHE WAS GONNA STAB US IN THE BACK!
MAYBE IT'S NOT WHAT YOU THINK!
DON'T MAKE EXCUSES FOR HER, MO.
BEEP.
LEON, JUST HEAR ME OUT--
L-LEON?! HELLO?
OH, COME ON, MAN!
LEON
CALL ENDED
I'M OUT!
I'M NOT STAYING HERE ON HER ORDERS FOR ANOTHER SECOND.
THAT TRAITOR! SOME "FRIEND" SHE TURNED OUT--
HEY, YOU!
YOU SHOULDN'T BE HERE!

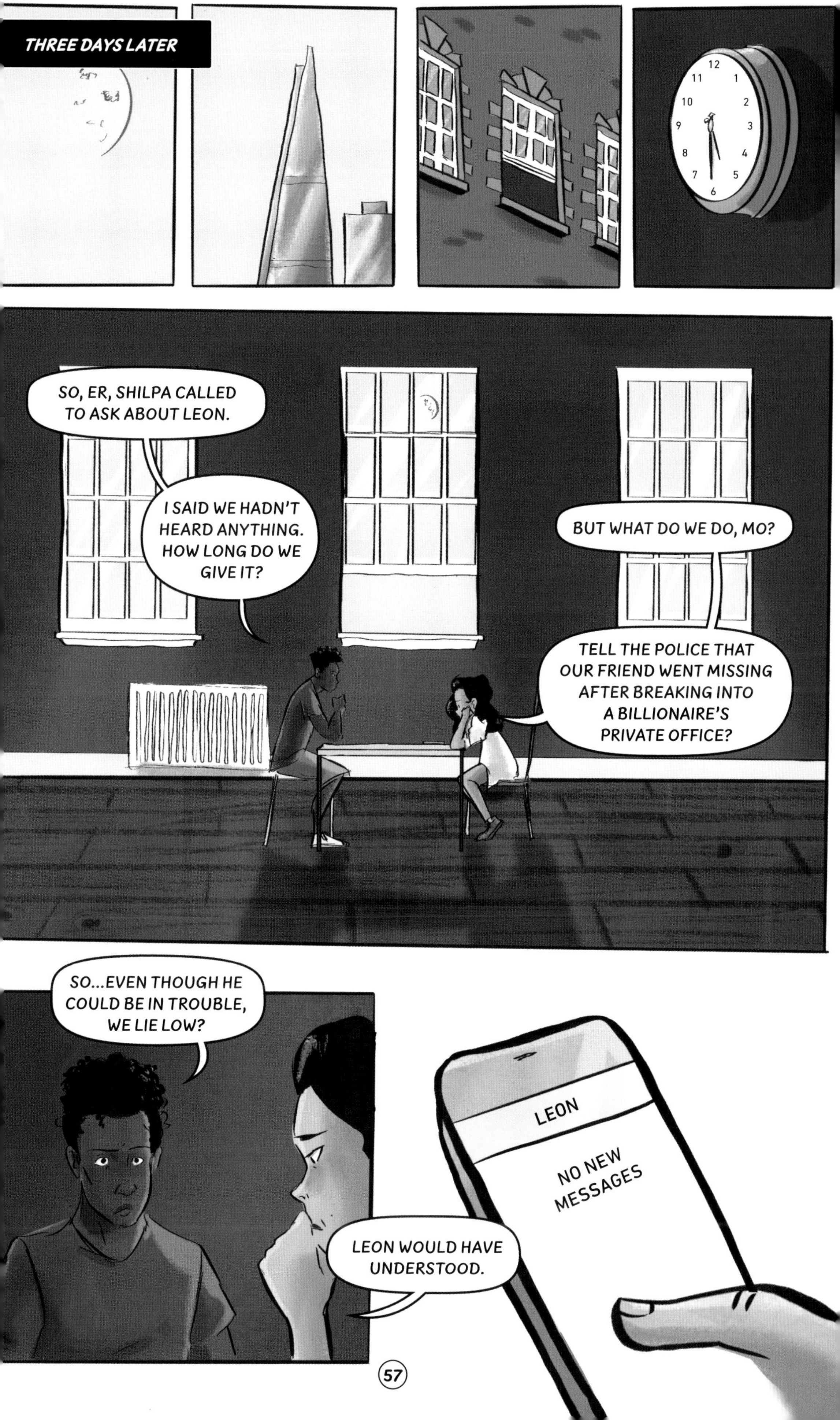
THREE DAYS LATER
SO, ER, SHILPA CALLED TO ASK ABOUT LEON.
I SAID WE HADN'T HEARD ANYTHING. HOW LONG DO WE GIVE IT?
BUT WHAT DO WE DO, MO?
TELL THE POLICE THAT OUR FRIEND WENT MISSING AFTER BREAKING INTO A BILLIONAIRE'S PRIVATE OFFICE?
SO...EVEN THOUGH HE COULD BE IN TROUBLE, WE LIE LOW?
LEON WOULD HAVE UNDERSTOOD.
LEON
NO NEW MESSAGES

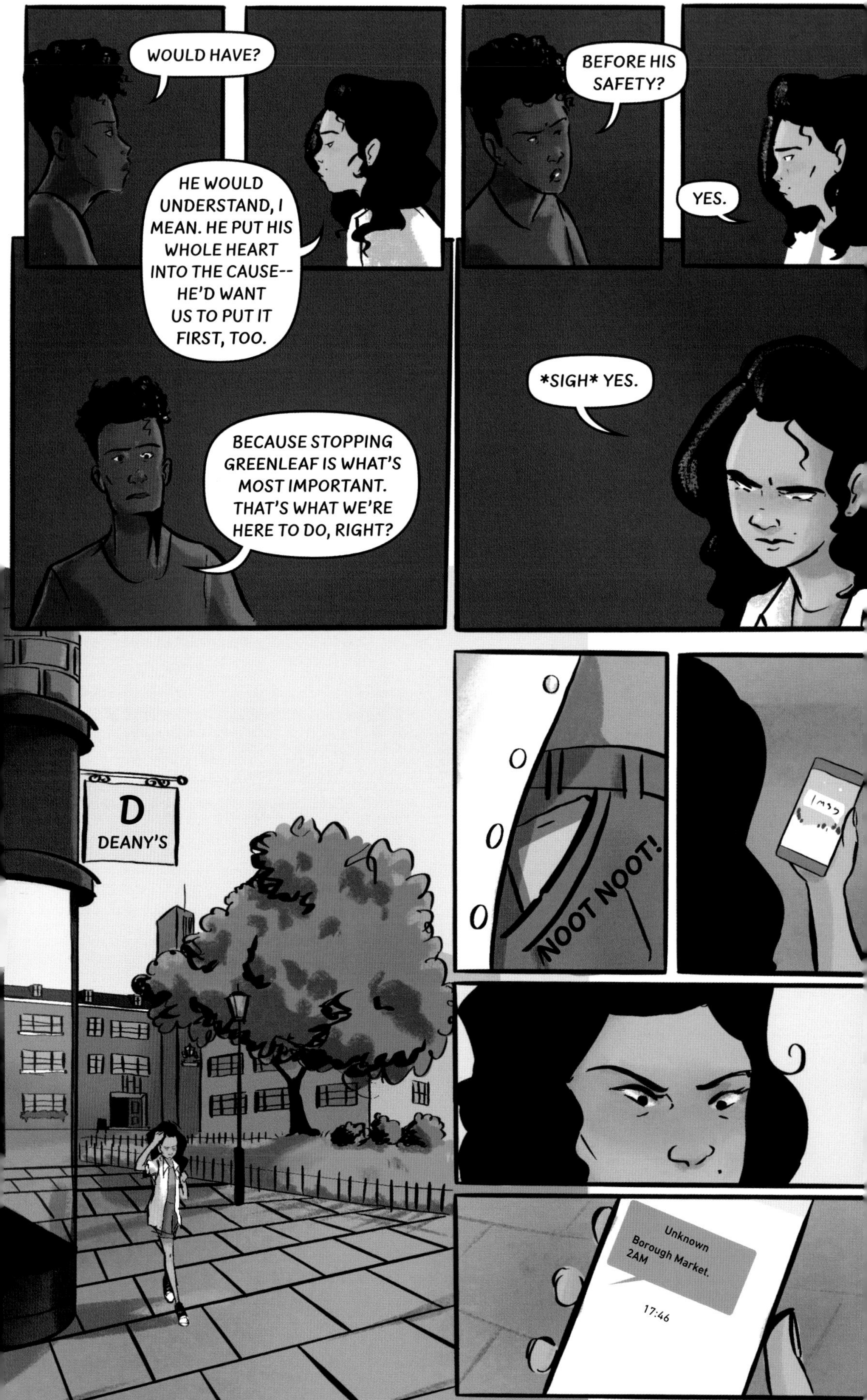
WOULD HAVE?
HE WOULD UNDERSTAND, I MEAN. HE PUT HIS WHOLE HEART INTO THE CAUSE--HE'D WANT US TO PUT IT FIRST, TOO.
BEFORE HIS SAFETY?
YES.
BECAUSE STOPPING GREENLEAF IS WHAT'S MOST IMPORTANT. THAT'S WHAT WE'RE HERE TO DO, RIGHT?
SIGH YES.
D
DEANY'S
NOOT NOOT!
Unknown
Borough Market.
2AM
17:46

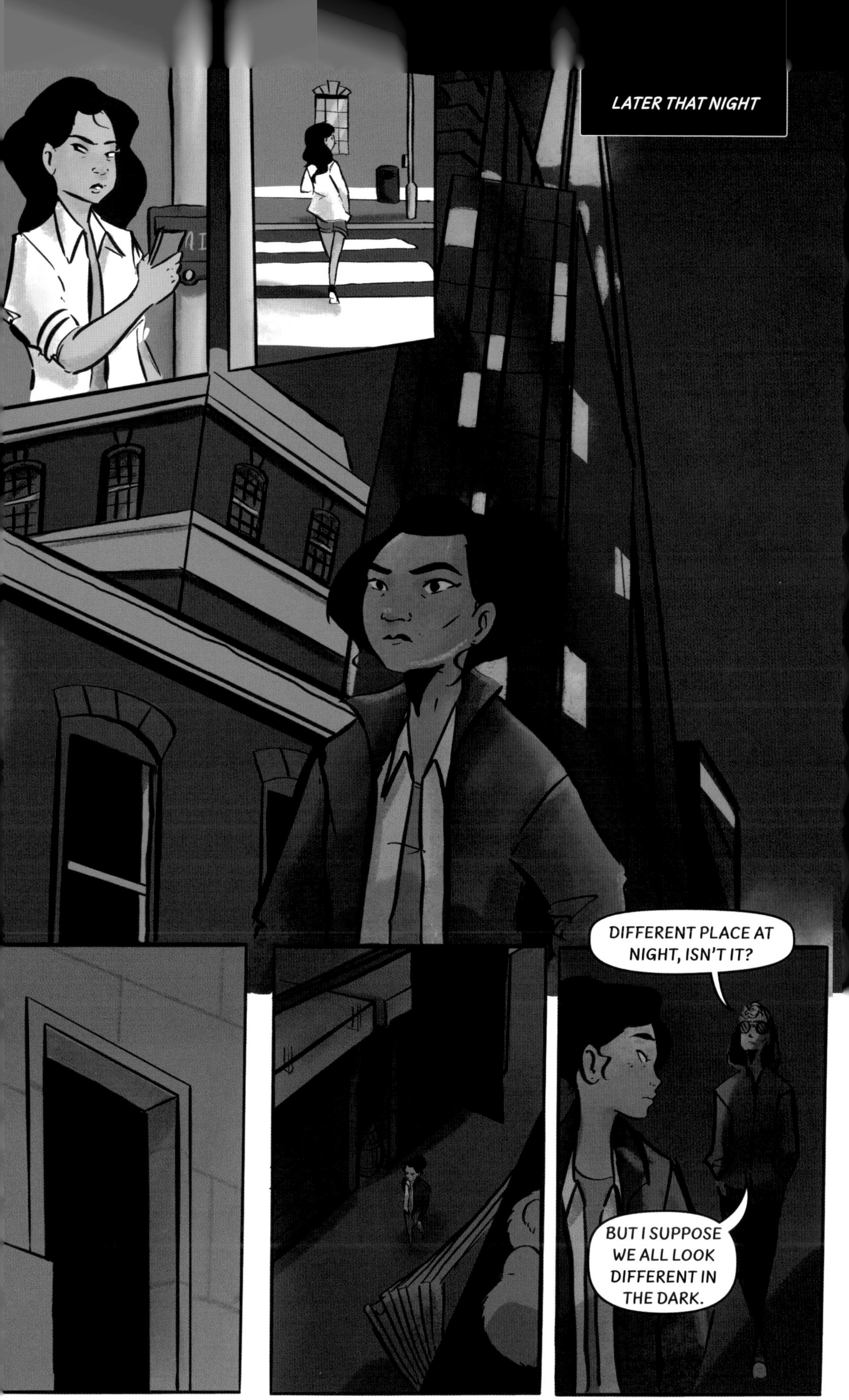
LATER THAT NIGHT
DIFFERENT PLACE AT NIGHT, ISN'T IT?
BUT I SUPPOSE WE ALL LOOK DIFFERENT IN THE DARK.

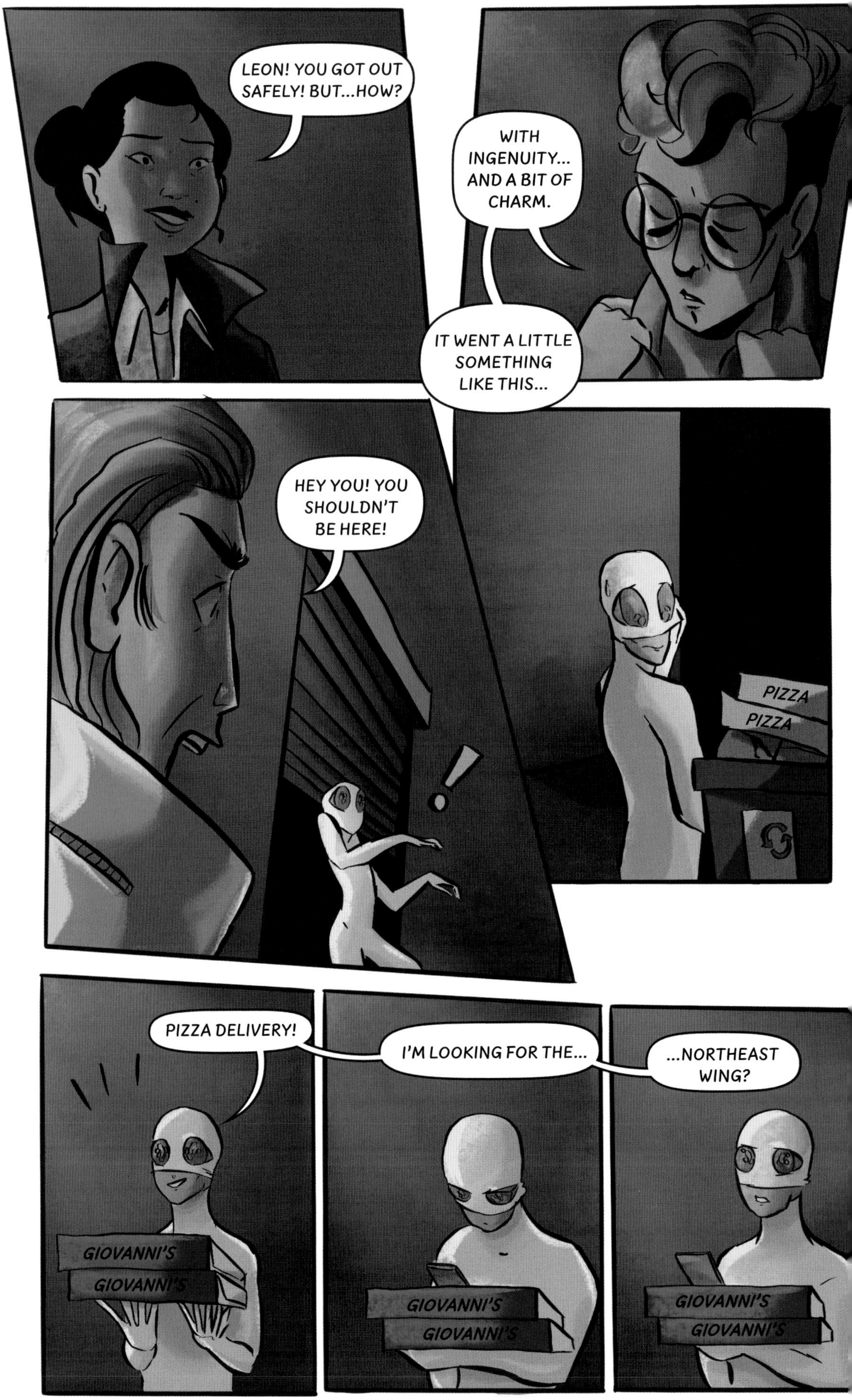
LEON! YOU GOT OUT SAFELY! BUT...HOW?
WITH INGENUITY... AND A BIT OF CHARM.
IT WENT A LITTLE SOMETHING LIKE THIS...
HEY YOU! YOU SHOULDN'T BE HERE!
PIZZA
PIZZA
PIZZA DELIVERY!
GIOVANNI'S
GIOVANNI'S
I'M LOOKING FOR THE...
GIOVANNI'S
GIOVANNI'S
...NORTHEAST WING?
GIOVANNI'S
GIOVANNI'S

WHAT'S WITH THE OUTFIT?
PIZZA
PIZZA
EH, STUPID HEALTH AND SAFETY RULES.
I WASN'T COMPLAINING. IT WORKS ON YOU.
GIOVANNI'S
GIOVANNI'S

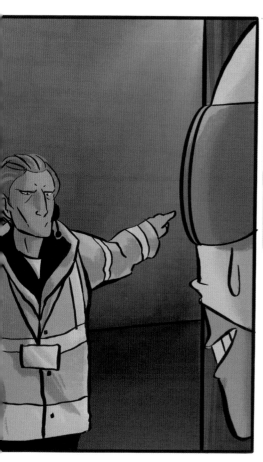

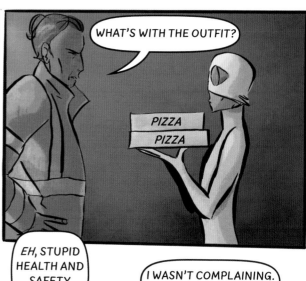

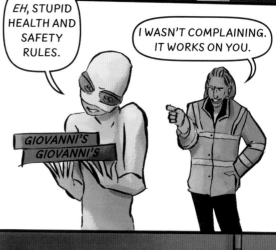

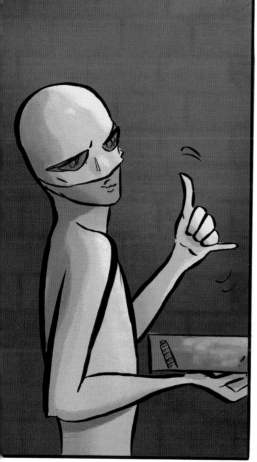

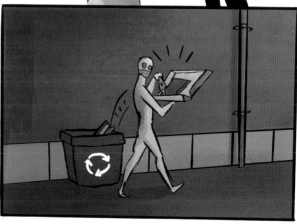

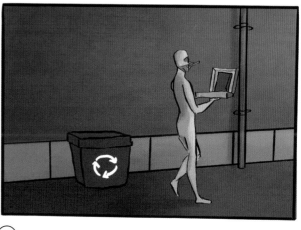

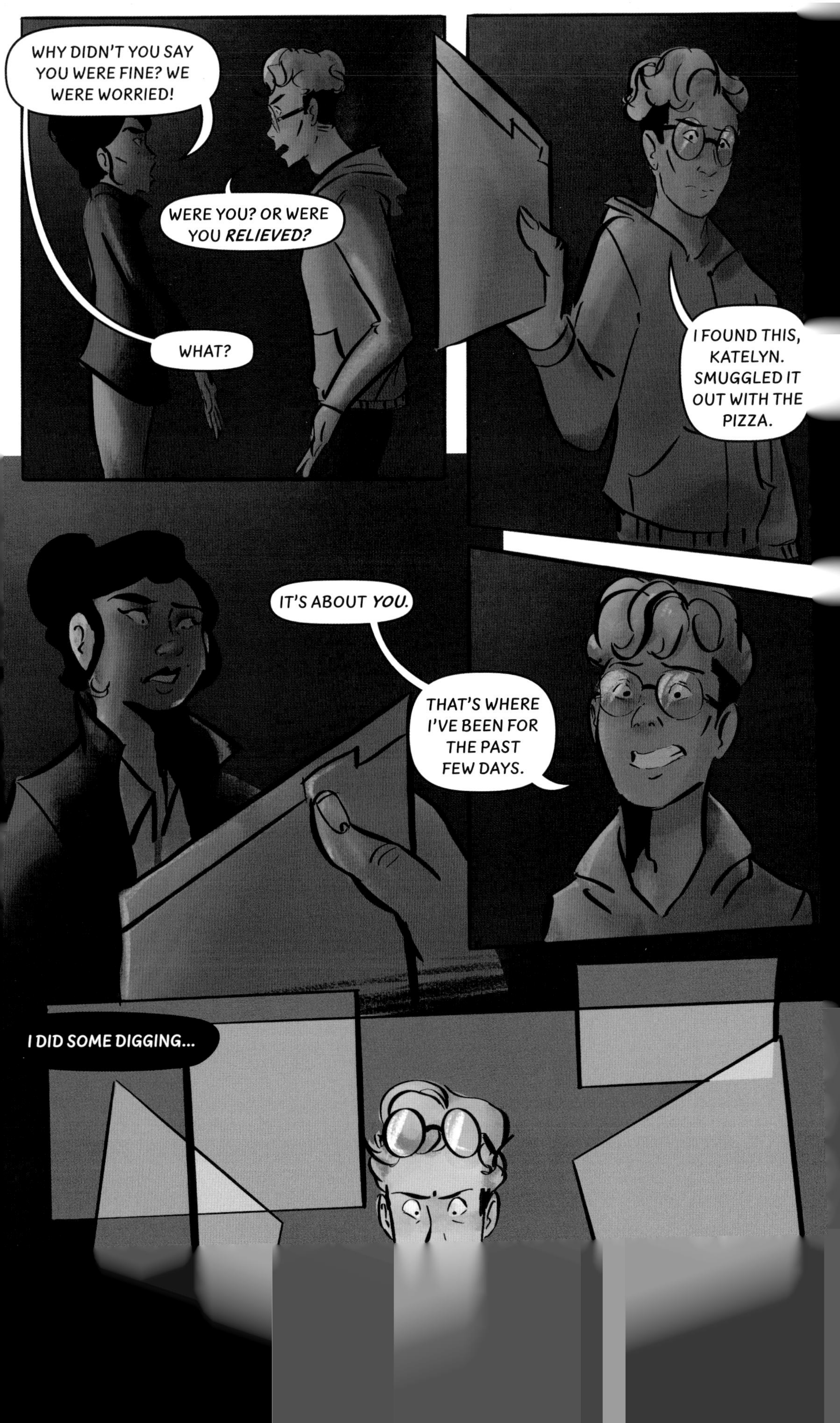
WHY DIDN'T YOU SAY YOU WERE FINE? WE WERE WORRIED!
WERE YOU? OR WERE YOU *RELIEVED?*
WHAT?
I FOUND THIS, KATELYN. SMUGGLED IT OUT WITH THE PIZZA.
IT'S ABOUT *YOU.*
THAT'S WHERE I'VE BEEN FOR THE PAST FEW DAYS.
I DID SOME DIGGING...

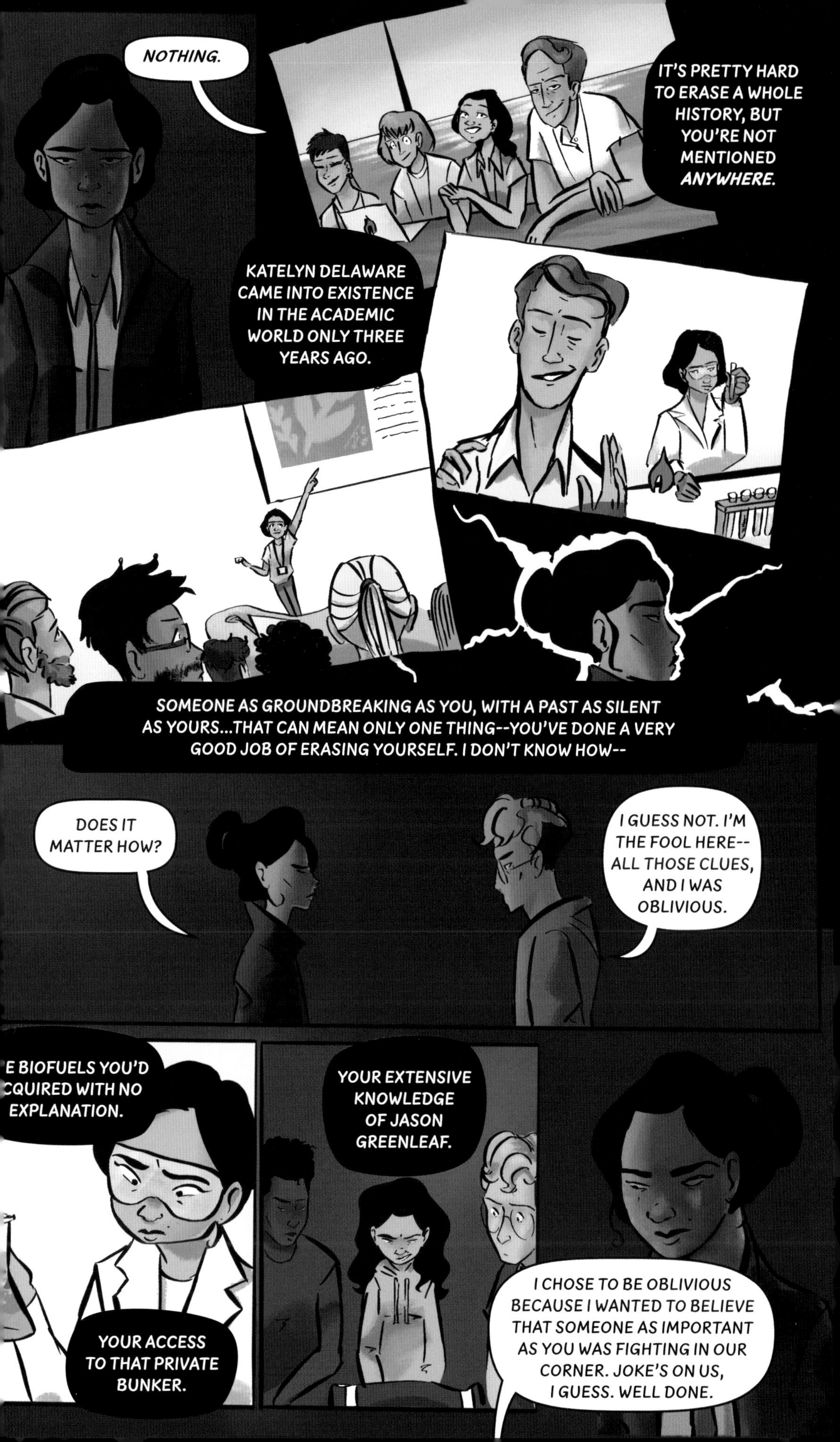
NOTHING.
IT'S PRETTY HARD TO ERASE A WHOLE HISTORY, BUT YOU'RE NOT MENTIONED *ANYWHERE*.
KATELYN DELAWARE CAME INTO EXISTENCE IN THE ACADEMIC WORLD ONLY THREE YEARS AGO.
SOMEONE AS GROUNDBREAKING AS YOU, WITH A PAST AS SILENT AS YOURS...THAT CAN MEAN ONLY ONE THING--YOU'VE DONE A VERY GOOD JOB OF ERASING YOURSELF. I DON'T KNOW HOW--
DOES IT MATTER HOW?
I GUESS NOT. I'M THE FOOL HERE--ALL THOSE CLUES, AND I WAS OBLIVIOUS.
E BIOFUELS YOU'D CQUIRED WITH NO EXPLANATION.
YOUR ACCESS TO THAT PRIVATE BUNKER.
YOUR EXTENSIVE KNOWLEDGE OF JASON GREENLEAF.
I CHOSE TO BE OBLIVIOUS BECAUSE I WANTED TO BELIEVE THAT SOMEONE AS IMPORTANT AS YOU WAS FIGHTING IN OUR CORNER. JOKE'S ON US, I GUESS. WELL DONE.

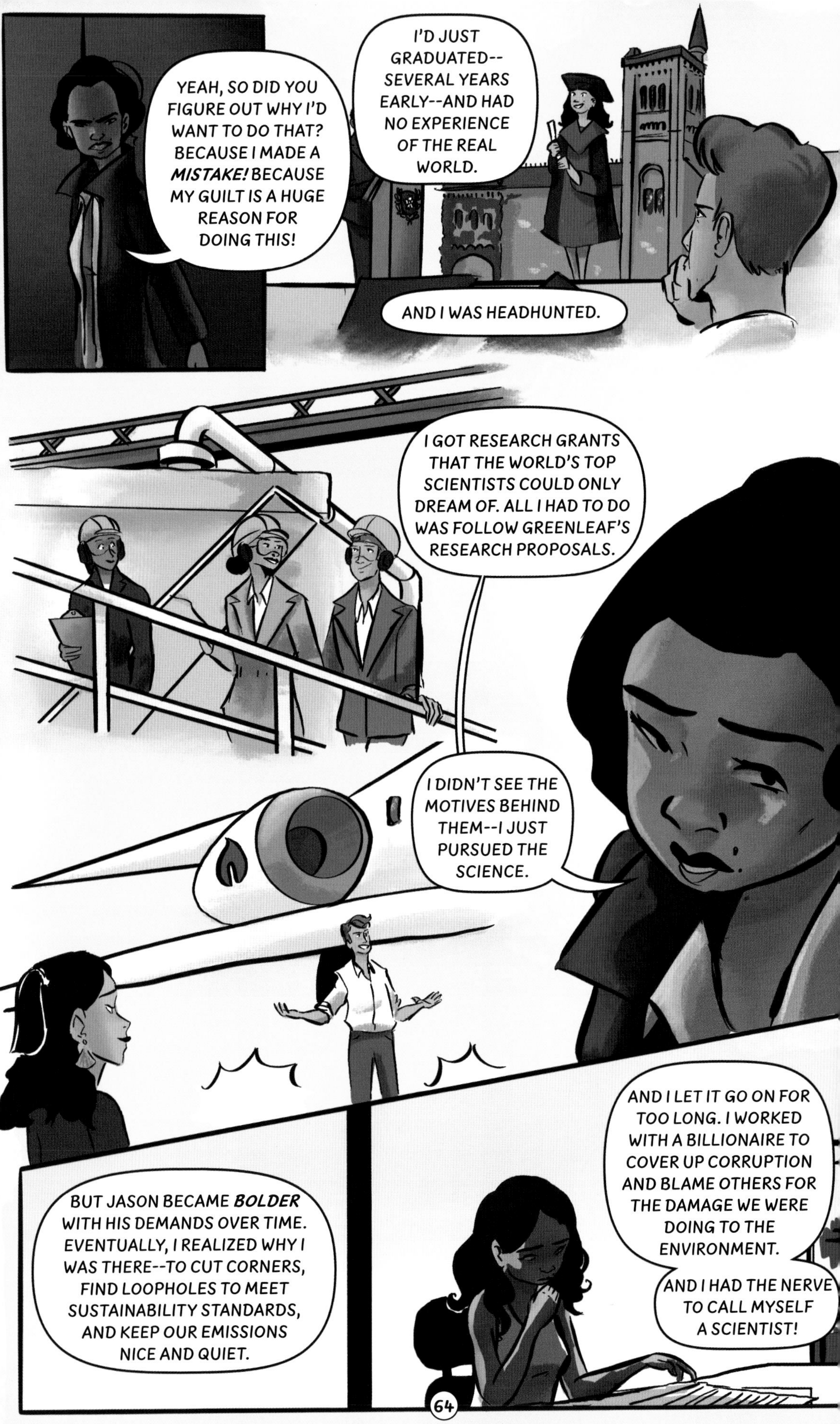
YEAH, SO DID YOU FIGURE OUT WHY I'D WANT TO DO THAT? BECAUSE I MADE A *MISTAKE!* BECAUSE MY GUILT IS A HUGE REASON FOR DOING THIS!
I'D JUST GRADUATED--SEVERAL YEARS EARLY--AND HAD NO EXPERIENCE OF THE REAL WORLD.
AND I WAS HEADHUNTED.
I GOT RESEARCH GRANTS THAT THE WORLD'S TOP SCIENTISTS COULD ONLY DREAM OF. ALL I HAD TO DO WAS FOLLOW GREENLEAF'S RESEARCH PROPOSALS.
I DIDN'T SEE THE MOTIVES BEHIND THEM--I JUST PURSUED THE SCIENCE.
BUT JASON BECAME *BOLDER* WITH HIS DEMANDS OVER TIME. EVENTUALLY, I REALIZED WHY I WAS THERE--TO CUT CORNERS, FIND LOOPHOLES TO MEET SUSTAINABILITY STANDARDS, AND KEEP OUR EMISSIONS NICE AND QUIET.
AND I LET IT GO ON FOR TOO LONG. I WORKED WITH A BILLIONAIRE TO COVER UP CORRUPTION AND BLAME OTHERS FOR THE DAMAGE WE WERE DOING TO THE ENVIRONMENT.
AND I HAD THE NERVE TO CALL MYSELF A SCIENTIST!

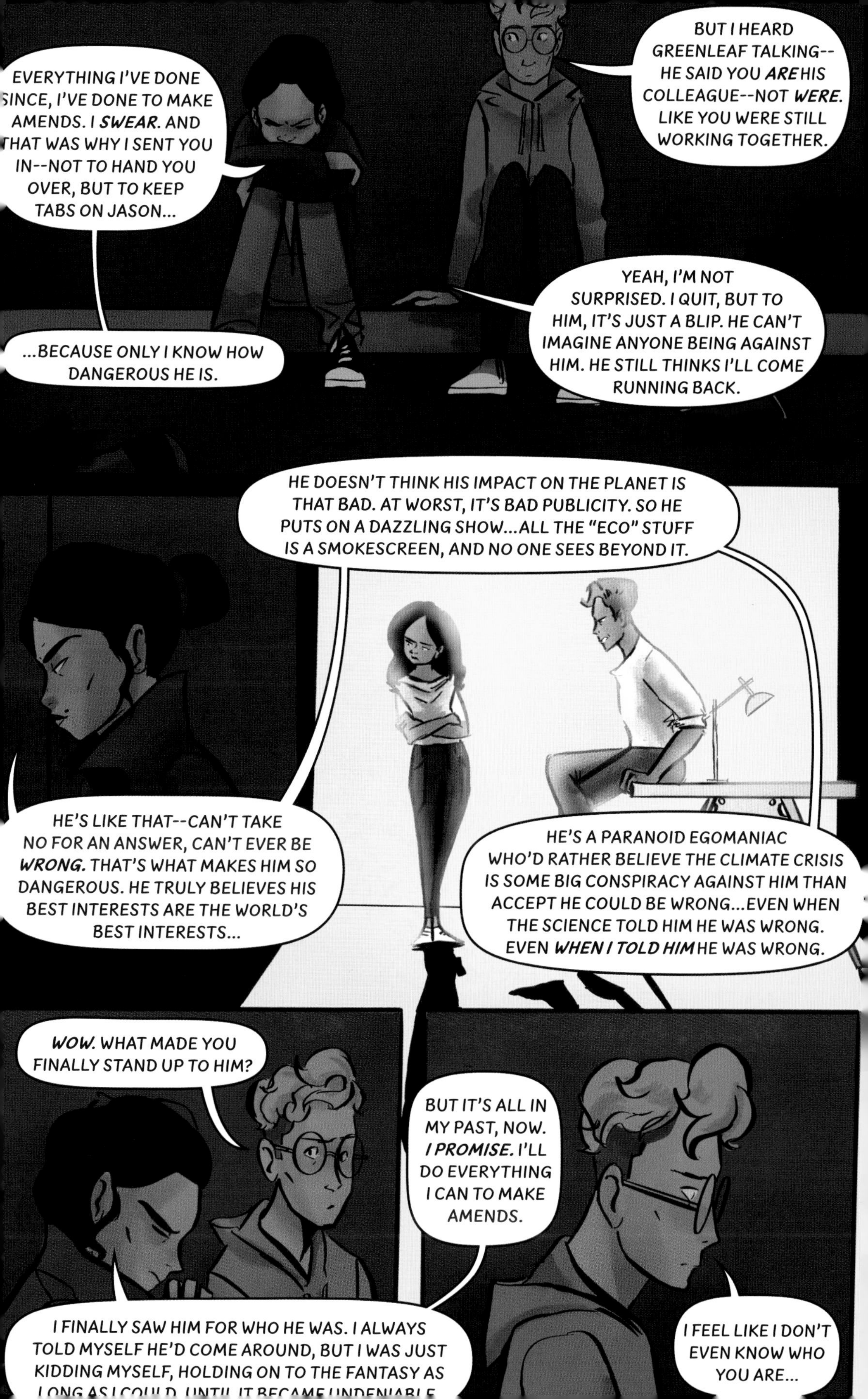
EVERYTHING I'VE DONE SINCE, I'VE DONE TO MAKE AMENDS. I ***SWEAR***. AND THAT WAS WHY I SENT YOU IN--NOT TO HAND YOU OVER, BUT TO KEEP TABS ON JASON...
...BECAUSE ONLY I KNOW HOW DANGEROUS HE IS.
BUT I HEARD GREENLEAF TALKING--HE SAID YOU ***ARE*** HIS COLLEAGUE--NOT ***WERE***. LIKE YOU WERE STILL WORKING TOGETHER.
YEAH, I'M NOT SURPRISED. I QUIT, BUT TO HIM, IT'S JUST A BLIP. HE CAN'T IMAGINE ANYONE BEING AGAINST HIM. HE STILL THINKS I'LL COME RUNNING BACK.
HE DOESN'T THINK HIS IMPACT ON THE PLANET IS THAT BAD. AT WORST, IT'S BAD PUBLICITY. SO HE PUTS ON A DAZZLING SHOW...ALL THE "ECO" STUFF IS A SMOKESCREEN, AND NO ONE SEES BEYOND IT.
HE'S LIKE THAT--CAN'T TAKE NO FOR AN ANSWER, CAN'T EVER BE ***WRONG.*** THAT'S WHAT MAKES HIM SO DANGEROUS. HE TRULY BELIEVES HIS BEST INTERESTS ARE THE WORLD'S BEST INTERESTS...
HE'S A PARANOID EGOMANIAC WHO'D RATHER BELIEVE THE CLIMATE CRISIS IS SOME BIG CONSPIRACY AGAINST HIM THAN ACCEPT HE COULD BE WRONG...EVEN WHEN THE SCIENCE TOLD HIM HE WAS WRONG. EVEN ***WHEN I TOLD HIM*** HE WAS WRONG.
WOW. WHAT MADE YOU FINALLY STAND UP TO HIM?
I FINALLY SAW HIM FOR WHO HE WAS. I ALWAYS TOLD MYSELF HE'D COME AROUND, BUT I WAS JUST KIDDING MYSELF, HOLDING ON TO THE FANTASY AS
BUT IT'S ALL IN MY PAST, NOW. ***I PROMISE.*** I'LL DO EVERYTHING I CAN TO MAKE AMENDS.
I FEEL LIKE I DON'T EVEN KNOW WHO YOU ARE...

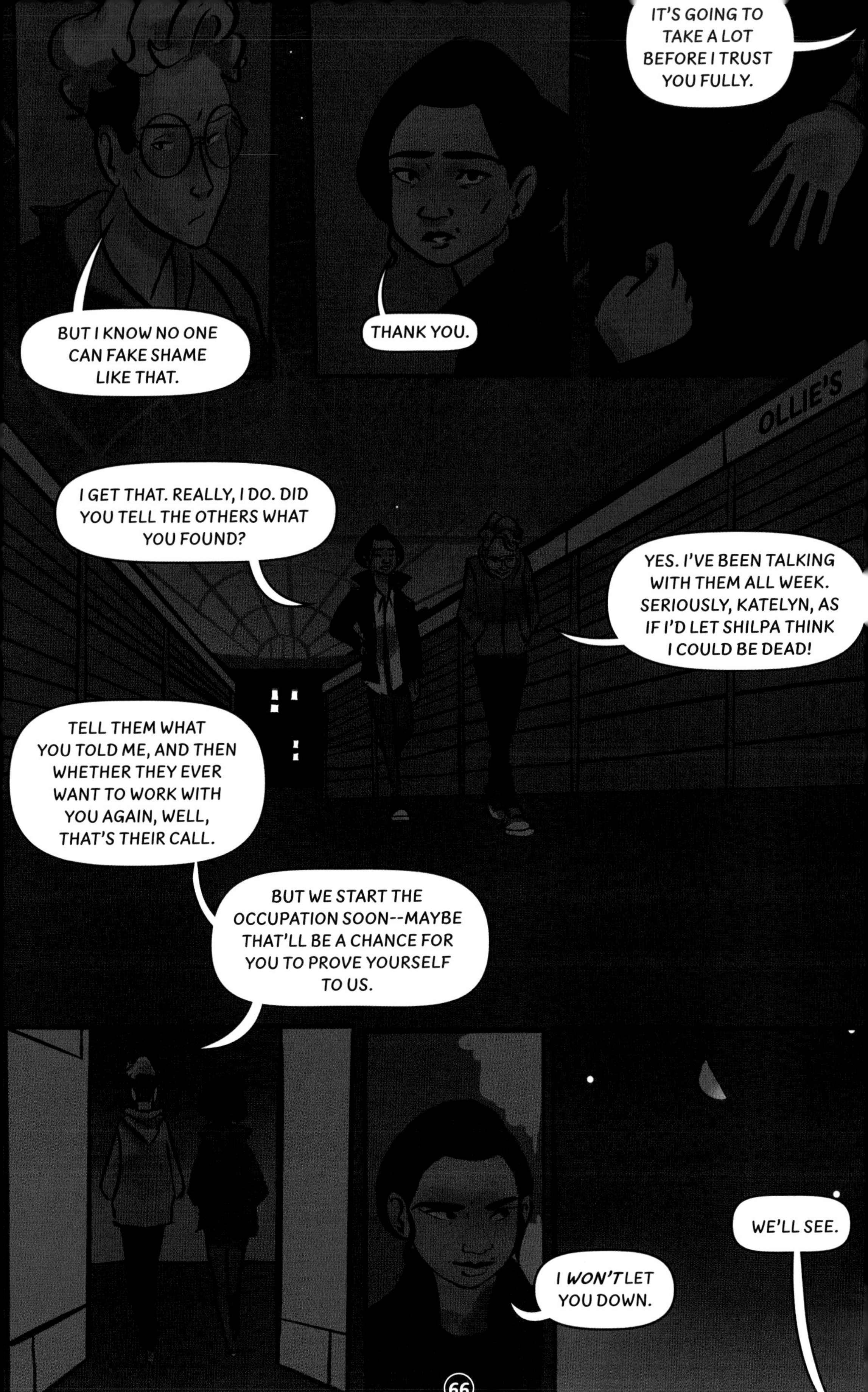
IT'S GOING TO TAKE A LOT BEFORE I TRUST YOU FULLY.
BUT I KNOW NO ONE CAN FAKE SHAME LIKE THAT.
THANK YOU.
OLLIE'S
I GET THAT. REALLY, I DO. DID YOU TELL THE OTHERS WHAT YOU FOUND?
YES. I'VE BEEN TALKING WITH THEM ALL WEEK. SERIOUSLY, KATELYN, AS IF I'D LET SHILPA THINK I COULD BE DEAD!
TELL THEM WHAT YOU TOLD ME, AND THEN WHETHER THEY EVER WANT TO WORK WITH YOU AGAIN, WELL, THAT'S THEIR CALL.
BUT WE START THE OCCUPATION SOON--MAYBE THAT'LL BE A CHANCE FOR YOU TO PROVE YOURSELF TO US.
WE'LL SEE.
I *WON'T* LET YOU DOWN.

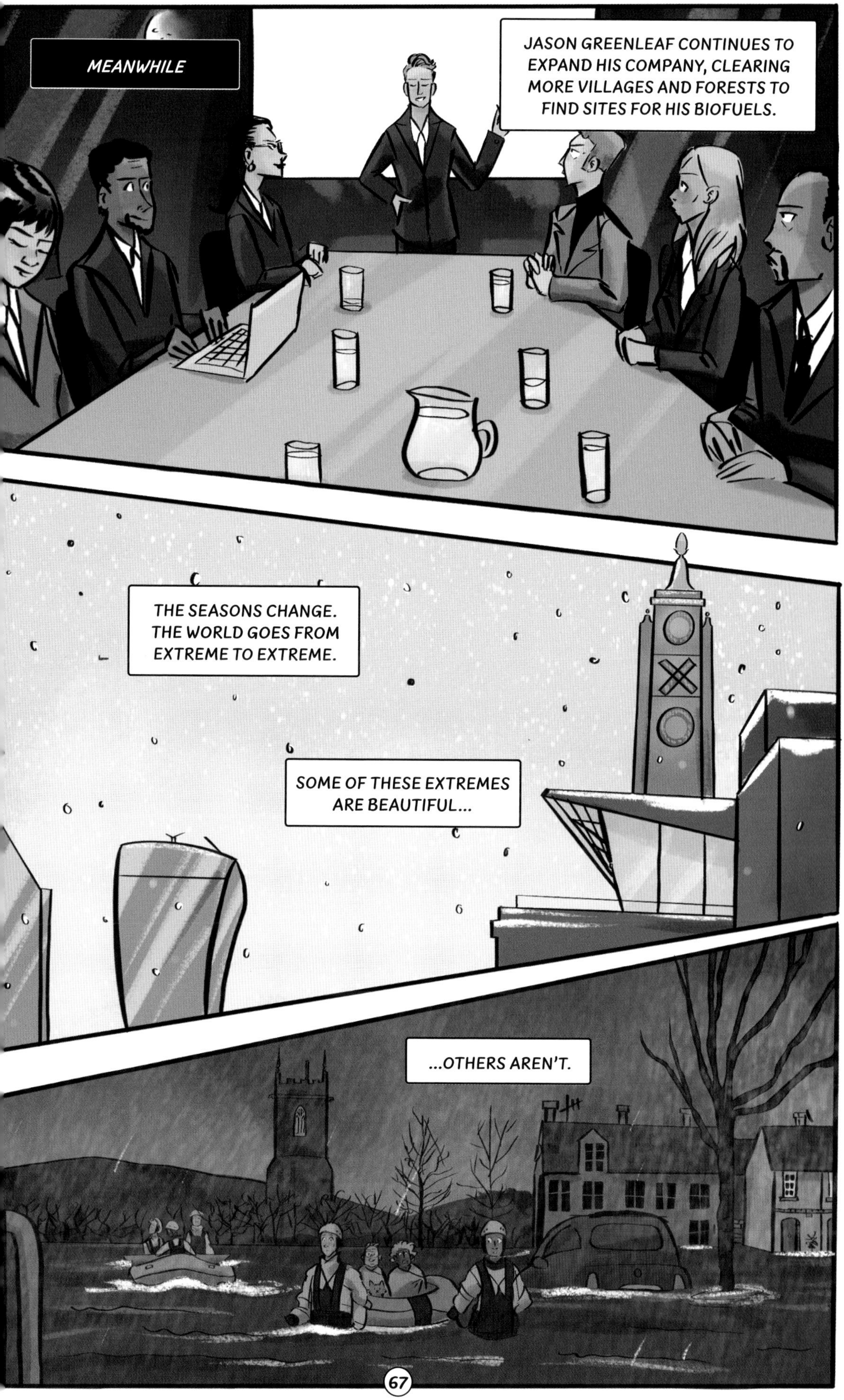
MEANWHILE
JASON GREENLEAF CONTINUES TO EXPAND HIS COMPANY, CLEARING MORE VILLAGES AND FORESTS TO FIND SITES FOR HIS BIOFUELS.
THE SEASONS CHANGE. THE WORLD GOES FROM EXTREME TO EXTREME.
SOME OF THESE EXTREMES ARE BEAUTIFUL...
...OTHERS AREN'T.

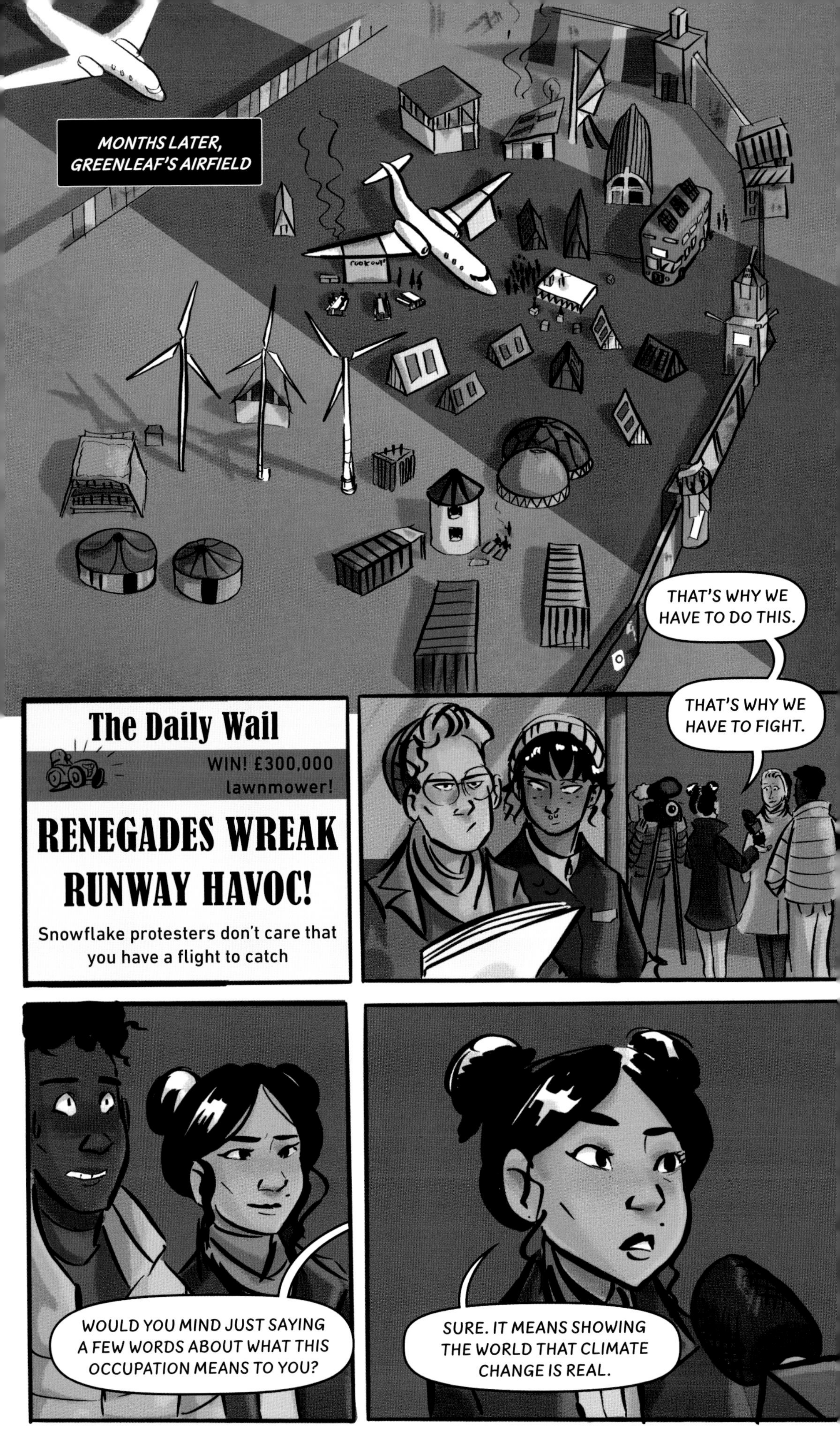
MONTHS LATER, GREENLEAF'S AIRFIELD
THAT'S WHY WE HAVE TO DO THIS.
The Daily Wail
WIN! £300,000 lawnmower!
RENEGADES WREAK RUNWAY HAVOC!
Snowflake protesters don't care that you have a flight to catch
THAT'S WHY WE HAVE TO FIGHT.
WOULD YOU MIND JUST SAYING A FEW WORDS ABOUT WHAT THIS OCCUPATION MEANS TO YOU?
SURE. IT MEANS SHOWING THE WORLD THAT CLIMATE CHANGE IS REAL.

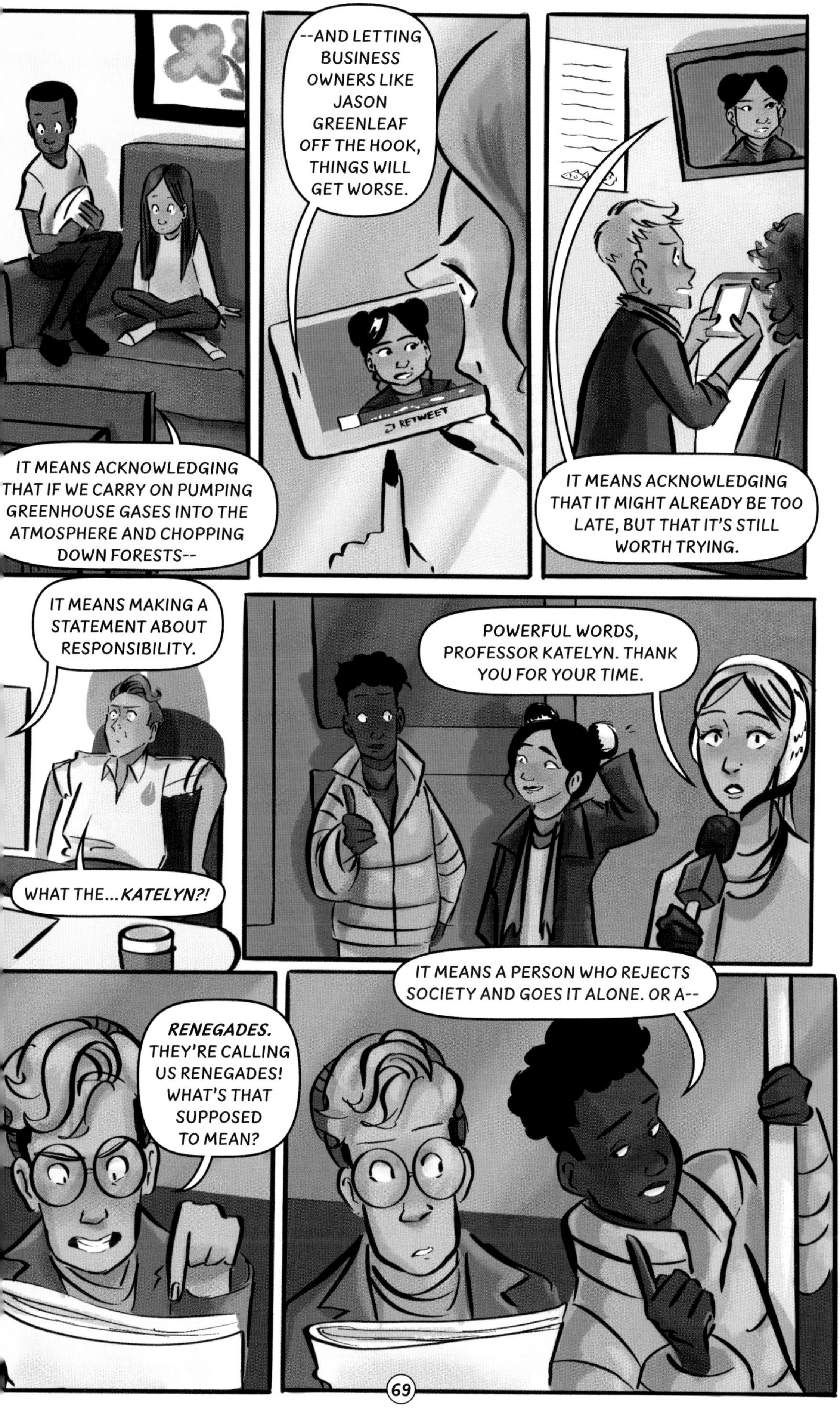
--AND LETTING BUSINESS OWNERS LIKE JASON GREENLEAF OFF THE HOOK, THINGS WILL GET WORSE.
RETWEET
IT MEANS ACKNOWLEDGING THAT IF WE CARRY ON PUMPING GREENHOUSE GASES INTO THE ATMOSPHERE AND CHOPPING DOWN FORESTS--
IT MEANS ACKNOWLEDGING THAT IT MIGHT ALREADY BE TOO LATE, BUT THAT IT'S STILL WORTH TRYING.
IT MEANS MAKING A STATEMENT ABOUT RESPONSIBILITY.
WHAT THE... *KATELYN?!*
POWERFUL WORDS, PROFESSOR KATELYN. THANK YOU FOR YOUR TIME.
RENEGADES. THEY'RE CALLING US RENEGADES! WHAT'S THAT SUPPOSED TO MEAN?
IT MEANS A PERSON WHO REJECTS SOCIETY AND GOES IT ALONE. OR A--

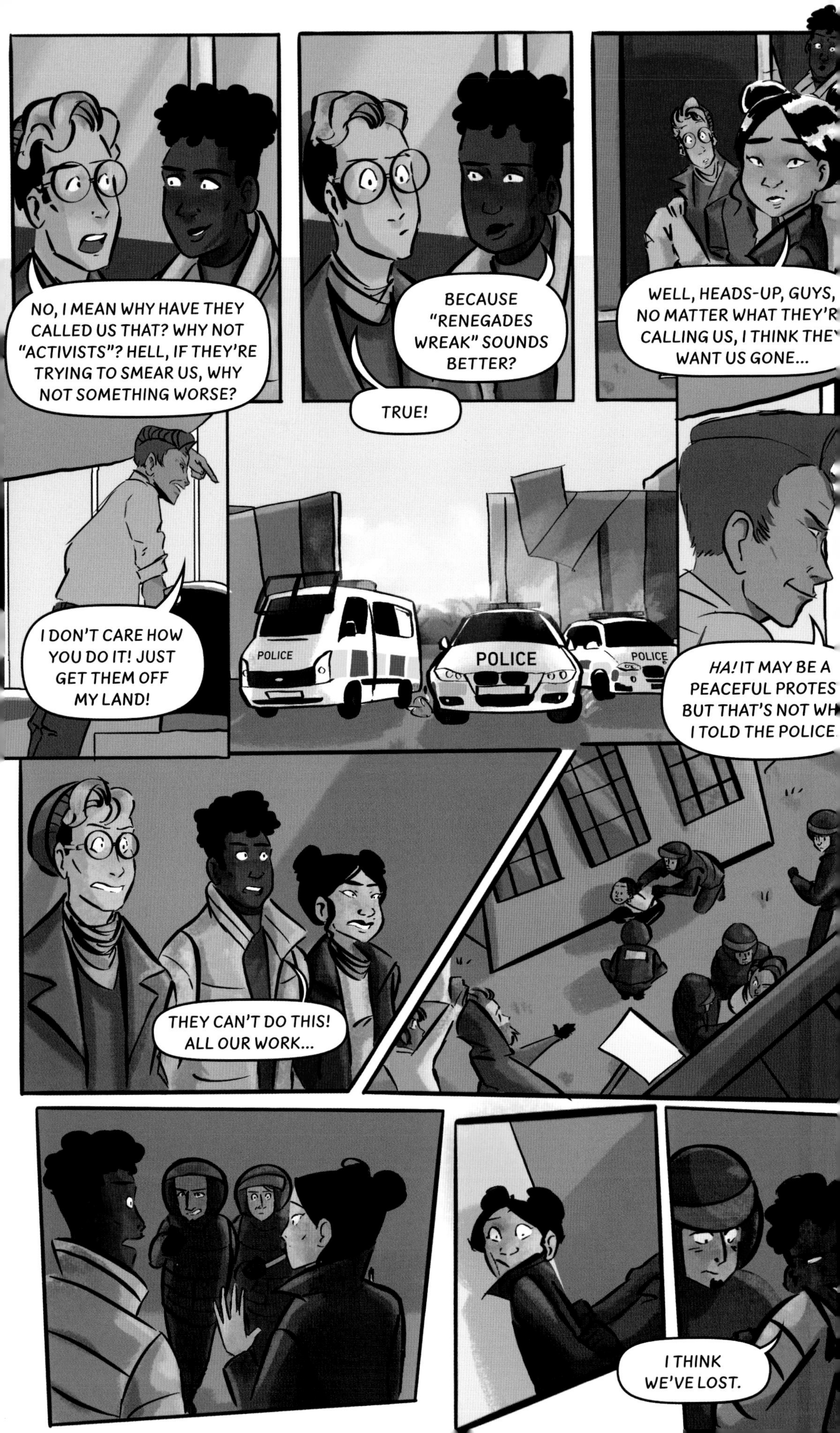
NO, I MEAN WHY HAVE THEY CALLED US THAT? WHY NOT "ACTIVISTS"? HELL, IF THEY'RE TRYING TO SMEAR US, WHY NOT SOMETHING WORSE?
BECAUSE "RENEGADES WREAK" SOUNDS BETTER?
TRUE!
WELL, HEADS-UP, GUYS, NO MATTER WHAT THEY'R CALLING US, I THINK THE WANT US GONE...
I DON'T CARE HOW YOU DO IT! JUST GET THEM OFF MY LAND!
POLICE
POLICE
POLICE
HA! IT MAY BE A PEACEFUL PROTES BUT THAT'S NOT WH I TOLD THE POLICE.
THEY CAN'T DO THIS! ALL OUR WORK...
I THINK WE'VE LOST.

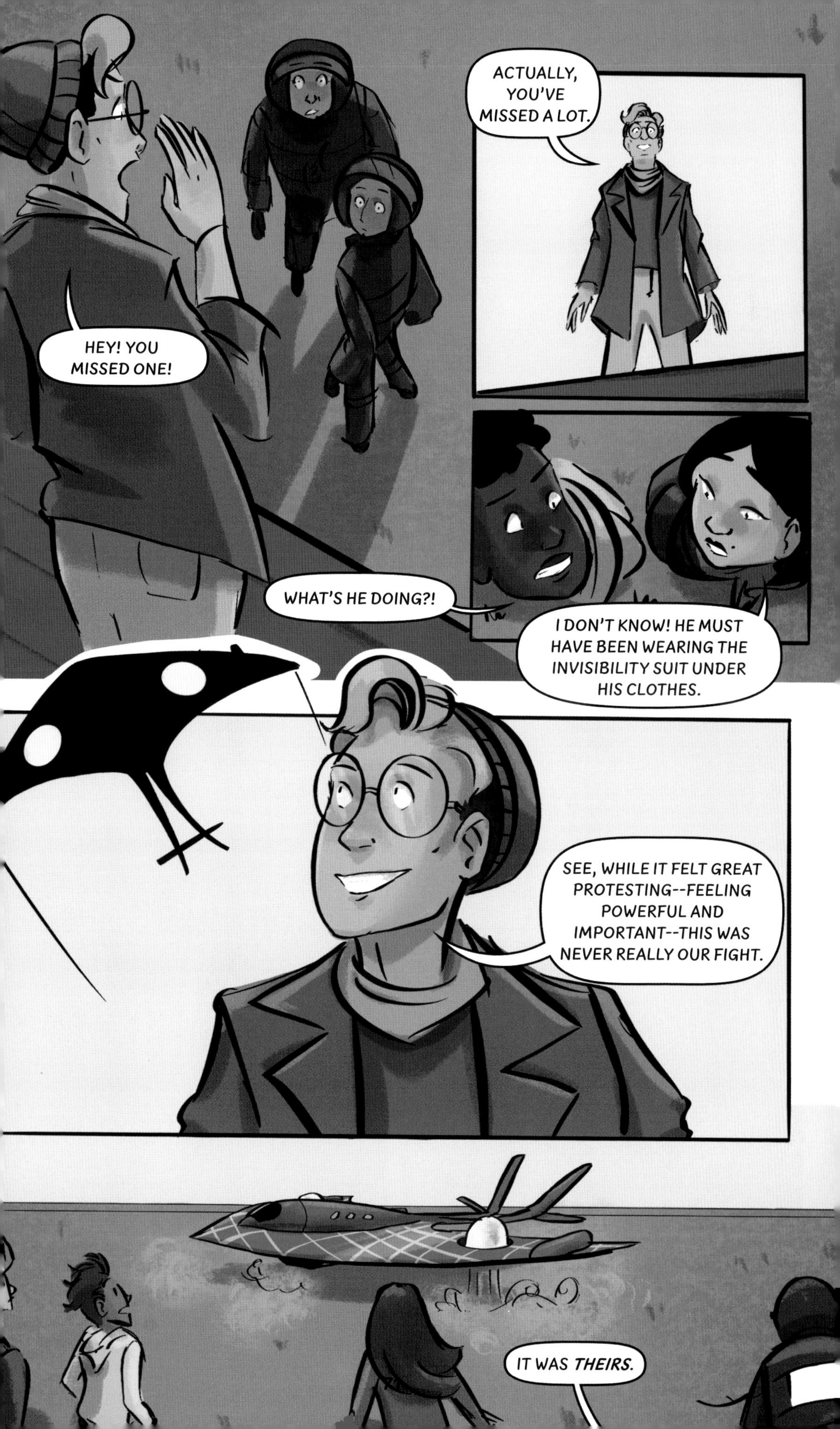
HEY! YOU MISSED ONE!
ACTUALLY, YOU'VE MISSED A LOT.
WHAT'S HE DOING?!
I DON'T KNOW! HE MUST HAVE BEEN WEARING THE INVISIBILITY SUIT UNDER HIS CLOTHES.
SEE, WHILE IT FELT GREAT PROTESTING--FEELING POWERFUL AND IMPORTANT--THIS WAS NEVER REALLY OUR FIGHT.
IT WAS *THEIRS*.

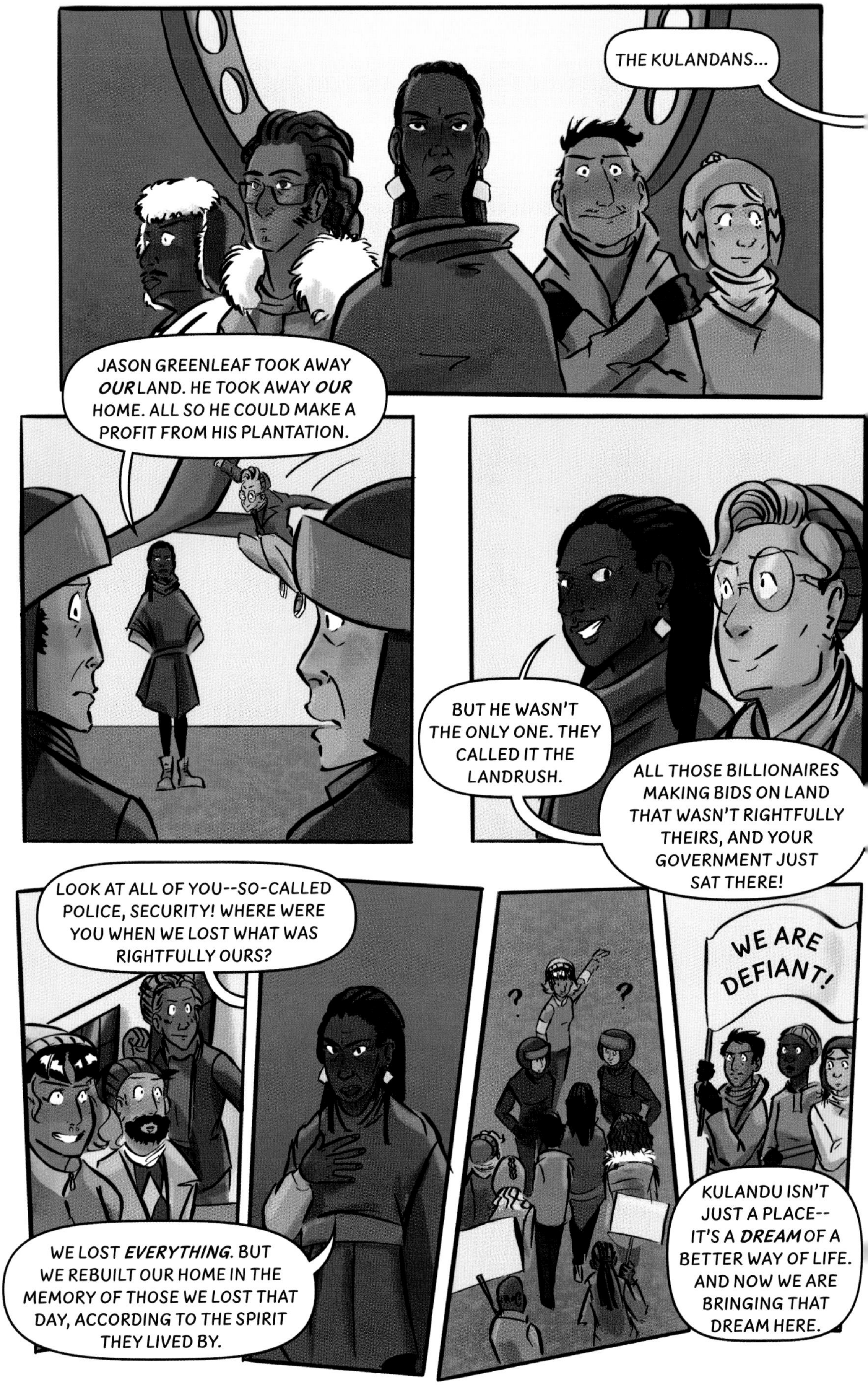
THE KULANDANS...
JASON GREENLEAF TOOK AWAY *OUR* LAND. HE TOOK AWAY *OUR* HOME. ALL SO HE COULD MAKE A PROFIT FROM HIS PLANTATION.
BUT HE WASN'T THE ONLY ONE. THEY CALLED IT THE LANDRUSH.
ALL THOSE BILLIONAIRES MAKING BIDS ON LAND THAT WASN'T RIGHTFULLY THEIRS, AND YOUR GOVERNMENT JUST SAT THERE!
LOOK AT ALL OF YOU--SO-CALLED POLICE, SECURITY! WHERE WERE YOU WHEN WE LOST WHAT WAS RIGHTFULLY OURS?
WE LOST *EVERYTHING*. BUT WE REBUILT OUR HOME IN THE MEMORY OF THOSE WE LOST THAT DAY, ACCORDING TO THE SPIRIT THEY LIVED BY.
WE ARE DEFIANT!
KULANDU ISN'T JUST A PLACE-- IT'S A *DREAM* OF A BETTER WAY OF LIFE. AND NOW WE ARE BRINGING THAT DREAM HERE.

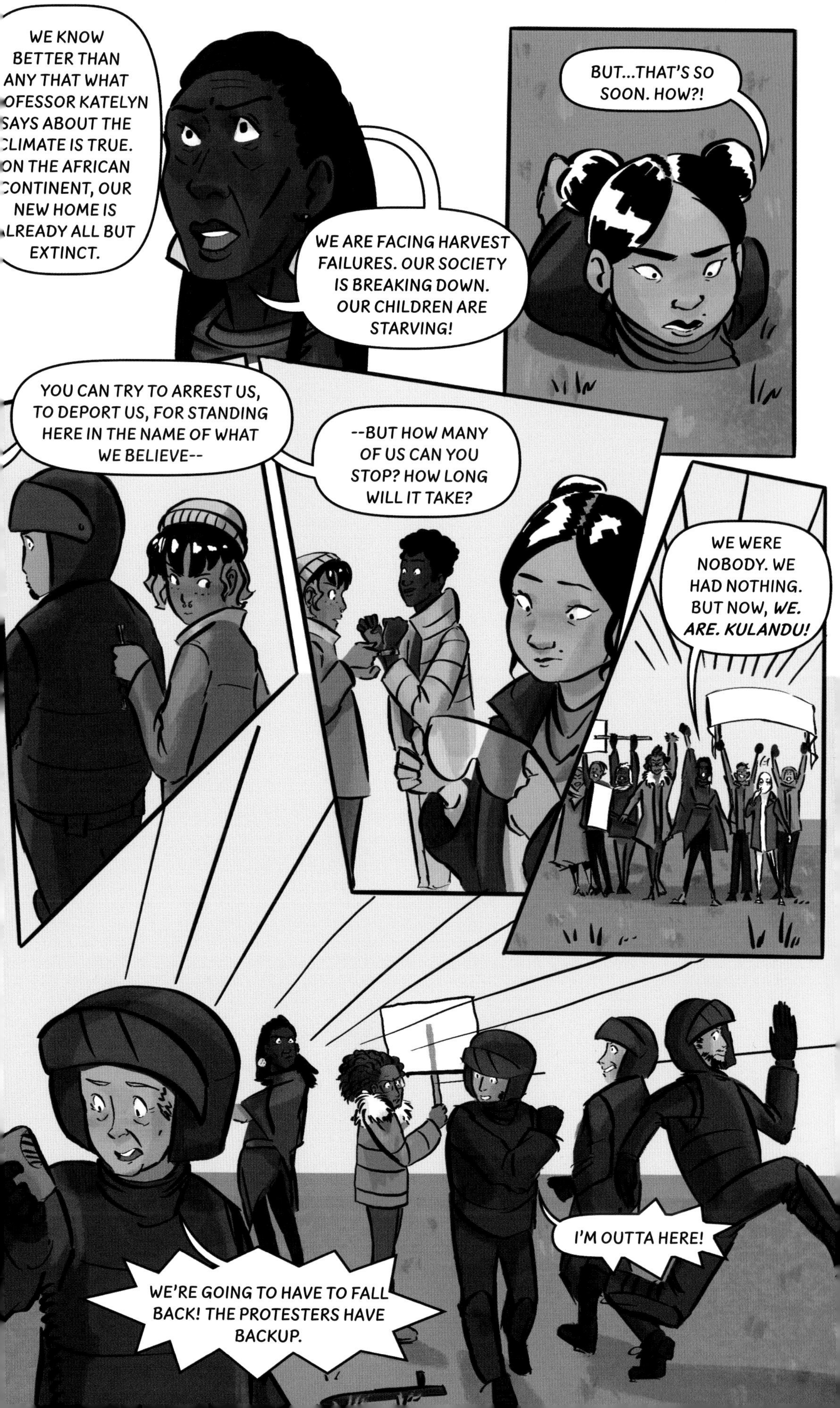
WE KNOW BETTER THAN ANY THAT WHAT OFESSOR KATELYN SAYS ABOUT THE CLIMATE IS TRUE. ON THE AFRICAN CONTINENT, OUR NEW HOME IS LREADY ALL BUT EXTINCT.
WE ARE FACING HARVEST FAILURES. OUR SOCIETY IS BREAKING DOWN. OUR CHILDREN ARE STARVING!
BUT...THAT'S SO SOON. HOW?!
YOU CAN TRY TO ARREST US, TO DEPORT US, FOR STANDING HERE IN THE NAME OF WHAT WE BELIEVE--
--BUT HOW MANY OF US CAN YOU STOP? HOW LONG WILL IT TAKE?
WE WERE NOBODY. WE HAD NOTHING. BUT NOW, *WE. ARE. KULANDU!*
I'M OUTTA HERE!
WE'RE GOING TO HAVE TO FALL BACK! THE PROTESTERS HAVE BACKUP.

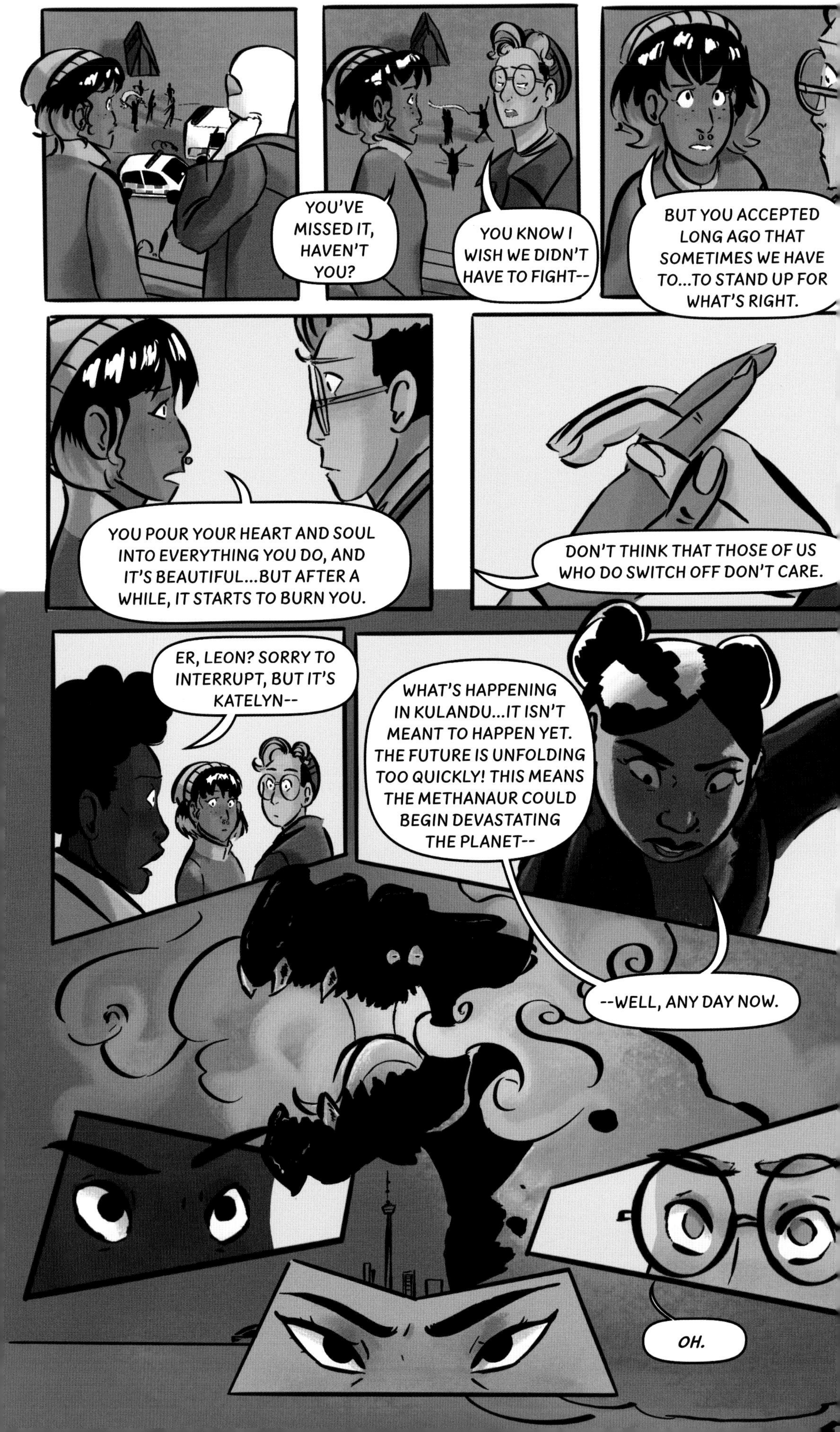
YOU'VE MISSED IT, HAVEN'T YOU?
YOU KNOW I WISH WE DIDN'T HAVE TO FIGHT--
BUT YOU ACCEPTED LONG AGO THAT SOMETIMES WE HAVE TO...TO STAND UP FOR WHAT'S RIGHT.
YOU POUR YOUR HEART AND SOUL INTO EVERYTHING YOU DO, AND IT'S BEAUTIFUL...BUT AFTER A WHILE, IT STARTS TO BURN YOU.
DON'T THINK THAT THOSE OF US WHO DO SWITCH OFF DON'T CARE.
ER, LEON? SORRY TO INTERRUPT, BUT IT'S KATELYN--
WHAT'S HAPPENING IN KULANDU...IT ISN'T MEANT TO HAPPEN YET. THE FUTURE IS UNFOLDING TOO QUICKLY! THIS MEANS THE METHANAUR COULD BEGIN DEVASTATING THE PLANET--
--WELL, ANY DAY NOW.
OH.

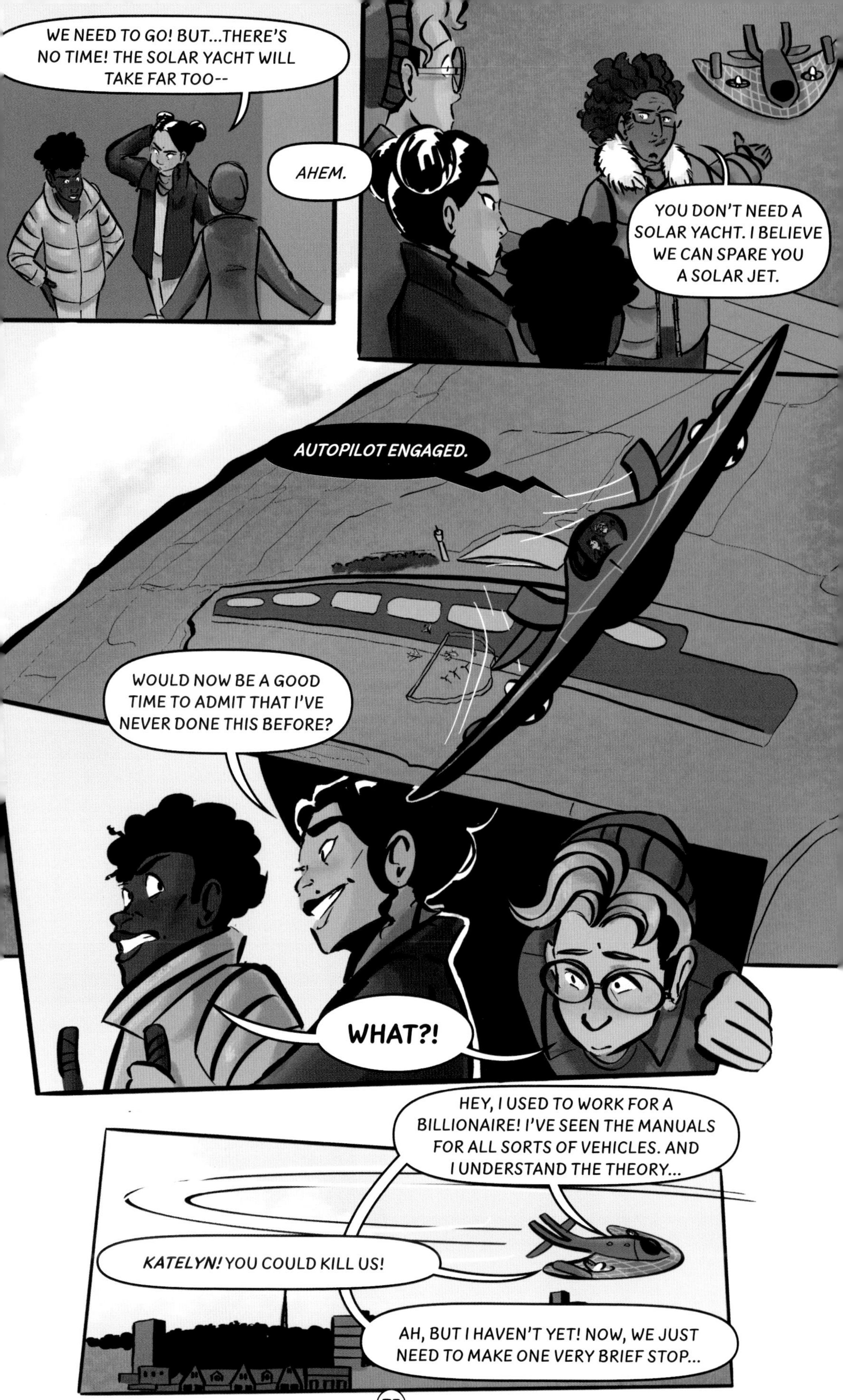
WE NEED TO GO! BUT...THERE'S NO TIME! THE SOLAR YACHT WILL TAKE FAR TOO--
AHEM.
YOU DON'T NEED A SOLAR YACHT. I BELIEVE WE CAN SPARE YOU A SOLAR JET.
AUTOPILOT ENGAGED.
WOULD NOW BE A GOOD TIME TO ADMIT THAT I'VE NEVER DONE THIS BEFORE?
WHAT?!
HEY, I USED TO WORK FOR A BILLIONAIRE! I'VE SEEN THE MANUALS FOR ALL SORTS OF VEHICLES. AND I UNDERSTAND THE THEORY...
KATELYN! YOU COULD KILL US!
AH, BUT I HAVEN'T YET! NOW, WE JUST NEED TO MAKE ONE VERY BRIEF STOP...

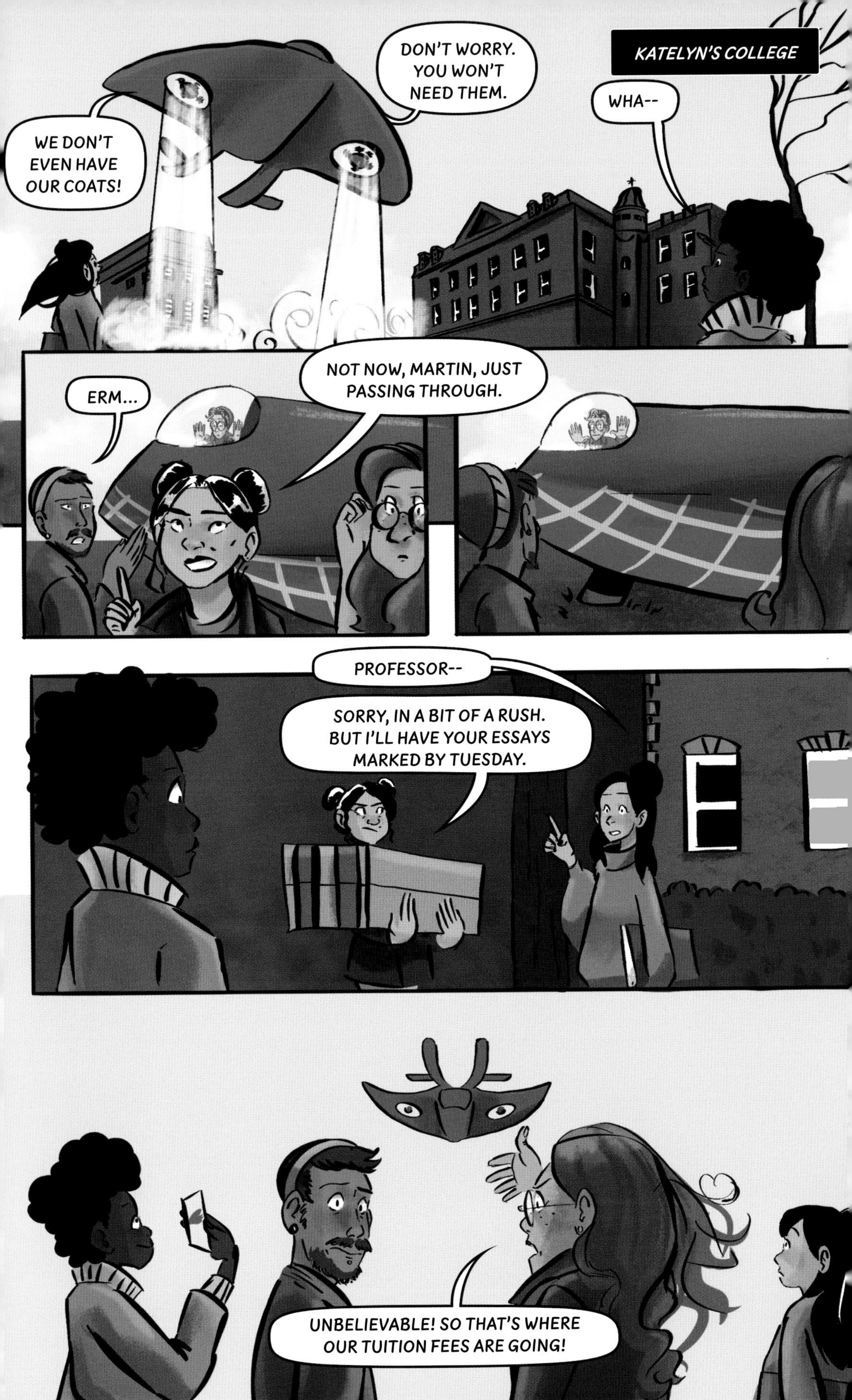
KATELYN'S COLLEGE
WE DON'T EVEN HAVE OUR COATS!
DON'T WORRY. YOU WON'T NEED THEM.
WHA--
ERM...
NOT NOW, MARTIN, JUST PASSING THROUGH.
PROFESSOR--
SORRY, IN A BIT OF A RUSH. BUT I'LL HAVE YOUR ESSAYS MARKED BY TUESDAY.
UNBELIEVABLE! SO THAT'S WHERE OUR TUITION FEES ARE GOING!

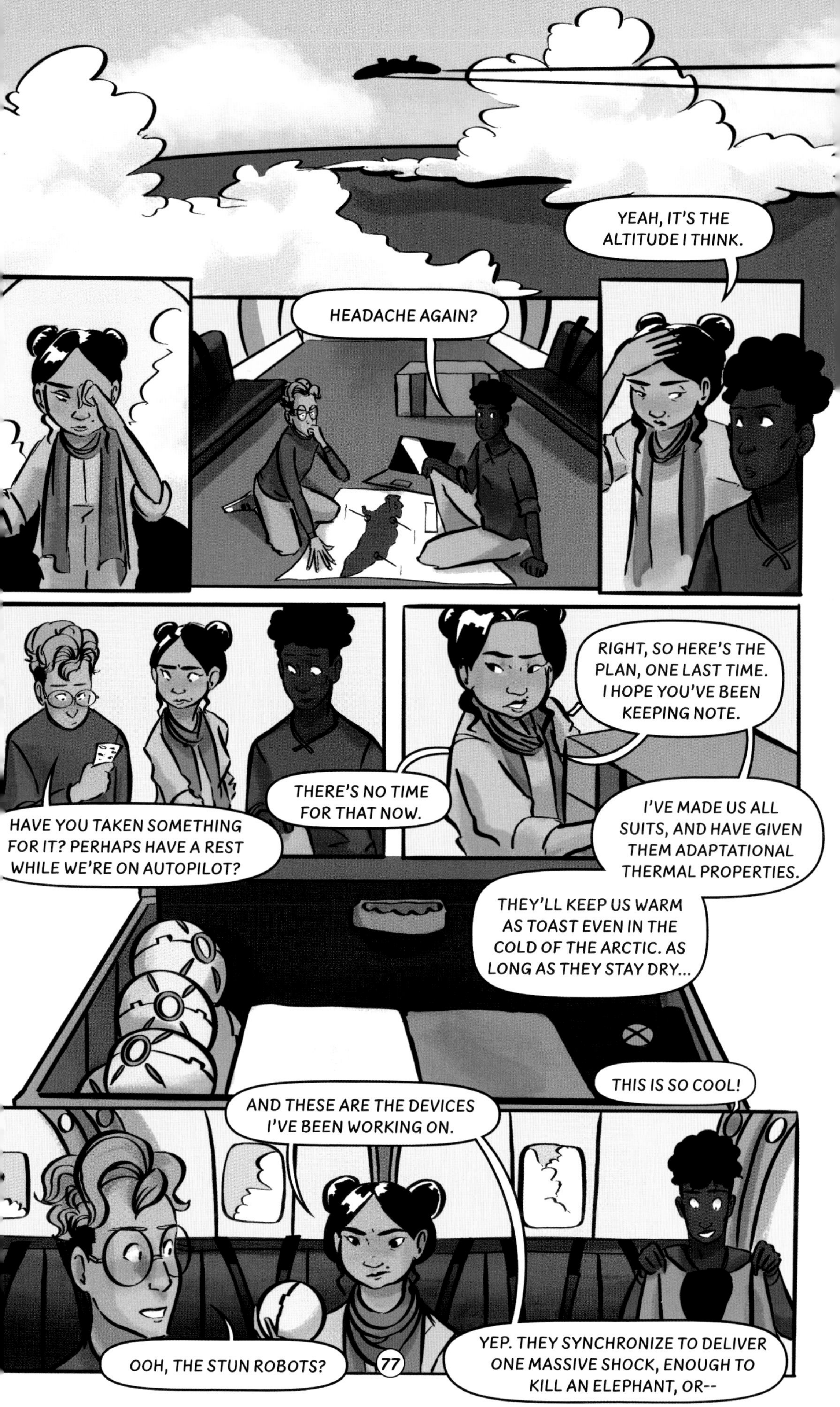
YEAH, IT'S THE ALTITUDE I THINK.
HEADACHE AGAIN?
HAVE YOU TAKEN SOMETHING FOR IT? PERHAPS HAVE A REST WHILE WE'RE ON AUTOPILOT?
THERE'S NO TIME FOR THAT NOW.
RIGHT, SO HERE'S THE PLAN, ONE LAST TIME. I HOPE YOU'VE BEEN KEEPING NOTE.
I'VE MADE US ALL SUITS, AND HAVE GIVEN THEM ADAPTATIONAL THERMAL PROPERTIES.
THEY'LL KEEP US WARM AS TOAST EVEN IN THE COLD OF THE ARCTIC. AS LONG AS THEY STAY DRY...
THIS IS SO COOL!
AND THESE ARE THE DEVICES I'VE BEEN WORKING ON.
OOH, THE STUN ROBOTS?
YEP. THEY SYNCHRONIZE TO DELIVER ONE MASSIVE SHOCK, ENOUGH TO KILL AN ELEPHANT, OR--

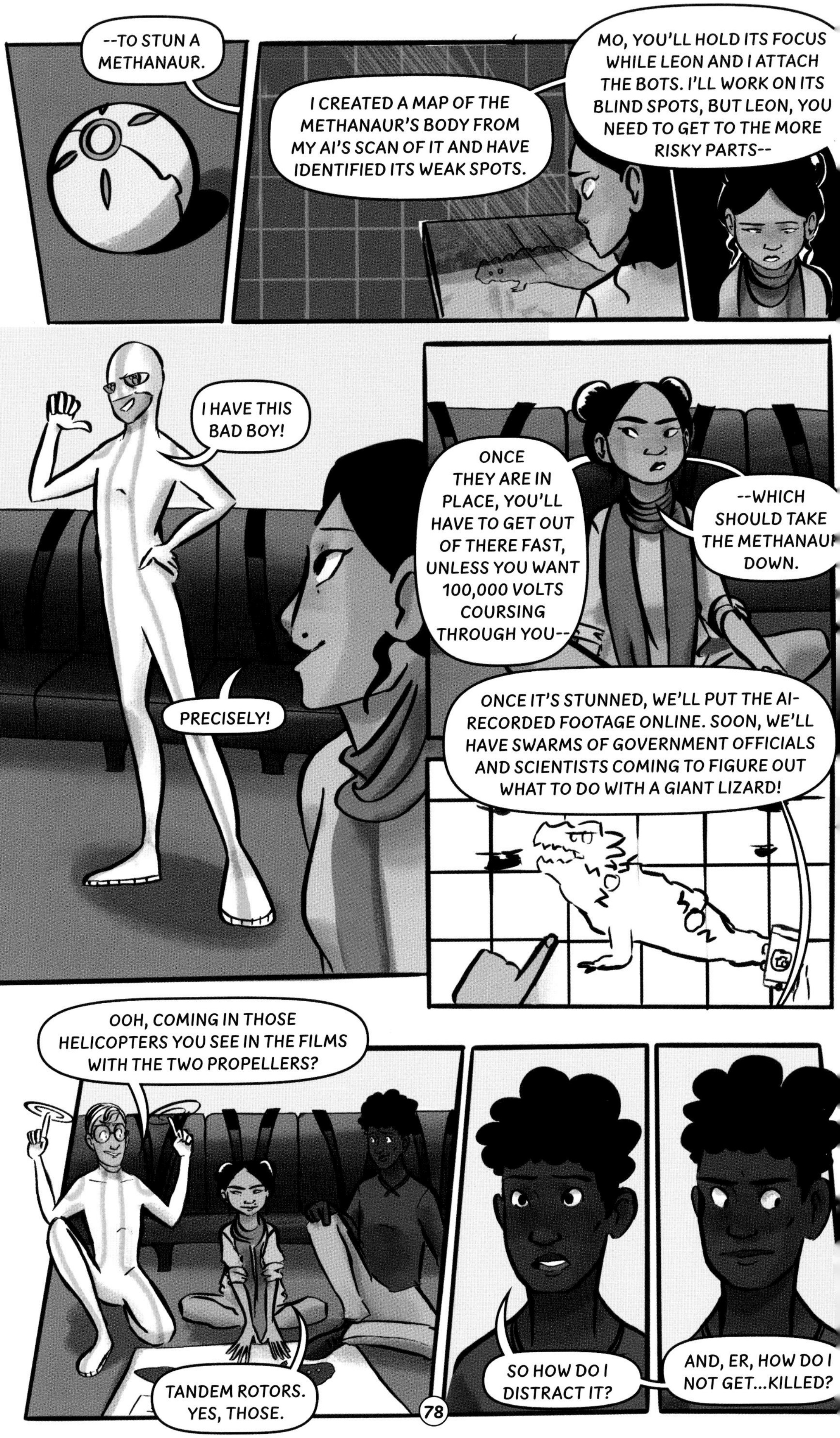
--TO STUN A METHANAUR.
I CREATED A MAP OF THE METHANAUR'S BODY FROM MY AI'S SCAN OF IT AND HAVE IDENTIFIED ITS WEAK SPOTS.
MO, YOU'LL HOLD ITS FOCUS WHILE LEON AND I ATTACH THE BOTS. I'LL WORK ON ITS BLIND SPOTS, BUT LEON, YOU NEED TO GET TO THE MORE RISKY PARTS--
I HAVE THIS BAD BOY!
PRECISELY!
ONCE THEY ARE IN PLACE, YOU'LL HAVE TO GET OUT OF THERE FAST, UNLESS YOU WANT 100,000 VOLTS COURSING THROUGH YOU--
--WHICH SHOULD TAKE THE METHANAUR DOWN.
ONCE IT'S STUNNED, WE'LL PUT THE AI-RECORDED FOOTAGE ONLINE. SOON, WE'LL HAVE SWARMS OF GOVERNMENT OFFICIALS AND SCIENTISTS COMING TO FIGURE OUT WHAT TO DO WITH A GIANT LIZARD!
OOH, COMING IN THOSE HELICOPTERS YOU SEE IN THE FILMS WITH THE TWO PROPELLERS?
TANDEM ROTORS. YES, THOSE.
SO HOW DO I DISTRACT IT?
AND, ER, HOW DO I NOT GET...KILLED?

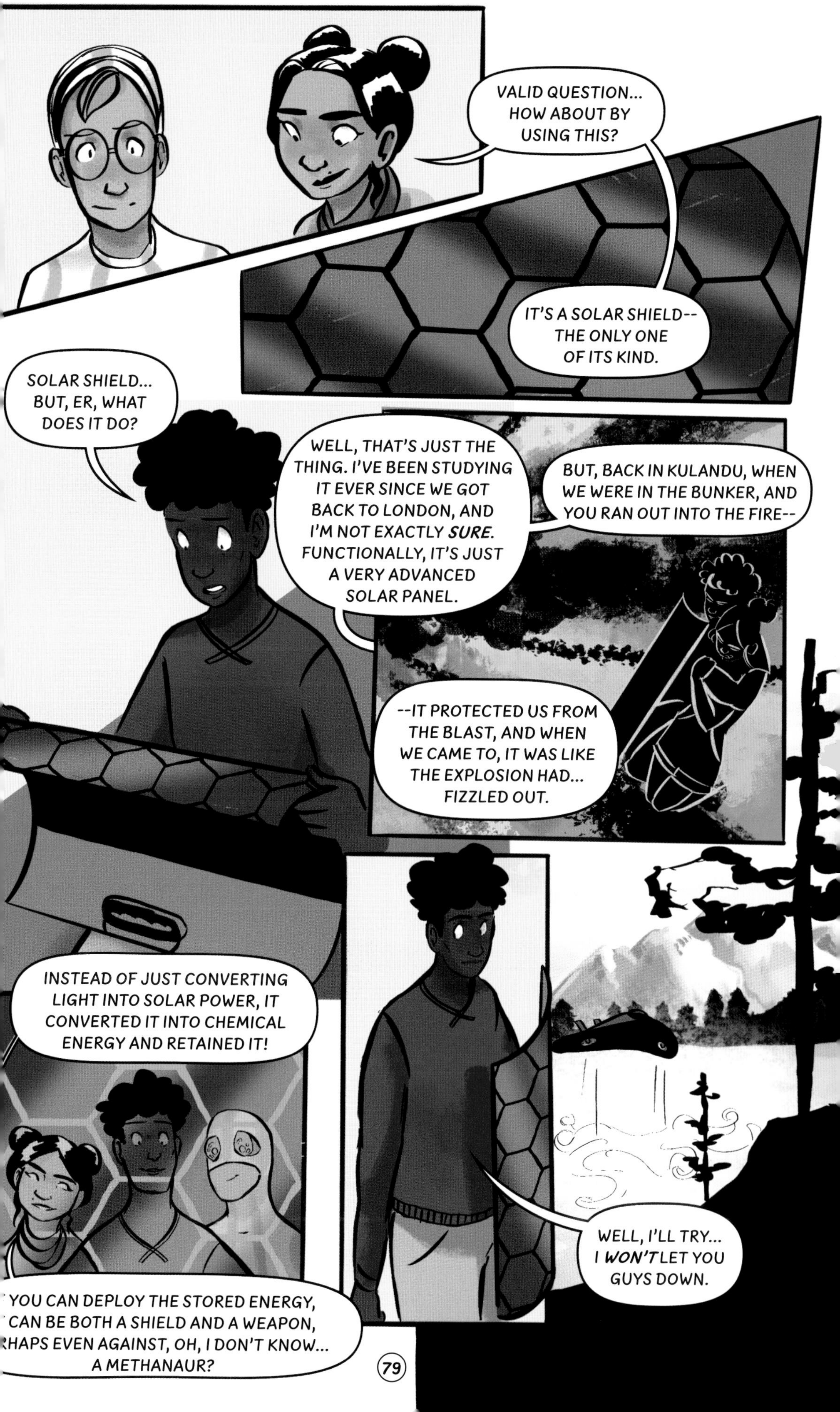
VALID QUESTION... HOW ABOUT BY USING THIS?
IT'S A SOLAR SHIELD-- THE ONLY ONE OF ITS KIND.
SOLAR SHIELD... BUT, ER, WHAT DOES IT DO?
WELL, THAT'S JUST THE THING. I'VE BEEN STUDYING IT EVER SINCE WE GOT BACK TO LONDON, AND I'M NOT EXACTLY *SURE*. FUNCTIONALLY, IT'S JUST A VERY ADVANCED SOLAR PANEL.
BUT, BACK IN KULANDU, WHEN WE WERE IN THE BUNKER, AND YOU RAN OUT INTO THE FIRE--
--IT PROTECTED US FROM THE BLAST, AND WHEN WE CAME TO, IT WAS LIKE THE EXPLOSION HAD... FIZZLED OUT.
INSTEAD OF JUST CONVERTING LIGHT INTO SOLAR POWER, IT CONVERTED IT INTO CHEMICAL ENERGY AND RETAINED IT!
YOU CAN DEPLOY THE STORED ENERGY, CAN BE BOTH A SHIELD AND A WEAPON, RHAPS EVEN AGAINST, OH, I DON'T KNOW... A METHANAUR?
WELL, I'LL TRY... I *WON'T* LET YOU GUYS DOWN.

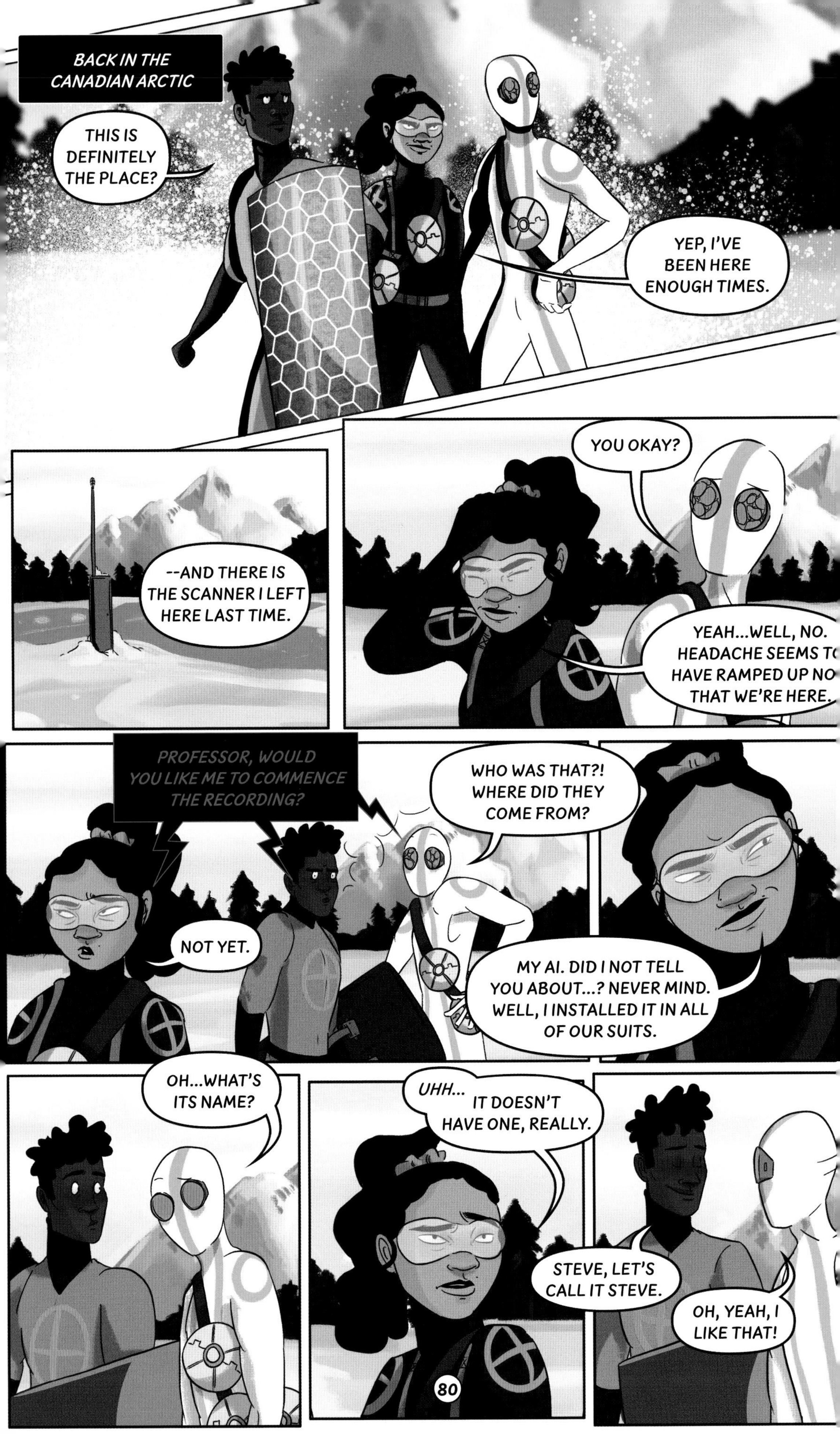

BACK IN THE CANADIAN ARCTIC
THIS IS DEFINITELY THE PLACE?
YEP, I'VE BEEN HERE ENOUGH TIMES.
--AND THERE IS THE SCANNER I LEFT HERE LAST TIME.
YOU OKAY?
YEAH...WELL, NO. HEADACHE SEEMS TO HAVE RAMPED UP NOW THAT WE'RE HERE.
PROFESSOR, WOULD YOU LIKE ME TO COMMENCE THE RECORDING?
NOT YET.
WHO WAS THAT?! WHERE DID THEY COME FROM?
MY AI. DID I NOT TELL YOU ABOUT...? NEVER MIND. WELL, I INSTALLED IT IN ALL OF OUR SUITS.
OH...WHAT'S ITS NAME?
UHH... IT DOESN'T HAVE ONE, REALLY.
STEVE, LET'S CALL IT STEVE.
OH, YEAH, I LIKE THAT!

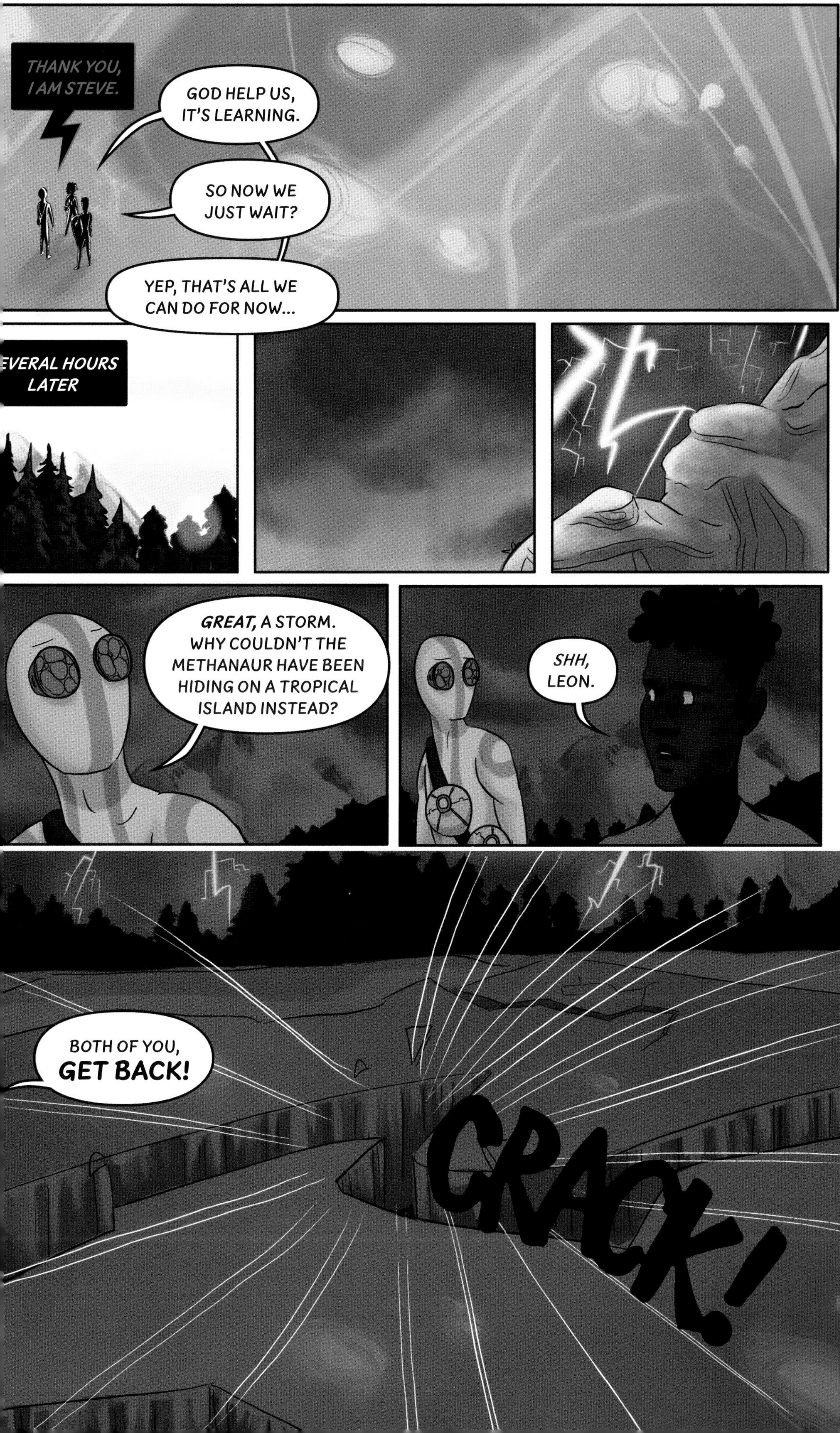
THANK YOU, I AM STEVE.
GOD HELP US, IT'S LEARNING.
SO NOW WE JUST WAIT?
YEP, THAT'S ALL WE CAN DO FOR NOW...
EVERAL HOURS LATER
GREAT, A STORM. WHY COULDN'T THE METHANAUR HAVE BEEN HIDING ON A TROPICAL ISLAND INSTEAD?
SHH, LEON.
BOTH OF YOU, **GET BACK!**
CRACK!

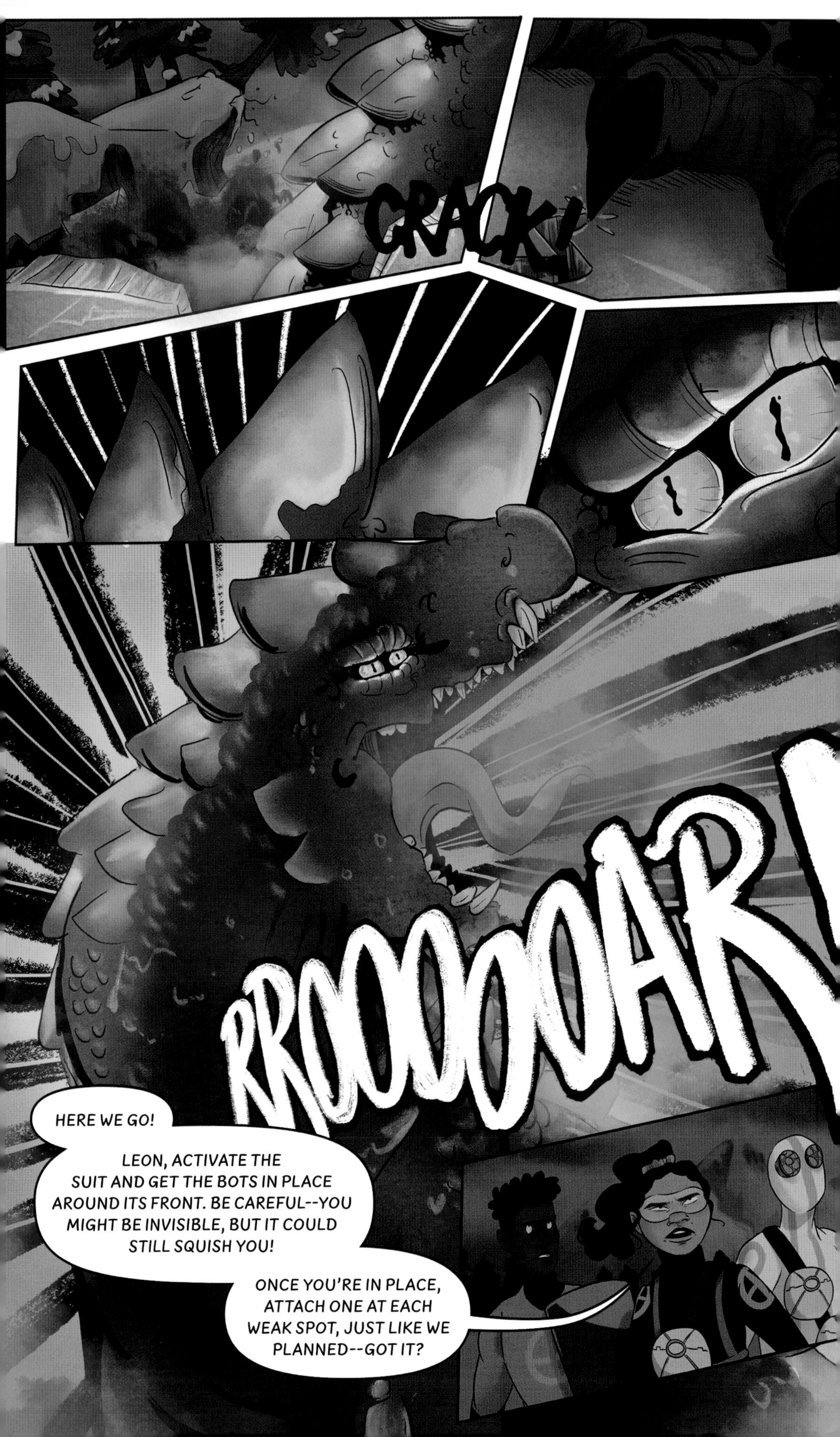
CRACK!
RROOOOOAR
HERE WE GO!
LEON, ACTIVATE THE SUIT AND GET THE BOTS IN PLACE AROUND ITS FRONT. BE CAREFUL--YOU MIGHT BE INVISIBLE, BUT IT COULD STILL SQUISH YOU!
ONCE YOU'RE IN PLACE, ATTACH ONE AT EACH WEAK SPOT, JUST LIKE WE PLANNED--GOT IT?

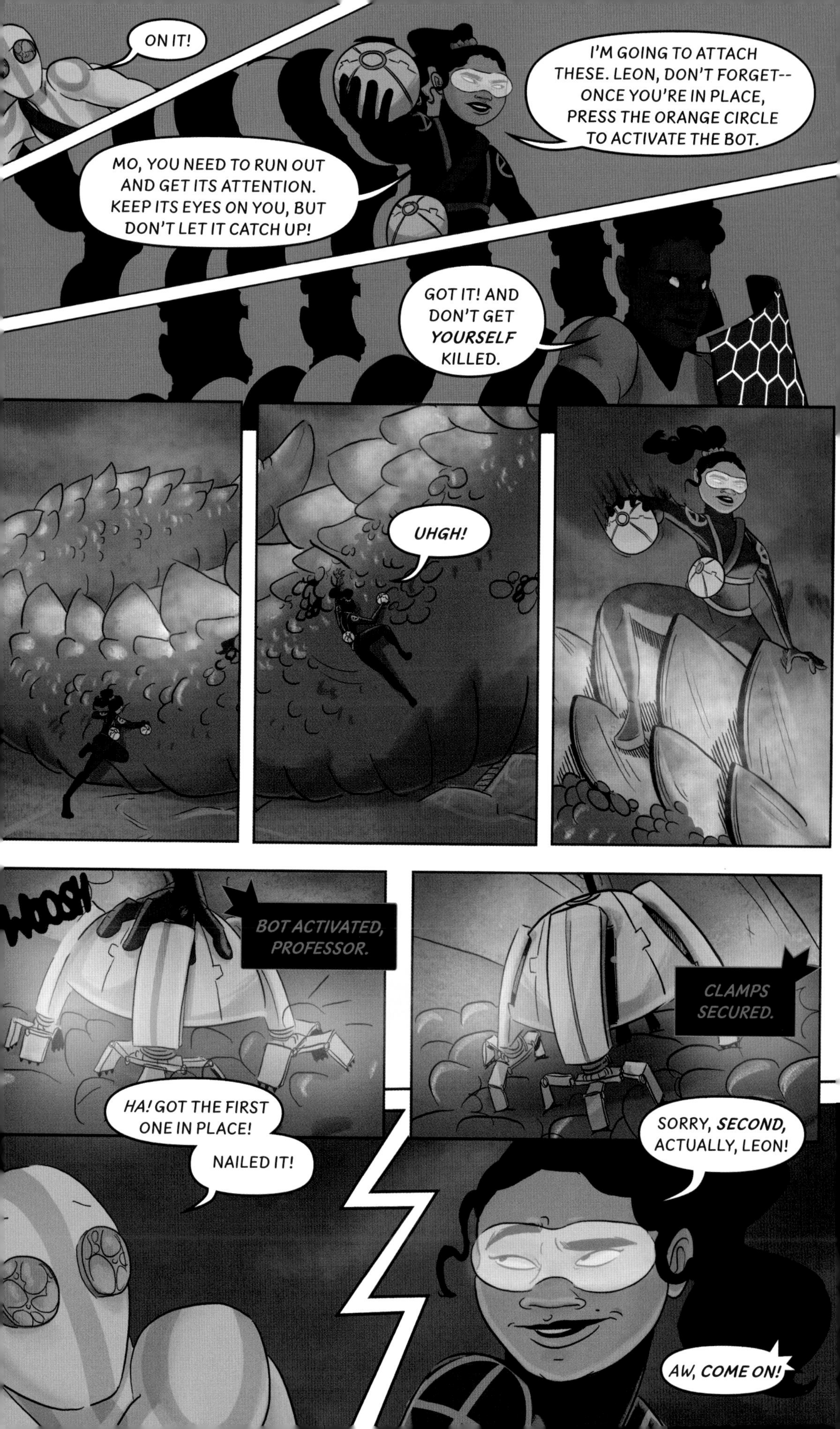
ON IT!
I'M GOING TO ATTACH THESE. LEON, DON'T FORGET-- ONCE YOU'RE IN PLACE, PRESS THE ORANGE CIRCLE TO ACTIVATE THE BOT.
MO, YOU NEED TO RUN OUT AND GET ITS ATTENTION. KEEP ITS EYES ON YOU, BUT DON'T LET IT CATCH UP!
GOT IT! AND DON'T GET *YOURSELF* KILLED.
UHGH!
WOOSH
BOT ACTIVATED, PROFESSOR.
CLAMPS SECURED.
HA! GOT THE FIRST ONE IN PLACE!
NAILED IT!
SORRY, *SECOND,* ACTUALLY, LEON!
AW, COME ON!

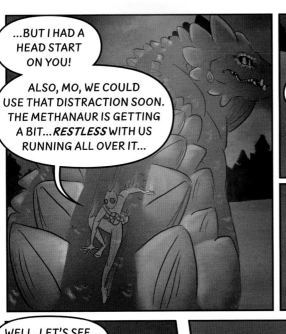

...BUT I HAD A HEAD START ON YOU!

ALSO, MO, WE COULD USE THAT DISTRACTION SOON. THE METHANAUR IS GETTING A BIT...*RESTLESS* WITH US RUNNING ALL OVER IT...

I'M IN POSITION, KATE. NOW WHAT?

THE SHIELD IS LIKE LEON'S SUIT--IT IN TUNE TO YOUR BOD SO IT SHOULD WORK F YOU. I DON'T KNOW EXACTLY HOW, BUT-

GREAT, EASY...

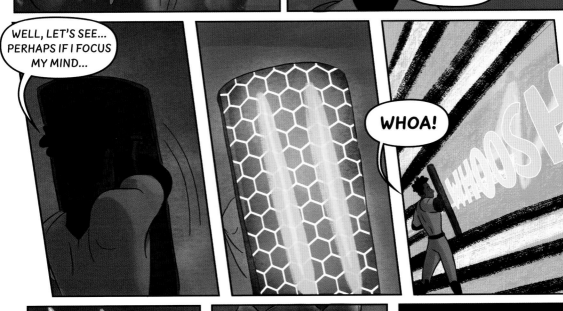

WELL, LET'S SEE... PERHAPS IF I FOCUS MY MIND...

WHOA!

WHOOSH

IT *WORKED!*

I GOT ITS ATTENTION. IT'S FOLLOWING ME!

OH MY GOD--IT'S FOLLOWING ME...

OOOAAR!

THAT'S THE PLAN!

YOU'RE DOING GREAT.

I'VE GOT ONE MORE BOT TO GO.

ME TOO.

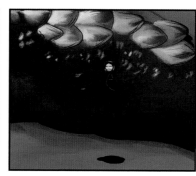

LAST ONE DOWN!

TIME TO GET MOVING THEN!

HUD

RIGHT BEHIND YOU!

OKAY...

...HERE GOES NOTHING. MO, YOU AT A SAFE DISTANCE?

YEAH!

GOOD, OKAY. STEVE, ACTIVATE THE BOTS.

GRRRRRROOOOAAR!

I THINK IT'S WORKING!

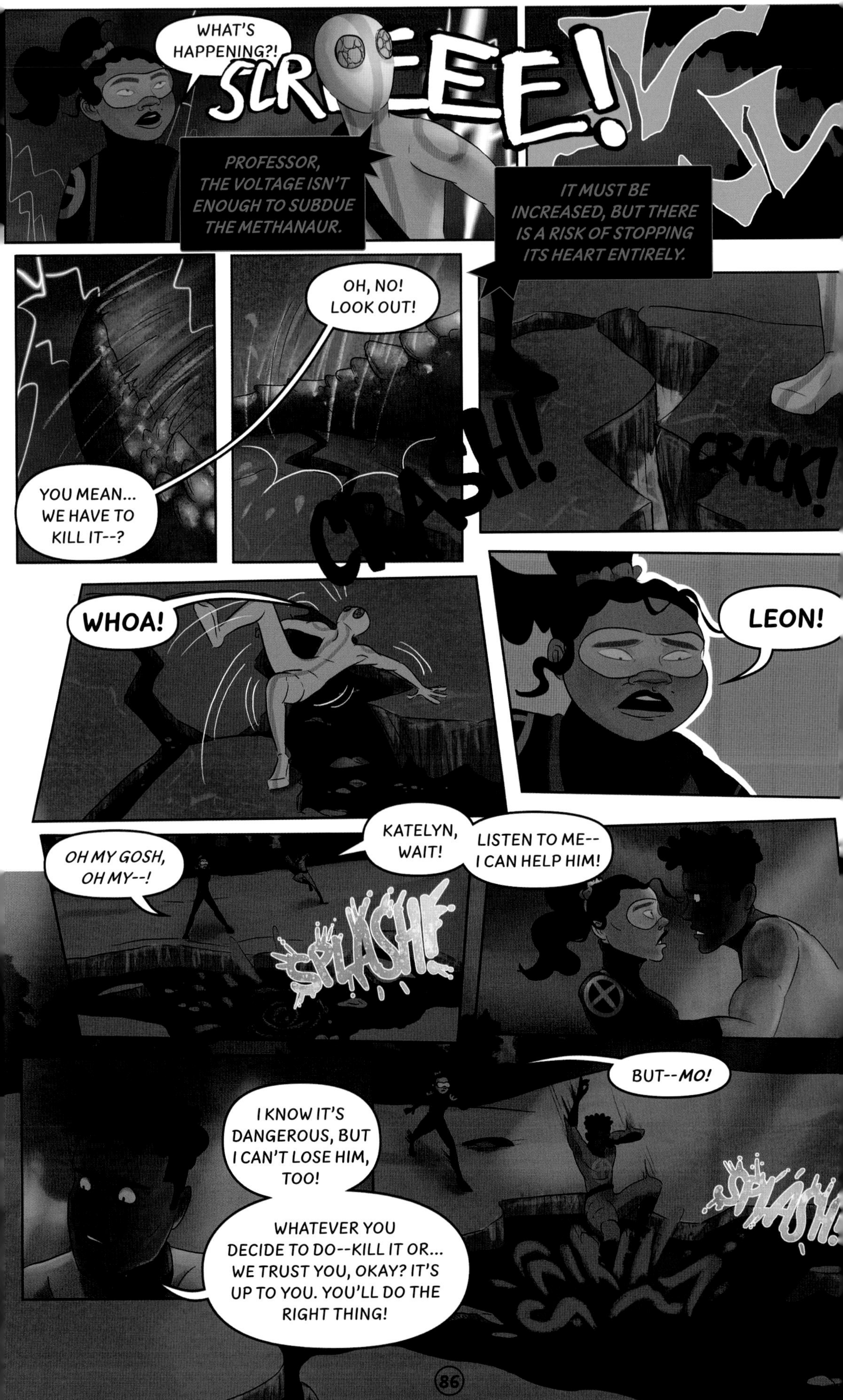
WHAT'S HAPPENING?!
SCREEEE!
PROFESSOR, THE VOLTAGE ISN'T ENOUGH TO SUBDUE THE METHANAUR.
IT MUST BE INCREASED, BUT THERE IS A RISK OF STOPPING ITS HEART ENTIRELY.
YOU MEAN... WE HAVE TO KILL IT--?
OH, NO! LOOK OUT!
CRASH!
CRACK!
WHOA!
LEON!
OH MY GOSH, OH MY--!
KATELYN, WAIT!
SPLASH!
LISTEN TO ME-- I CAN HELP HIM!
BUT--MO!
I KNOW IT'S DANGEROUS, BUT I CAN'T LOSE HIM, TOO!
WHATEVER YOU DECIDE TO DO--KILL IT OR... WE TRUST YOU, OKAY? IT'S UP TO YOU. YOU'LL DO THE RIGHT THING!
SPLASH!

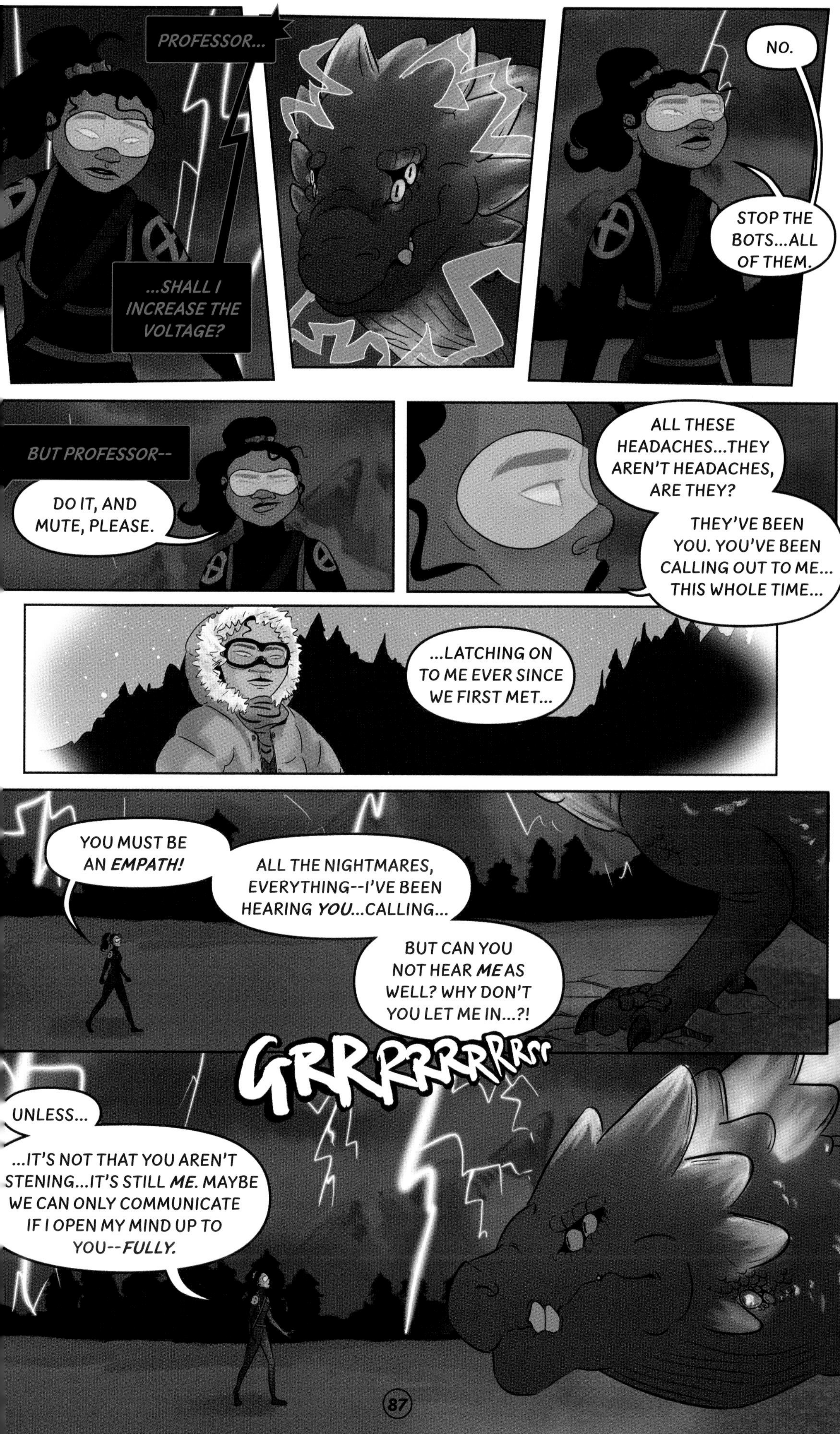

PROFESSOR...
...SHALL I INCREASE THE VOLTAGE?
NO.
STOP THE BOTS...ALL OF THEM.
BUT PROFESSOR--
DO IT, AND MUTE, PLEASE.
ALL THESE HEADACHES...THEY AREN'T HEADACHES, ARE THEY?
THEY'VE BEEN YOU. YOU'VE BEEN CALLING OUT TO ME... THIS WHOLE TIME...
...LATCHING ON TO ME EVER SINCE WE FIRST MET...
YOU MUST BE AN EMPATH!
ALL THE NIGHTMARES, EVERYTHING--I'VE BEEN HEARING YOU...CALLING...
BUT CAN YOU NOT HEAR ME AS WELL? WHY DON'T YOU LET ME IN...?!
GRRRRRRRrrr
UNLESS...
...IT'S NOT THAT YOU AREN'T STENING...IT'S STILL ME. MAYBE WE CAN ONLY COMMUNICATE IF I OPEN MY MIND UP TO YOU--FULLY.

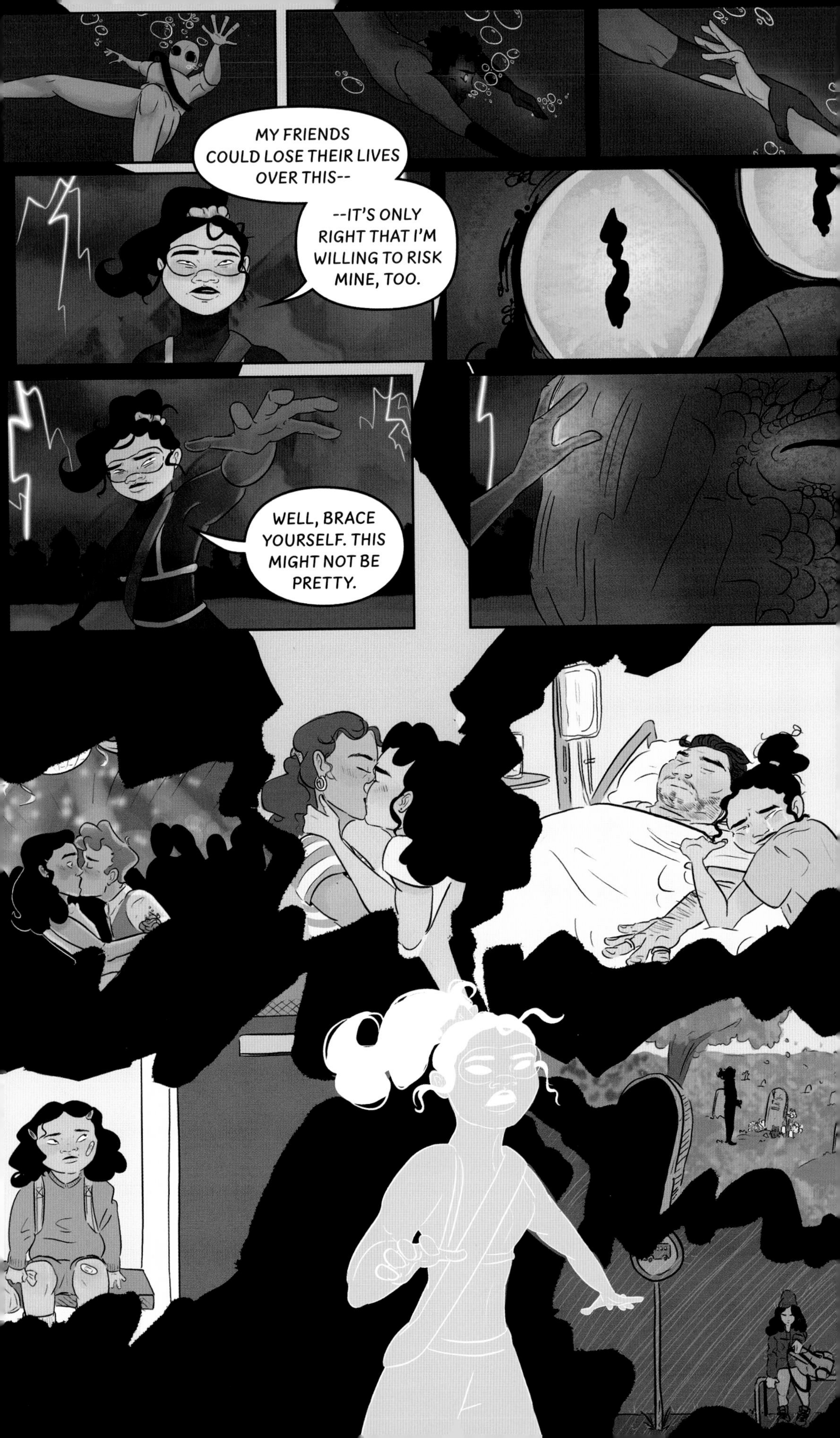
MY FRIENDS COULD LOSE THEIR LIVES OVER THIS--
--IT'S ONLY RIGHT THAT I'M WILLING TO RISK MINE, TOO.
WELL, BRACE YOURSELF. THIS MIGHT NOT BE PRETTY.

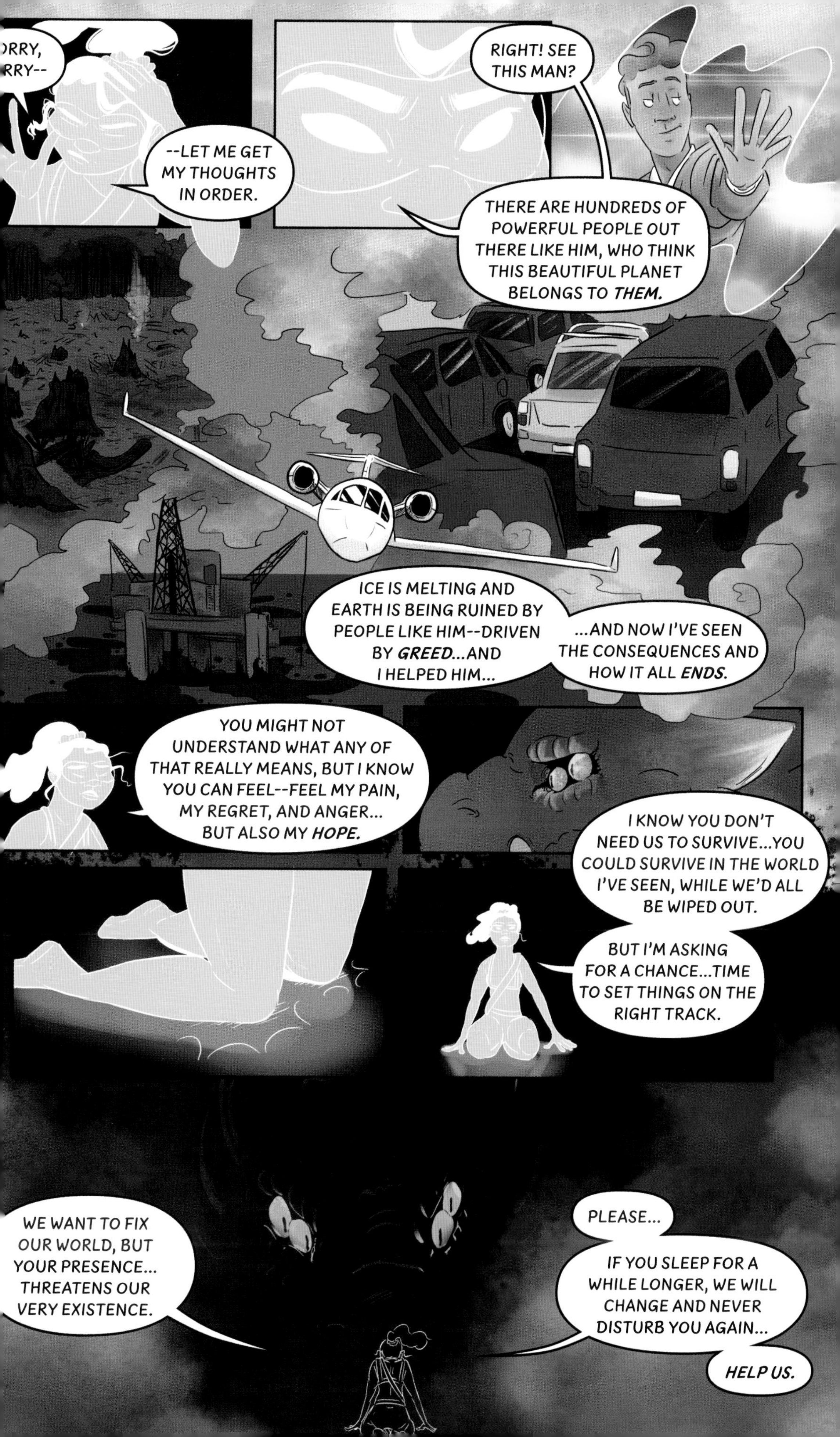
ORRY, RRY--
--LET ME GET MY THOUGHTS IN ORDER.
RIGHT! SEE THIS MAN?
THERE ARE HUNDREDS OF POWERFUL PEOPLE OUT THERE LIKE HIM, WHO THINK THIS BEAUTIFUL PLANET BELONGS TO *THEM.*
ICE IS MELTING AND EARTH IS BEING RUINED BY PEOPLE LIKE HIM--DRIVEN BY ***GREED***...AND I HELPED HIM...
...AND NOW I'VE SEEN THE CONSEQUENCES AND HOW IT ALL *ENDS.*
YOU MIGHT NOT UNDERSTAND WHAT ANY OF THAT REALLY MEANS, BUT I KNOW YOU CAN FEEL--FEEL MY PAIN, MY REGRET, AND ANGER... BUT ALSO MY *HOPE.*
I KNOW YOU DON'T NEED US TO SURVIVE...YOU COULD SURVIVE IN THE WORLD I'VE SEEN, WHILE WE'D ALL BE WIPED OUT.
BUT I'M ASKING FOR A CHANCE...TIME TO SET THINGS ON THE RIGHT TRACK.
WE WANT TO FIX OUR WORLD, BUT YOUR PRESENCE... THREATENS OUR VERY EXISTENCE.
PLEASE...
IF YOU SLEEP FOR A WHILE LONGER, WE WILL CHANGE AND NEVER DISTURB YOU AGAIN...
HELP US.

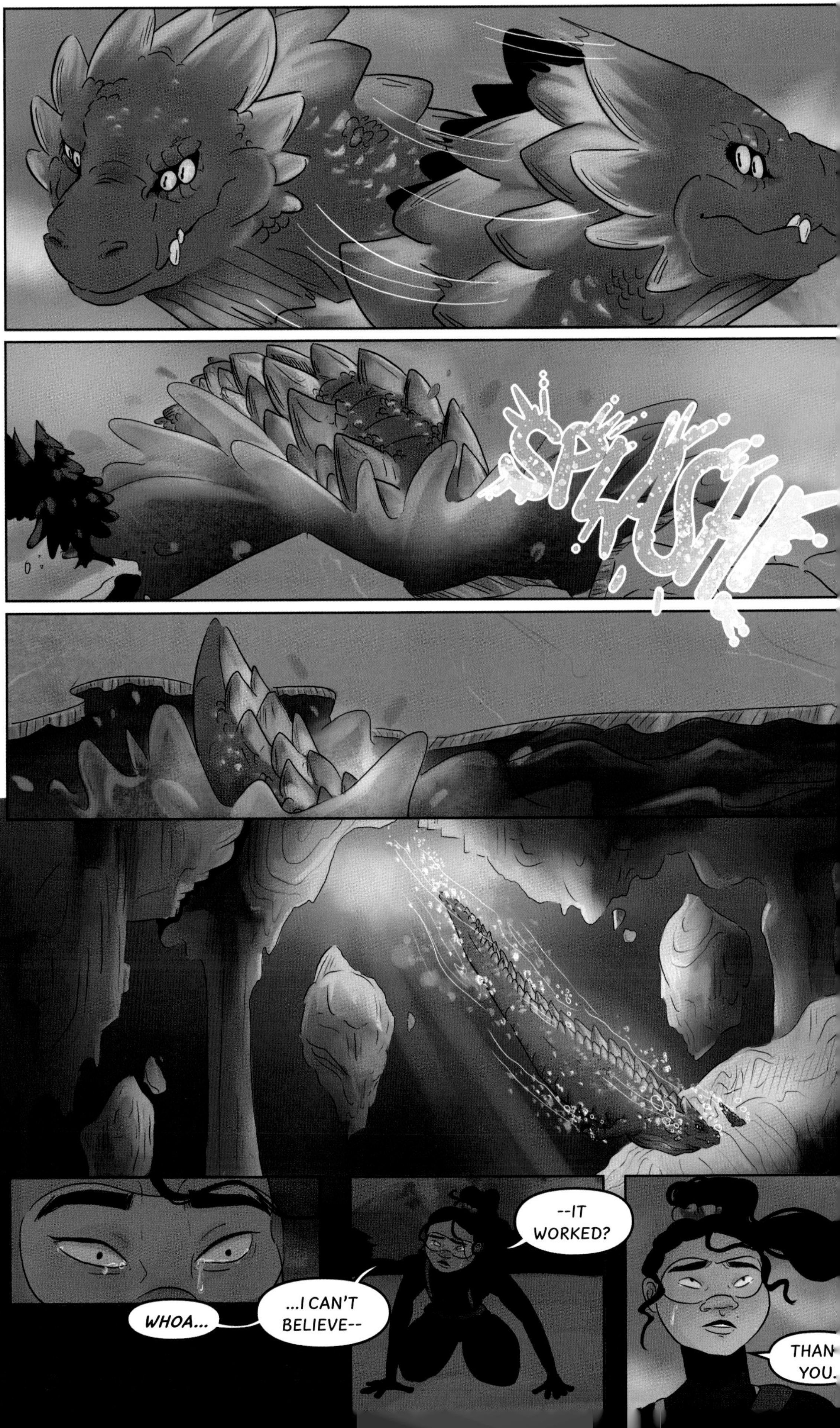
SPLASH!
WHOA...
...I CAN'T BELIEVE--
--IT WORKED?
THAN
YOU.

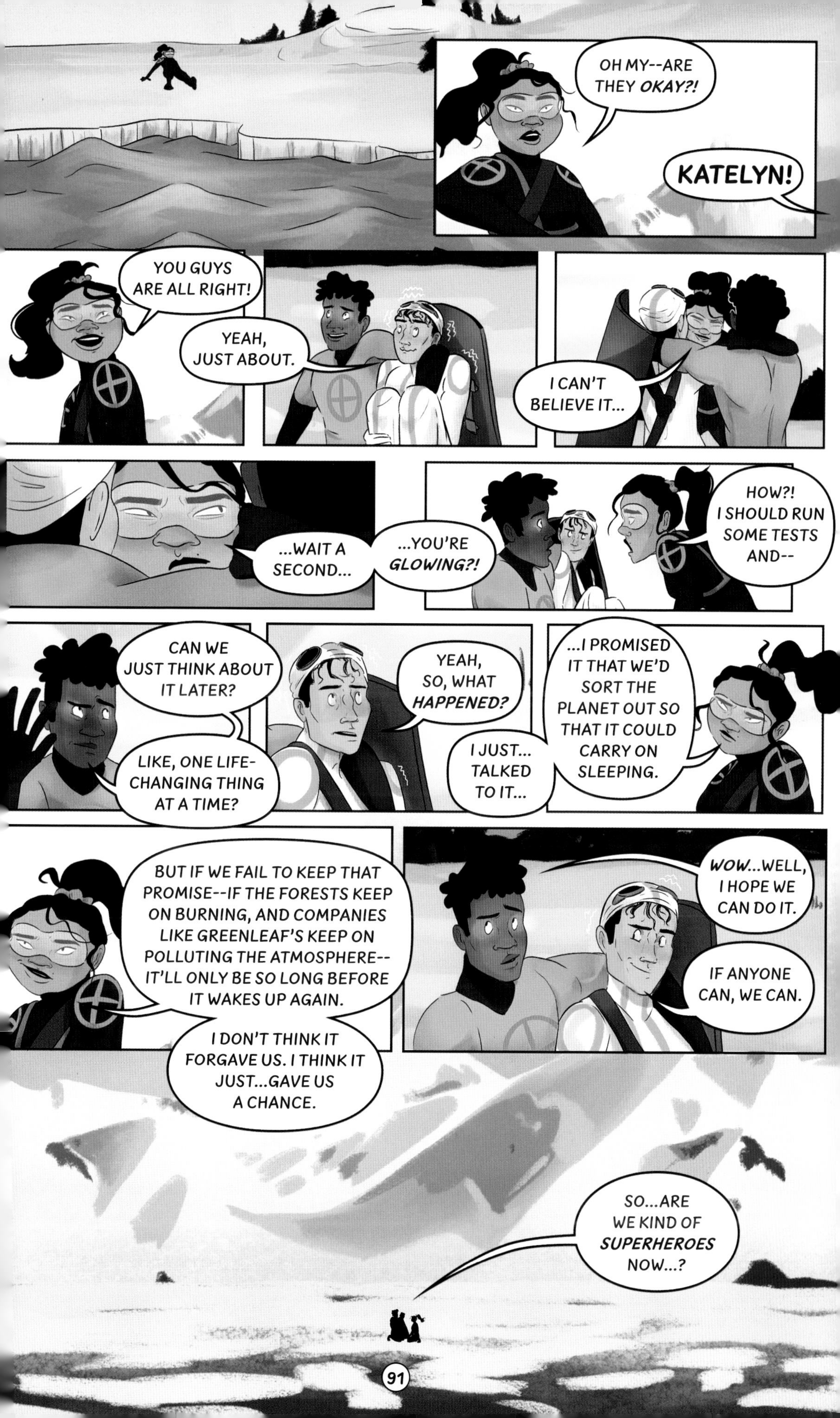
OH MY--ARE THEY *OKAY?!*
KATELYN!
YOU GUYS ARE ALL RIGHT!
YEAH, JUST ABOUT.
I CAN'T BELIEVE IT...
...WAIT A SECOND...
...YOU'RE *GLOWING?!*
HOW?! I SHOULD RUN SOME TESTS AND--
CAN WE JUST THINK ABOUT IT LATER?
LIKE, ONE LIFE-CHANGING THING AT A TIME?
YEAH, SO, WHAT *HAPPENED?*
I JUST... TALKED TO IT...
...I PROMISED IT THAT WE'D SORT THE PLANET OUT SO THAT IT COULD CARRY ON SLEEPING.
BUT IF WE FAIL TO KEEP THAT PROMISE--IF THE FORESTS KEEP ON BURNING, AND COMPANIES LIKE GREENLEAF'S KEEP ON POLLUTING THE ATMOSPHERE--IT'LL ONLY BE SO LONG BEFORE IT WAKES UP AGAIN.
I DON'T THINK IT FORGAVE US. I THINK IT JUST...GAVE US A CHANCE.
WOW...WELL, I HOPE WE CAN DO IT.
IF ANYONE CAN, WE CAN.
SO...ARE WE KIND OF *SUPERHEROES* NOW...?

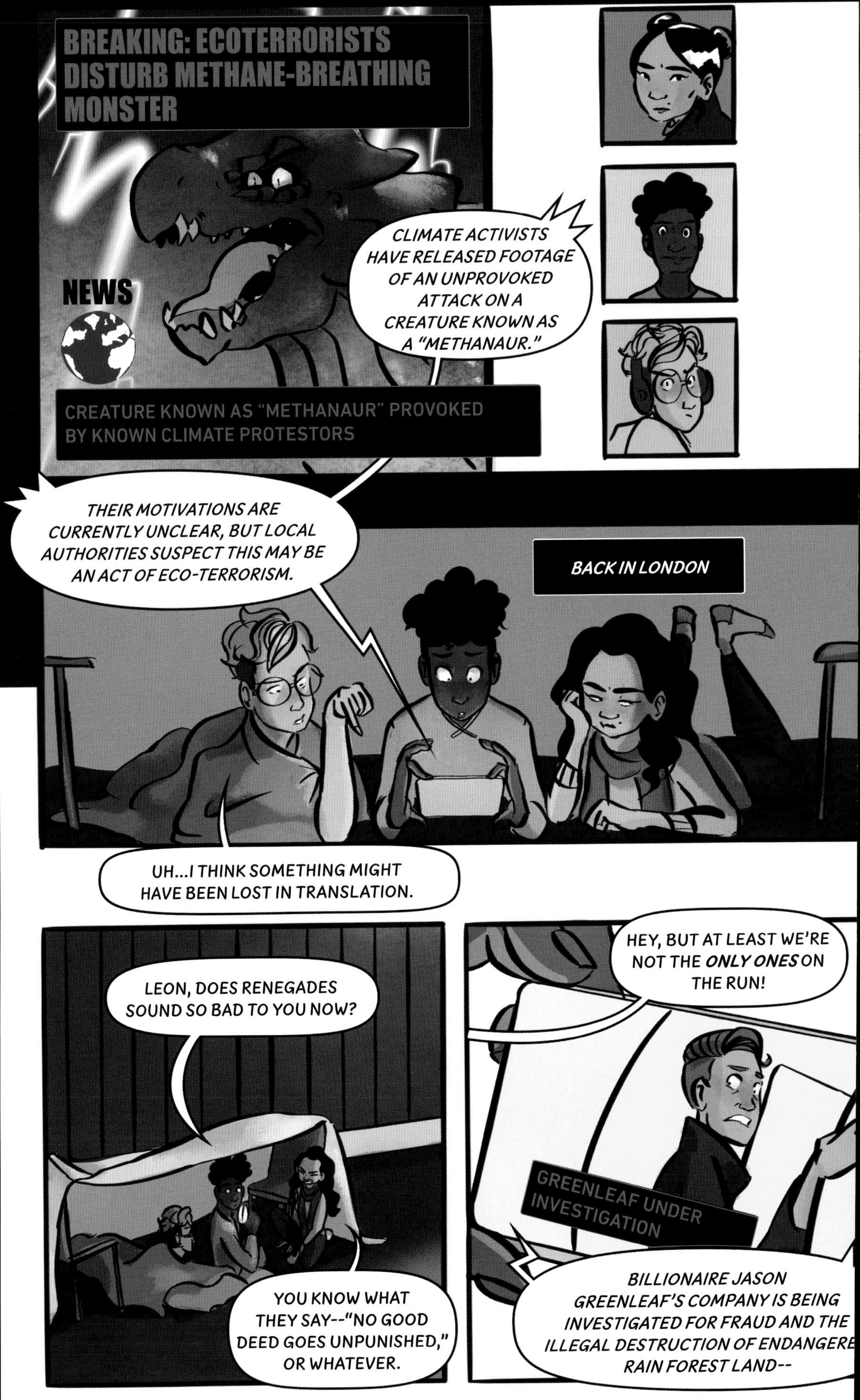
BREAKING: ECOTERRORISTS DISTURB METHANE-BREATHING MONSTER
NEWS
CLIMATE ACTIVISTS HAVE RELEASED FOOTAGE OF AN UNPROVOKED ATTACK ON A CREATURE KNOWN AS A "METHANAUR."
CREATURE KNOWN AS "METHANAUR" PROVOKED BY KNOWN CLIMATE PROTESTORS
THEIR MOTIVATIONS ARE CURRENTLY UNCLEAR, BUT LOCAL AUTHORITIES SUSPECT THIS MAY BE AN ACT OF ECO-TERRORISM.
BACK IN LONDON
UH...I THINK SOMETHING MIGHT HAVE BEEN LOST IN TRANSLATION.
LEON, DOES RENEGADES SOUND SO BAD TO YOU NOW?
YOU KNOW WHAT THEY SAY--"NO GOOD DEED GOES UNPUNISHED," OR WHATEVER.
HEY, BUT AT LEAST WE'RE NOT THE ONLY ONES ON THE RUN!
GREENLEAF UNDER INVESTIGATION
BILLIONAIRE JASON GREENLEAF'S COMPANY IS BEING INVESTIGATED FOR FRAUD AND THE ILLEGAL DESTRUCTION OF ENDANGERE RAIN FOREST LAND--

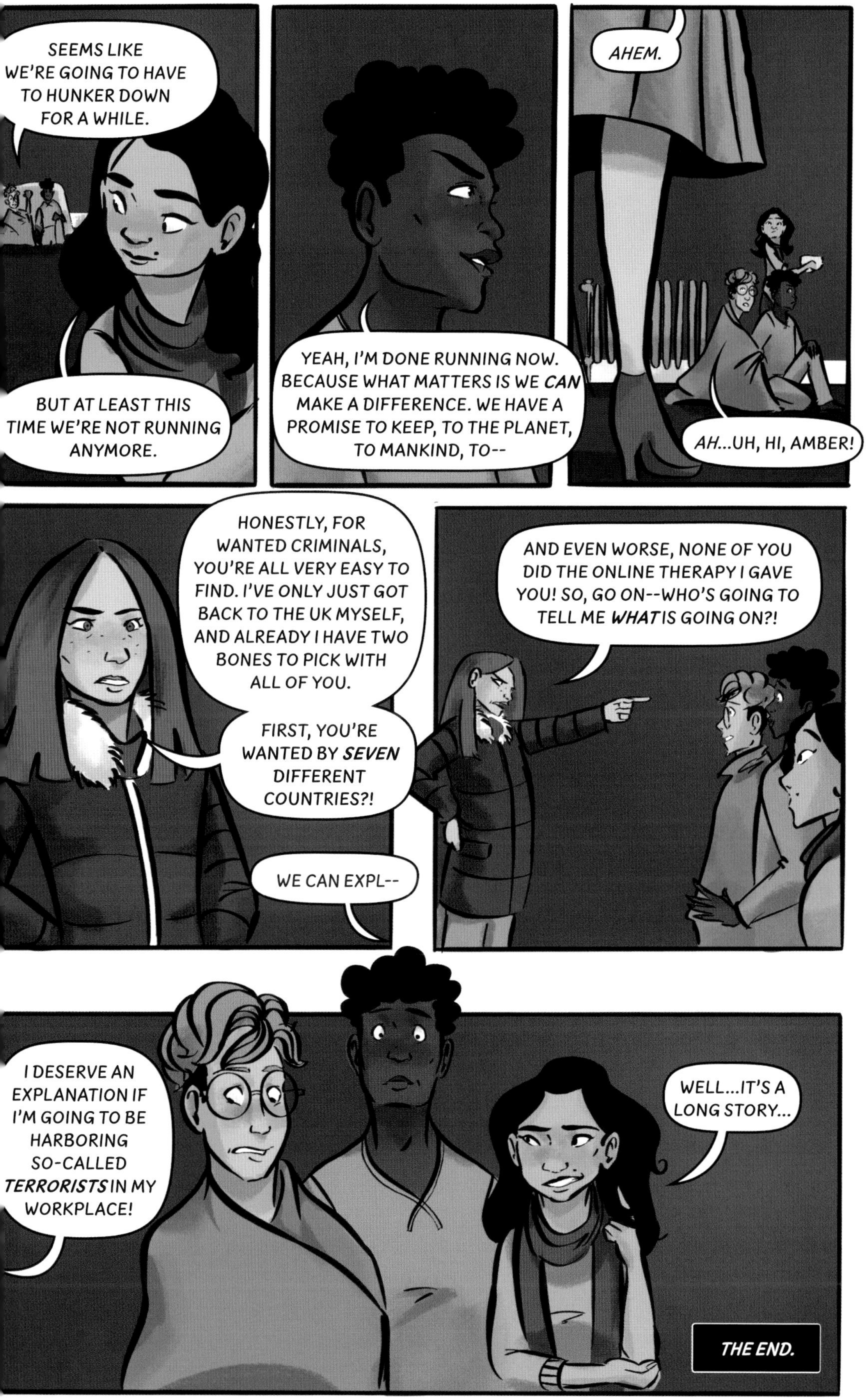
SEEMS LIKE WE'RE GOING TO HAVE TO HUNKER DOWN FOR A WHILE.
BUT AT LEAST THIS TIME WE'RE NOT RUNNING ANYMORE.
YEAH, I'M DONE RUNNING NOW. BECAUSE WHAT MATTERS IS WE *CAN* MAKE A DIFFERENCE. WE HAVE A PROMISE TO KEEP, TO THE PLANET, TO MANKIND, TO--
AHEM.
AH...UH, HI, AMBER!
HONESTLY, FOR WANTED CRIMINALS, YOU'RE ALL VERY EASY TO FIND. I'VE ONLY JUST GOT BACK TO THE UK MYSELF, AND ALREADY I HAVE TWO BONES TO PICK WITH ALL OF YOU.
FIRST, YOU'RE WANTED BY ***SEVEN*** DIFFERENT COUNTRIES?!
WE CAN EXPL--
AND EVEN WORSE, NONE OF YOU DID THE ONLINE THERAPY I GAVE YOU! SO, GO ON--WHO'S GOING TO TELL ME ***WHAT*** IS GOING ON?!
I DESERVE AN EXPLANATION IF I'M GOING TO BE HARBORING SO-CALLED ***TERRORISTS*** IN MY WORKPLACE!
WELL...IT'S A LONG STORY...
THE END.

THE CLIMATE EMERGENCY

WHILE A GIANT METHANAUR MAY BE A WORK OF FICTION, THE THREAT OF CLIMATE CHANGE IS VERY REAL AND AFFECTS US ALL. TO HAVE ANY CHANCE OF PREVENTING THE PLANET FROM WARMING FURTHER, WE NEED TO ACT NOW, SO IT'S IMPORTANT TO UNDERSTAND THE SCIENCE OF CLIMATE CHANGE-- THE CAUSES, THE EFFECTS, AND WHAT WE CAN ALL DO ABOUT IT.

WHAT IS CLIMATE CHANGE?

The climate of our planet changes slowly, over long periods of time, but human activity is causing it to warm faster than usual. This is affecting both the climate and life on Earth. For example, when Arctic ice melts, it means a loss of habitat for many animals.

WHY IS IT HAPPENING?

Earth is warmed by a layer of gases in the atmosphere that trap heat from the sun. Many human activities release gases, such as carbon dioxide and methane, known as greenhouse gases because they build up in the atmosphere trapping more heat, like the glass of a greenhouse.

WHAT ARE THE CAUSES?

Rising consumption is increasing the demand for energy to power industry and our homes, for transportation, and for food. Burning fossil fuels (coal, oil, and gas), deforestation, and farming all emit greenhouse gases. The actions of the super-rich—such as traveling in private jets, like Jason Greenleaf's—can be especially harmful. The average private jet flight emits around 150 times more greenhouse gases than a similar journey by high-speed train.

WHAT ABOUT BIOFUELS?

Fuels made from plants are called biofuels. When they burn, they emit greenhouse gases, but this is offset to some degree by the fact that they absorb carbon dioxide as they grow. Biofuels used to be considered a more sustainable alternative to fossil fuels, but they are often the cause of severe deforestation.

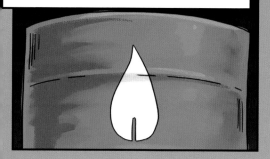

WHY ARE FORESTS IMPORTANT?

Forests are known as "carbon sinks" because trees take in and store carbon dioxide to get energy. When a forest is cleared and burned—for grazing cattle or growing biofuels for example—not only is this carbon dioxide released into the atmosphere, but also a carbon sink is lost. Biofuels made of crop waste are therefore much more sustainable than those made of crops grown for biofuel.

WHAT ARE THE CONSEQUENCES?

Climate change is having a big impact on our planet. A rise in temperature of a few degrees might not seem much, but it has caused ice to melt and sea levels to rise. The change in temperature has also led to more extreme weather events, including tropical cyclones like Cyclone Idai in 2019, which tragically killed more than 1,000 people in Mozambique, Zimbabwe, and Malawi.

ARCTIC ICE AND METHANE

Global warming is causing huge areas of ice in the Arctic to melt. Some of this ice forms part of frozen lakes and frozen earth, called permafrost, in which methane gas is trapped. When these areas thaw, methane—a far more potent greenhouse gas than carbon dioxide—is released. This begins a vicious cycle of global warming—as the planet warms, more ice melts and more methane is released.

WHAT CAN WE DO?

We can all take individual action to cut emissions, by eating less meat and using greener ways to travel. But to make a real impact, big companies and governments must act, too. We need to speak up to insist the climate emergency becomes a priority. School strikes, letters to politicians, and peaceful protest are all useful ways we can help make our voices heard. History shows this can lead to victory. Like in our story, plans for an airport near Nantes, France, were scrapped in 2018, due to activists occupying the site with an ecocamp.

MEET THE TEAM

IT'S GOING TO TAKE A SUPERHUMAN EFFORT TO SLOW DOWN CLIMATE CHANGE, SO A TEAM OF STUDENTS AND YOUNG ILLUSTRATORS GOT TOGETHER TO CREATE SOME COMIC BOOK SUPERHEROES TO HELP "SAVE THE WORLD". WE'RE GOING TO NEED ALL THE HELP WE CAN GET!

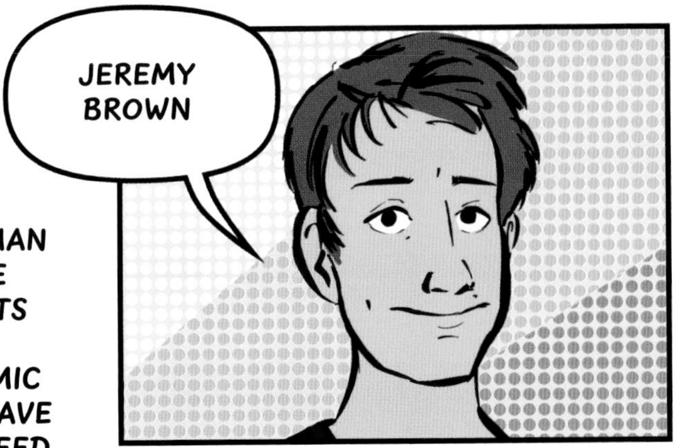
JEREMY BROWN

THE RENEGADES WAS COFOUNDED BY JEREMY WHILE STUDYING A MASTER'S IN CLIMATE CHANGE AT KING'S COLLEGE LONDON. ALONGSIDE DREAMING UP THE CHARACTERS AND STORY ARCS, HE ENJOYS A SPOT OF POLITICS AND STAND-UP COMEDY.

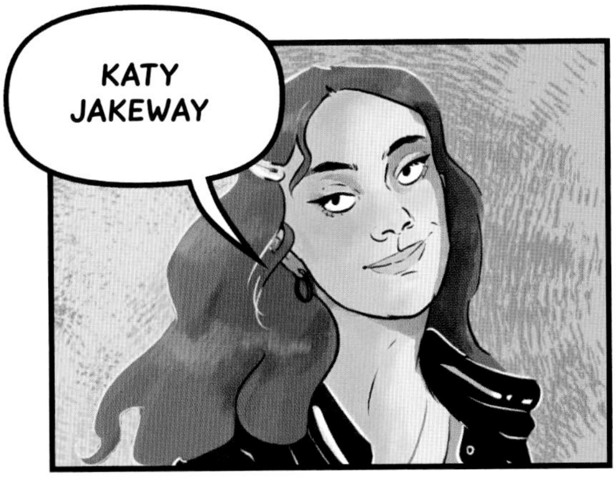
KATY JAKEWAY

WHILE CREATING *THE RENEGADES*, KATY WAS ALSO STUDYING AT KING'S COLLEGE LONDON. KATY JOINED THE PROJECT IN ITS EARLY DAYS, USING HER PASSION FOR ART AND WRITING TO HELP BRING JEREMY'S INITIAL IDEAS TO LIFE.

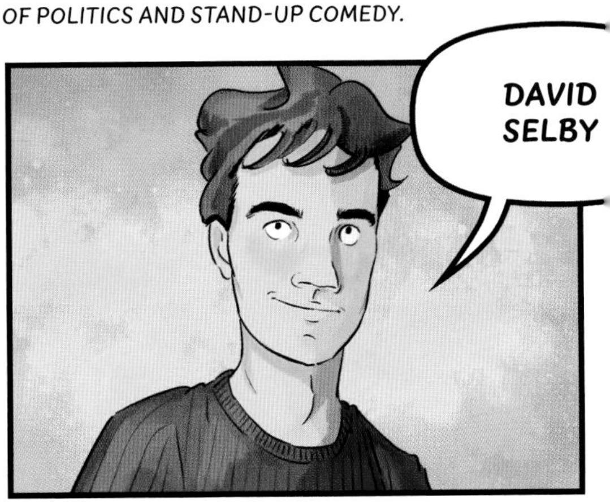
DAVID SELBY

CO-SCRIPTWRITER OF *THE RENEGADES* AND FELLOW KING'S COLLEGE LONDON STUDENT, DAVID WAS EAGER TO BUILD ON JEREMY AND KATY'S IDEAS AND HOPES TO SEE THE PROJECT RAISE AWARENESS ABOUT CLIMATE CHANGE.

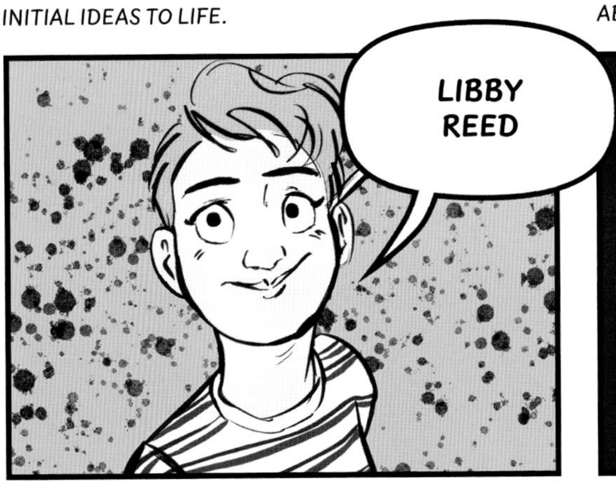
LIBBY REED

LIBBY SPENDS MOST OF HER TIME DRAWING AND MAKING UP STORIES. SHE LOVES ANIMALS, ESPECIALLY REPTILES, AND USES HER ARTWORK TO SHOW THE BEAUTY OF THE NATURAL WORLD.

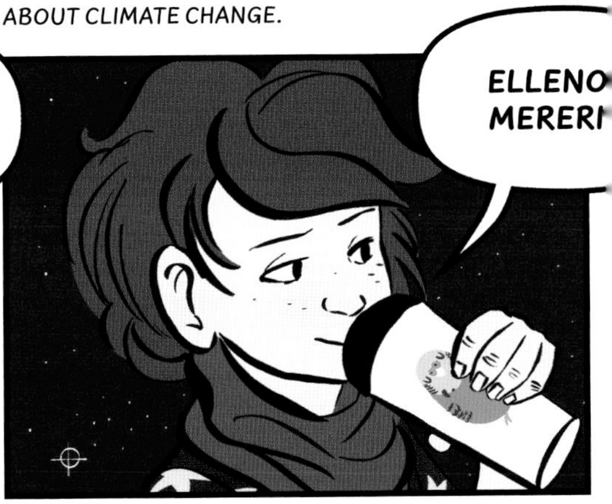
ELLENO
MERER

ELLENOR IS INSPIRED BY DAVID ATTENBOROUGH AND CHARLES DARWIN; PEOPLE WHO HAVE SHOWN THE MIGHT AND MIRACLE OF OUR PLANET TO MILLIONS OF PEOPLE. ELLENOR LIKES FOLKLORE AND STARGAZING.

ACKNOWLEDGMENTS SPECIAL THANKS TO SUFFOLK FRIEND AND COMIC GEEK, MISCHA PEARSON, FOR PIONEERING THE GUARDIANS OF THE PLANET (THE PREDECESSOR TO THE RENEGADES). MUCH CREDIT TO COURSEMATES JONATHAN HYDE, TOM HAMBLEY, AND ELIAS YASSIN FOR THEIR GEOGRAPHICAL WISDOM, BOLD ACTIVISM, AND LOYAL FRIENDSHIP, WHICH ALL VERY MUCH HELPED SHAPE THE COMIC. THERE ARE TOO MANY TO LIST HERE, BUT A BIG THANK YOU ALSO TO JAMES PORTER, GEORGE ADAMSON, ODHRAN LINSEY, MICHAEL BARNARD, AND ALL THE LOVELY CREW AT DK FOR THEIR ENTHUSIASM, PATIENCE, AND COMMITMENT TO PROTECTING THE PLANET THROUGH STORYTELLING.

DK WOULD LIKE TO THANK HAZEL BEYNON FOR PROOFREADING